The Secret She Kept

#1 National Bestselling and NAACP Image Award–Winning Author of *Say Amen, Again*

ReShonda Ta[...]

READERS GUIDE

LEY

“tack ***The Florida Times-Union*****) in her bestselling novels featuring high-spirited Rachel Jackson Adams and the Houston congregation that critics and readers adore!**

SAY AMEN, AGAIN

Winner of the NAACP Image Award for Outstanding Literary Work

“Heartfelt. . . . A fast-paced story filled with vivid characters.”

—*Publishers Weekly*

EVERYBODY SAY AMEN

A *USA Today* Top Ten Summer Sizzler!

“A fun, redemptive book, packed with colorful characters, drama, and scandal.”

—*RT Book Reviews*

LET THE CHURCH SAY AMEN

#1 *Essence* magazine bestseller

One of *Library Journal*’s Best Christian Books for 2004

“Billingsley infuses her text with just the right dose of humor to balance the novel’s serious events.”

—*Library Journal* (starred review)

“Amen to *Let the Church Say Amen*. . . . [A] well-written novel.”

—*Indianapolis Recorder*

“Emotionally compelling. . . . Full of palpable joy, grief, and soulful characters.”

—*The Jacksonville Free Press*

“Her community of very human saints will win readers over with their humor and verve.”

"Faith-based fiction doesn't get better than Billingsley's," raves *Publishers Weekly,* praising how this gifted author entwines circumstances and characters "that many readers, Christian or not, can identify with."

A GOOD MAN IS HARD TO FIND

"Billingsley's engaging voice will keep readers turning the pages and savoring each scandalous revelation."

—*Publishers Weekly* (starred review)

HOLY ROLLERS

"Sensational. . . . [Billingsley] masterfully weaves together her trademark style of humor, girl-next-door drama, faith, and romance . . . [and] makes you fall in love with these characters."

—*RT Book Reviews*

THE DEVIL IS A LIE

"Steamy, sassy, sexy. . . . An entertaining dramedy."

—*Ebony*

"A romantic page-turner dipped in heavenly goodness."

—*Romantic Times* (4½ stars)

"Fast moving and hilarious."

—*Publishers Weekly*

CAN I GET A WITNESS?

A *USA Today* 2007 Summer Sizzler

"An emotional ride."

—*Ebony*

"Billingsley serves up a humdinger of a plot."

—*Essence*

THE PASTOR'S WIFE

"Billingsley has done it again. . . . A true page-turner."

—Urban-Reviews.com

I KNOW I'VE BEEN CHANGED

#1 *Dallas Morning News* bestseller

"Grabs you from the first page and never lets go. . . . Bravo!"

—Victoria Christopher Murray

"An excellent novel with a moral lesson to boot."

—Zane, *New York Times* bestselling author

"Emotionally charged . . . will not easily be forgotten."

—*Romantic Times* (4½ stars, Gold Medal, Top Pick)

"Compelling, heartfelt."

—*Booklist*

MY BROTHER'S KEEPER

"This is a keeper."

—*The Daily Oklahoman*

"Poignant, captivating, emotional, and intriguing. . . . A humorous and heart-wrenching look at how deep childhood issues can run."

—*The Mississippi Link*

Also by ReShonda Tate Billingsley

Sinners & Saints
(with Victoria Christopher Murray)
Say Amen, Again
A Good Man Is Hard to Find
Holy Rollers
The Devil Is a Lie
Can I Get a Witness?
The Pastor's Wife
Everybody Say Amen
I Know I've Been Changed
Help! I've Turned Into My Mother
Let the Church Say Amen
My Brother's Keeper
Have a Little Faith
(with Jacquelin Thomas, J. D. Mason, and Sandra Kitt)

And Check Out ReShonda's Young Adult Titles

Drama Queens
Caught Up in the Drama
Friends 'Til the End
Fair-Weather Friends
Getting Even
With Friends Like These
Blessings in Disguise
Nothing But Drama

the secret she kept

ReShonda Tate Billingsley

G

GALLERY BOOKS

New York London Toronto Sydney New Delhi

GALLERY BOOKS
A Division of Simon & Schuster, Inc.
1230 Avenue of the Americas
New York, NY 10020

First Gallery Books trade paperback edition July 2012

GALLERY BOOKS and colophon are registered trademarks of Simon & Schuster, Inc.

For information about special discounts for bulk purchases, please contact Simon & Schuster Special Sales at 1-866-506-1949 or business@simonandschuster.com.

The Simon & Schuster Speakers Bureau can bring authors to your live event. For more information or to book an event contact the Simon & Schuster Speakers Bureau at 1-866-248-3049 or visit our website at www.simonspeakers.com.

Manufactured in the United States of America

10 9 8 7 6 5 4 3 2 1

Library of Congress Cataloging-in-Publication Data

Billingsley, ReShonda Tate.
The secret she kept / ReShonda Tate Billingsley. — First Gallery Books trade paperback ed.
p. cm.
1. Dating (Social customs)—Fiction. 2. Married people—Fiction. 3. Women—Mental health—Fiction. 4. Mental illness—Fiction. I. Title.
PS3602.I445S43 2012
813'.6—dc23 2011053379

ISBN 978-1-4516-3965-0
ISBN 978-1-4516-3968-1 (ebook)

To Those Who Suffer

and

Those Who Suffer with Them

Prologue

"Crazy leaves clues."

Lance Kingston stared at his tell-it-like-it-is grandmother, wondering where in the world she got such outlandish sayings.

"You hear me, boy?" she repeated.

"Yeah, I heard you, Grandma, 'crazy leaves clues.'" Lance sighed heavily, reminding himself that his grandmother was eighty-six and had long ago lost that filter between her brain and her mouth. Nowadays, if she thought it, she said it. "But I'll ask you again, please don't call her crazy," Lance said wearily.

"Humph," his grandmother muttered, wobbling her petite frame over to the marble kitchen table in his mother's West Houston home. It had been an emotionally draining day, and Lance wanted nothing more than to just go home and try to get his head together about what had happened. But his mother had insisted that he shouldn't be alone. "Those clues were like a bread-crumb trail that led you straight to crazy, so I don't know what else you wanna call it," his grandmother said pointedly. "You can try to fancy it up all you want, but it is what it is." She eased down into one of the wooden chairs. "I told you, I spotted something about that girl from the beginning—the way her eyes darted all over the place sometimes, the way her family was too quick to get her married, the way she seemed to withdraw into herself." His grandmother shook her head as if she'd been warning him all along.

Lance loved his grandmother to death, but right about now he would give anything just to shut her up. This wasn't some stranger she was talking about. This was his wife. His pregnant wife. And Lance had just made the most difficult decision of his life.

Finally, his mother, Beverly, stepped in. "Ignore your grandmother. You know how she gets." Beverly walked over and gently squeezed his shoulder. He was grateful that she wasn't giving him a hard time as well. After all, she was no fan of his wife's either. "I know this is difficult on you, Son, but you did the right thing."

Lance looked up at his mother as she stood over him. Tears slowly filled his eyes. "I did the right thing? Really? Then why does it feel so wrong?"

She slid into the chair across from him at the kitchen table. "Because you love her and you love your unborn child." Beverly patted his hand gently. "But she's not well, sweetie. You've tried, Lord knows you've had the patience of Job. You didn't have any other choice. You're doing what you have to do."

"Mama, she said she hated me and wishes she had never met me." Lance's thoughts drifted back to just three hours ago. The absolute lowest he'd ever gone.

He had lied to persuade Tia to come with him. Told her they were going to another hospital for an early delivery because she was so ready to have the baby. If she'd been thinking clearly, she'd have known that wasn't possible. She'd have realized that just twenty-four hours earlier, she'd been trying to cut the baby out of her stomach herself. But that's the way their life had been for the past seven months—up and down. Moments of peace and moments of madness. It was why he no longer had a choice.

"So, why are we in here?" Tia had asked, looking around the doctor's office. "Why didn't they put us in a room?" She rubbed her stomach absently. She was confused enough to think they really were going in for a scheduled C-section. "I need this baby out."

Lance turned to face her. "You know I love you, right?"

The slack look on her face faded away, and she smiled lovingly at him. Her beautiful golden-brown hair framed her oval face, giving her an almost angelic look. She looked almost . . . sane. "Yeah, I know that."

It pained his heart for him to be in this awful position. Tia was a beautiful gift from God. His heart and his soul. But he, alone, couldn't heal what ailed her.

Lance stroked the side of her face. "But you're sick, baby."

Her brow narrowed crossly. "Lance, I know I have some episodes and it's been kinda rough on you. I even know sometimes I get a little mixed up, but really, I'm okay." She flashed another smile, this one forced.

He managed one of his own as he struggled not to tear up. "No, you're not, but we're going to get you better." Just then two orderlies marched into the room. The attending physician, Dr. Berry, stood behind them. Tia's eyes darted toward them, then back at her husband.

"What's going on, Lance?"

"I'm sorry, baby. These people are going to take care of you." Lance swallowed the lump in his throat as he tried desperately to keep his composure.

"Are you having me committed?" she asked in disbelief.

"It's for your own good."

He might as well have pushed the manic button. "You can't do that! I'm an attorney. I know my rights!" she yelled, jumping up from her seat. Lance swiftly pulled a piece of paper out of his jacket pocket. "I hate to tell you, but this is a court order allowing me to commit you. It's signed by the judge."

He held the paper out for her to inspect. Tia knocked the paper from his hand.

"I don't give a damn who signed it! You're not locking me up in some psych ward!"

All of her signs of wildness were blazing on full. "Please understand, it's just until you get better."

"You can't do this."

"I'm sorry, baby. Yes, I can."

The doctor motioned for the orderlies to move toward Tia. Just before they reached her, she flew into an uncontrollable rage. "Are you out of your mind?" She grabbed a glass-dome paperweight off the doctor's desk and flung it at him, hitting him in the chest. It hurt, but he hardly noticed because he was watching her carefully. "I can't believe you're doing this to me! You bastard!" she screamed. "I'm not staying here! I'm sick of you trying to run my life." She reached over and grabbed a letter opener off the doctor's desk, then lunged toward Lance.

"Tia, noooo!" he cried, diving out of the way just in time. The orderlies tried to tackle her, but as a former track star, Tia was quick on her feet and literally slipped through their arms and backed into the corner.

"Get away from me!" she shouted. She had a crazed look in her eyes. Lance knew the look all too well.

"Mrs. Kingston, you don't want to do this," Dr. Berry said, his voice calm.

"Go to hell!" she spat. "You don't know what I want."

Lance wished that he had listened when his mother had offered to come with him. He wished he had some support here. It was heartbreaking watching Tia so out of control.

Lance was about to say something when Tia reversed the letter opener and pointed it at her stomach.

"I should kill this baby. I'm gonna kill her. I swear, if you leave me here, I will kill her."

"Don't!" Lance cried, his arms outstretched toward his wife. His heart raced as Tia pressed the tip of the sharp opener into her skin. "That's our baby. You don't want to hurt her." A thousand thoughts were whirling through his head. "But, sweetie, this is why I want you to get better," he said slowly, his voice cracking. "Why you *have* to get better. She needs you. *We* need you. You don't want to hurt her."

This wasn't the first time Tia had threatened their child. The last time she'd done it, Lance had finally broken down. Admitted that his wife needed help. Luckily, she'd barely pierced the amniotic sac, but Lance knew he could not take any more chances. Too much was at stake.

As he watched his hysterical wife once again turn into someone he didn't know, Lance couldn't help but wonder how he'd ended up so low and if he'd ever be able to climb back out.

Chapter 1

Fourteen Months Earlier

"All this talk about how women want a good man is a bunch of bull."

Lance leaned back against the barstool. He was tired, frustrated, and ready to go home. Absolutely nothing about this happy hour was happy. The women here were all on the prowl, had been doing nothing but prowling.

"Come on, it can't be that bad," his assistant said, shaking her head as if she were disgusted with her boss. Ruby had insisted that he appear at this First Friday event on behalf of *Epiphany,* the magazine that he ran. At thirty-three, Lance was every woman's dream—a great job, great personality, handsome, caring, and committed. So why was he so lonely?

"All these women here and you don't want to give anyone

a chance," Ruby said. In addition to being a great assistant, she was the consummate matchmaker.

"Yeah, I tried that," Lance said, motioning to the woman at the end of the bar who had asked him to buy her a drink. Lance didn't like forward women, and that she had been able to tell that his shoes cost $400 was an immediate turnoff.

"I know what I think," Ruby said, leaning back on the bar. "I think you're still bitter about Crystal."

"Please don't go there with Crystal." That was his ex-girlfriend. They'd broken up nine months ago after he'd found out she had cheated on him. She'd begged for forgiveness, and he'd forgiven her. He just couldn't take her back. He prided himself on being faithful, and he expected any woman he was with to be the same.

"I know that's your girl," Lance replied, for what had to be the hundredth time. Ruby and Crystal had gotten close during the three years that Crystal and he had dated. "But remember, we agreed that in order for us to stay effective at work, Crystal is not to be discussed."

Ruby threw her hands up in surrender. "Sorry."

"Besides, I'm done with Crystal. I know she's trying to get back together, but I can't go back." That wasn't a lie. Crystal had begged, pleaded, and called for months. She'd even gone to his mother and grandmother—whom she knew from church—and had them side with her, but Lance didn't want to hear it. That part of his life was closed. He was ready to move on. The problem was that he hadn't found anyone worth moving on with.

Lance caught Ruby looking at him sideways, a small smirk on her face. "What?"

"I thought we weren't talking about Crystal."

He put up his hands. "We're not." He sipped the last of his drink, then set the glass back down. "Okay, boss lady, can I go now?" he playfully asked.

Ruby shook her head as if he were a lost cause. "Well, I guess you've done your civic duty, made your appearance for the magazine, so I guess it's okay for you to leave."

"Thank you very much." He stood. "It's amazing how you work for me, but it seems like I'm always taking orders from you." He gave Ruby an assessing look and, for a moment, found himself wondering what-if. *No,* he quickly shook that thought off. He wasn't about to cross a line and face a sexual harassment lawsuit. She was also the most effective assistant he'd ever had, and replacing her would be extremely difficult. He didn't need to mess up his work life by trying to jump-start his love life.

"Okay, I'll see you Monday," Ruby said, handing him a sheet of paper. "Here's your itinerary for the beginning of the week. Don't forget you have a meeting with the folks at Coca-Cola at nine a.m."

"I won't forget."

Lance headed out of the bar area and had just reached the lobby when he stopped in his tracks. He was mesmerized by the woman ahead of him heading toward the rotating glass doors. She was an absolute vision of loveliness in a short, off-the-shoulder, coral-colored dress. She wasn't too heavy or too thin.

Beautiful, thick, golden-brown hair flowed down her back. Her shapely legs were evidence of an athletic past.

"Now, that's someone I'd like to meet," he mumbled as he quickened his pace to catch up with her.

The woman had just exited the revolving door when her three-inch heel got stuck in a rubber strip and her bare foot popped out. Frustration filled her face, making Lance glad as he swooped down for the shoe.

"Here you go, Cinderella," he said, bowing as he handed it to her.

She narrowed her eyes and looked at him as if he were crazy.

Suddenly, Lance felt extremely corny. "Umm, I was just saying, you know, I was um, acting like your prince, you know, bringing your shoe as you fled before midnight." He pointed to the large grandfather clock on the bank building across the street. "Because, umm, it's eight fifty-eight, which is kinda close to midnight." If he could've disappeared at that moment, Lance would have. He cursed himself for that second glass of Cîroc he'd had.

"Thank you," she said sharply as she took her shoe and slipped it on her foot. She continued on to the parking lot.

"I'm sorry," Lance said, following her. "I didn't catch your name."

"That's because I didn't throw it," she said over her shoulder, not breaking her stride.

"Look, maybe I came across the wrong way." He was surprised at himself. He didn't usually chase women. He didn't have to. But something about this woman was pulling him with an irresistible force.

She stopped, took a deep breath, then turned around to face him. "Look, um . . ."

"Lance, Lance Kingston," he said with a smile.

"Look, Lance Kingston. Thanks a bunch for retrieving my shoe," she said curtly, "but I'm not interested in anything you're trying to sell. I'm not interested in being your latest conquest, nor am I interested in your lies about happily ever after."

Lance took a step back and held his hands up. "Whoa. I just asked for a name. I wasn't looking for a wife, or a bed partner. Just a name, and maybe a phone number," he added with a grin.

She lowered her eyes. "I'm sorry. I've had all kinds of lame come-ons tonight, and each of them ended with an offer of me in their bed."

"Well, I admit, I may have sorta come off a little lame."

"Sorta?" she said, finally breaking a smile.

"Okay, I was *real* lame, but seriously, I just thought you were beautiful and wanted to ask for your number to maybe take you for coffee or something. So let me try this again. I'm Lance. Nice to meet you." He extended his hand.

She hesitated, but then offered up her own. "I'm Tia, Tia Jiles."

She was even more beautiful up close. "Well, Tia Jiles, did you enjoy the event?"

"I was here working, just finished giving a speech."

"Oh, really? Here? With all these tipsy folks?"

She rolled her eyes. "Tell me about it. It's something new the First Friday organizers are trying to do. The idea is to incorporate productive seminars into the program. But obviously, these people here are only interested in drinking and flirting with the opposite sex." She sounded exasperated.

"So, what do you do?"

Suddenly she lost her smile. "Um, yeah, this," she said, motioning between the two of them, "not really trying to do this little get-to-know-each-other thing, so thanks again for the shoe." She nodded, then turned and walked on toward her car.

Lance was speechless as he watched her leave.

"You can give that one up, dude."

Lance turned to see one of the bartenders from inside the event. He had a cigarette in his hand and was obviously taking a smoke break.

"What do you mean?" Lance asked.

The bartender motioned in Tia's direction. "Meaning, every guy in town has tried to talk to her. She isn't having it."

"Why? Is she married?"

The bartender shook his head. "Nope, she's just not interested. At least that's what I heard her tell someone. No, make that, that's what she tells everyone," he added, laughing.

"Do you know her?" The bartender seemed so sure that Lance didn't have a chance of getting with her.

"She works for some law firm downtown."

"Which one?"

The bartender shrugged as he puffed on his cigarette. "Don't know. Only seen her in here a couple of times. But I saw her picture on a sign outside the room she was speaking in. Maybe it has her company name." He shook his head doubtfully. "But if I were you, I wouldn't waste my ti—"

Lance didn't let him finish but darted back inside. He looked around until he spotted the easel holding Tia's sign: JOIN TIA JILES, PRESIDENT OF PAY IT FORWARD, AS SHE DISCUSSES WAYS TO GIVE BACK TO THE COMMUNITY.

Lance was even more impressed. Pay It Forward was a well-known charitable organization that encouraged professionals to make time to make a difference in low-income communities. They'd been after him to become a member, but he never had the time.

He would make time now. Lance felt a tinge of guilt that it took a beautiful woman for him to find the desire to give back. But he was determined, and if that meant he had to put in some volunteer hours, he would—because Lance knew he wouldn't rest until Tia Jiles was his.

Chapter 2

Tia gazed out the window of her nineteenth-floor office. She hadn't been able to get her mind off the man she'd met at the hotel three days ago. She had so wanted to give him her number. She knew all about Lance Kingston. As CEO of *Epiphany* magazine, he'd be a perfect mentor for Pay It Forward, she had thought. She'd been trying to get him to join for the last two years, but he never returned her letters or e-mails. Seeing him in person, though, and seeing his instant attraction to her, had ignited a different kind of flame.

Tia pulled up the article she'd found about him in *USA Today* on her computer. Lance was a power broker, a mover and shaker. The article didn't have any personal information, but she assumed that a man that good-looking, and that successful, had a wife and kids at home.

Then why did he ask for your number?

"Probably because he's like most men, a no-good dog, trying to hook up with a woman on the side while his wife is slaving away at home," she mumbled. But Tia's gut feeling told her that wasn't the case.

She shook off the thought. Whatever this attraction was to Lance Kingston, Tia needed to get rid of it. She'd long ago resolved that she'd never be able to last in a healthy relationship with a man like that. She'd given up on that dream because every relationship she'd had, had fallen apart. So Tia concentrated on work. She was the first one to arrive at Anderson, Logan, and Smith and the last one to leave. She billed more hours than any of the other associates or even partners. And when she wasn't working here, she was volunteering with Pay It Forward or doing pro bono work.

"Knock, knock."

Tia looked up and smiled at her paralegal, Lucinda Rivera, standing in the doorway. As always, she looked ready to party. "Hey, girl, come on in," Tia said, closing the window on her computer.

Lucinda sashayed into the room, looking like a prettier version of Jennifer Lopez. Tia didn't know how she even moved in that supertight miniskirt, which was highly inappropriate for work. "Hey, *mamacita,* a couple of us are going for drinks after work. Just thought I'd see if you wanted to come," Lucinda said. Over the last two years she and Tia had become good friends. Even though they didn't have much in common outside of work, they shared a common drive to succeed. Each was determined to climb the ladder of success so that she never had to go back to the poverty of her childhood.

Tia smiled apologetically. "Now, you know—"

Lucinda held up her hand. "Let me guess, you're swamped with work?"

Tia chuckled. "Yep."

"Same story, different day." Lucinda plopped down in the maroon leather chair in front of Tia's desk. "Come on, all you do is freakin' work, then go home to an empty apartment, where you work some more. You barely even sleep. You need to loosen up. Let's get out and have some fun."

"On a Monday night?" Tia retorted.

"Yes, the party is whenever you make it!"

"For your information, I went out Friday."

Lucinda clicked her teeth. "Yeah, because you were conducting a workshop—for free, I might add—not because you wanted to enjoy yourself. Did you even have a drink?"

"I was working."

Lucinda groaned and gave Tia a pitying look. "Uggh, one of these days, I'm going to take you to Vegas and help you let your hair down."

"I know how to let my hair down," Tia protested. "And remember, I went to Miami with you for that conference last year. My letting my hair down and your letting your hair down are two totally different things."

"Okay, fine, whatever," Lucinda said sarcastically. "Far be it from me to try to get you to enjoy life."

A knock on the door stopped Tia from responding. Tia was

actually grateful for the interruption because Lucinda could be relentless.

"Come in," Tia said.

Tia's assistant, Vicki, stuck her head in the door. "Miss Jiles, there's someone here with a delivery for you."

"Okay," Tia replied, eyeing her friend in confusion.

Vicki stepped aside and let a short, stocky guy in a too tight FTD shirt pass her. He was carrying a huge bouquet of rainbow roses. It was the most beautiful bouquet Tia had ever seen.

"Wow," Lucinda marveled as she admired the roses. "Those are gorgeous."

"Are you sure those are for me?" Tia asked, standing up to inspect the flowers.

The deliveryman looked at the name on his paper. "Are you Tia Jiles?"

"I am."

"Then they're for you." He set the flowers down on her desk.

"Well, thank you," Tia said, grabbing a $10 bill out of her purse and handing it to the man.

He nodded his appreciation. "My pleasure. You ladies have a nice day."

"Okay, somebody has been holding out on me," Lucinda said, tapping a long, lacquered fingernail. "Maybe you're not such a workaholic after all since you're getting unique flowers and all." She sniffed them. "Dang, look at these colors. This isn't some run-of-the-mill dude. This is a first-class arrangement. Who sent them?"

"I have no idea who these are from," Tia said, impressed by the bouquet's bountiful size.

"Then, how about we see?" Lucinda plucked the card from the middle of the roses.

"Can I do that?" Tia held her hand out for Lucinda to give her the card.

"Naw, since you don't know who it is, I need to open it." Lucinda tore the card from the envelope and began reading. "'Would love to take you to dinner. Won't be so corny this time. Prince Charming.'" Lucinda looked at her friend with her mouth open wide. "Well, dang, you *are* holding out."

"Shut up." Tia snatched the card from her. Tia's stomach was actually fluttering.

"Who is Prince Charming?" Lucinda paused. "Umm, never mind." She pulled a business card out of the envelope. "Lance Kingston. Where have I heard that name before?"

"He runs *Epiphany* magazine," Tia said nonchalantly.

Lucinda's eyes widened in shock. "Whoa. Isn't that like the biggest magazine next to *People*? Where did you meet him?"

"At the First Friday event I went to. He asked for my phone number."

"And of course you gave it to him, right?"

"No." Tia tossed the card on her desk. "I am not entertaining that man. He's probably married with kids."

Lucinda shook her head. "Well, obviously, he's not happily married if he's trying to get your number."

"Please. You know that doesn't mean anything."

Lucinda went around behind the desk to Tia's computer. "Girl, what am I going to do with you?"

"What are you doing?" Tia asked as Lucinda sat down in Tia's seat.

"Just hang on." Lucinda started tapping on the keys.

"What are you doing?" Tia repeated.

Lucinda ignored her and kept tapping. She peered at the computer screen, reading. "Good," she said, snatching up Tia's cell phone. She handed it to Tia.

"What is this for?"

"Call him. And if you don't, I will."

"Lucinda, you're married."

"I don't care." She pointed at the computer. "He's single, no kids, a good job with benefits. Girl, it doesn't get any better than that. Trust me, I know," Lucinda said in a dig toward her husband, who had the baby mama from hell.

Tia hesitated. "You really think I should call him?"

"I don't think; I know." Lucinda stopped, then her tone changed as she studied her friend. "Why do you look, I don't know, terrified?"

Tia wrung her fingers together. "What if I really like him?"

"Then great."

"Even worse, what if he really likes me?" Just the idea of being with a man like Lance Kingston made Tia nervous. She took small, deep breaths—something she always did when anxiety started to overtake her.

"Even better." Lucinda looked as if she didn't understand what the problem was. "You want to find someone who loves you more than you love him."

Tia relaxed a little. "Okay, you and your shade-tree philosophy."

Lucinda headed toward the door. "Stop sweating the small stuff, girl. Call the man; go out with him. See where it goes. If you don't click, you don't go out with him again. And if you do, then you just snagged you a good one." As Lucinda left the office, her words lingered in the air.

Tia sighed heavily. She picked up the phone on her desk to call, but quickly slammed it down. No, as bad as she wanted to call, she had learned a long time ago that she was destined never to enjoy the love of a good man. Anytime she thought otherwise, her feelings ended up hurt because the man never stayed. That was her curse and she'd finally made peace with it, so there was no sense in even dreaming about a different outcome.

She gave the bouquet a last longing look, then turned to the case files stacked on her desk. At lunchtime she would give the bouquet away, just to get it out of her sight.

Chapter 3

Lance was sure the flowers would grab her. But so far he hadn't heard from the woman who had been consuming his thoughts for the last four days. He knew the flowers had been delivered because he checked first thing this morning. But she hadn't called and it was almost five o'clock. Maybe this was going to be a little harder than he thought.

Lance was so drawn to this woman. All the research he'd dug up on her just made him more intrigued. That she was so committed to her pro bono work, despite her hectic schedule, spoke volumes. He wondered how she was able to handle all the things she did.

Finding out the name of Tia's law firm had been easy, but he'd had to pull a few strings to get her direct line. He'd been hesitant to call because he didn't want to come across as a stalker. But he was tired of waiting and was ready to make the next move.

His heart raced as someone picked up on the other end of the line.

"This is Tia Jiles."

"Hi," he stammered.

"Hello," she replied curtly. "How may I help you?"

"Hi, it's Lance Kingston . . . from the other night."

She paused, and for a moment he thought she was going to demand to know how he got her direct number, but instead she said, "Thank you for the flowers."

"I didn't know if you liked them."

She took a deep breath. "I liked them a lot."

It was his turn to hesitate, but he was determined not to blow it this time. "Look, we're both busy people, so let me get straight to the point. I was attracted to you from the first moment I saw you and I would love to take you to dinner. I'm not asking for anything more than dinner. You decide where you want to go from there."

Silence filled the phone; then suddenly she said, "Okay."

A smile spread across his face. "Okay?"

"Yes, when?" He could tell she was apprehensive, but he was determined to win her over.

"Tomorrow night," he said, hoping he didn't appear desperate.

"Then tomorrow night it is."

They exchanged information and made plans to meet at a Galleria-area restaurant.

After they hung up, Lance was on cloud nine. He hadn't felt so giddy since his first date with Crystal. No, not going there. He shook away any thoughts of the woman who broke his heart. He had plenty to do. He returned to reviewing the budget report his CFO had submitted. After a few minutes, his assistant came on the intercom.

"Mr. Kingston, your mother is on line one."

"Thank you, Ruby," Lance said, picking up the phone. "Hello, Mother."

"How is my darling son?"

"I'm fine." He leaned back in his chair. "How are you today? I was gonna call you to see how you were holding up."

His mother inhaled noisily and he could tell she'd been crying. "I'm okay. Mama's here trying to keep me busy so I don't think about your brother. She was supposed to go on an outing with the senior center, but she thinks I don't need to be alone, so she's here getting on my nerves."

Lance's heart went out to his mother. Today marked the two-year anniversary of his brother's death. He'd died after being shot by some crazed drug addict who was robbing a convenience store. Paul had been studying for the bar exam and had just gone into the store to get an energy drink. As the baby of the family, Paul was admired, respected, and loved by everyone, so his death had been devastating—for both Lance and his mother. Lance's younger sister, Patricia, lived in London, where she worked as a singer in some nightclub. So the burden of checking on his mother and grandmother fell entirely on Lance.

"Well, tell Gram I'll be by after work, so I'll take over from there."

"Please," his mother said, tsking, "I don't need babysitting. I'll be fine. Besides," she said, her voice turning softer, "Crystal is coming by."

Lance shot up in his chair. "Excuse me? Why is my ex coming over there?"

"Don't start. Just because you broke up with Crystal doesn't mean she can't check on me. She said she wanted to come bring me dinner because she knew today would be difficult."

Give me a break, Lance thought. While he had no doubt Crystal cared for his mom, and he knew that she'd loved Paul, she had to have an ulterior motive for going over to his mother's. She probably knew Lance would visit and was just using that as an excuse to see him since he had been refusing to take her calls.

"So, are you still gonna come? I think that would be nice. You, me, and Crystal, like old times."

Lance knew he needed to nip this notion in the bud—once and for all. He and Crystal were history, especially if tomorrow night worked out with Tia the way he hoped. "Mother, there will be no revisiting of old times. Crystal and I are over, okay? I appreciate her coming to see you, but if that's the case, I'll just come by tomorrow."

"Lance, why are you being so difficult? Crystal is a sweet girl. And I want some grandkids." He envisioned his mother sitting in her recliner, lamenting that she still didn't have grandchildren. She'd been working on him since he started dating Crystal. That's because his sister had made it clear that she had no desire to have children.

The thought of Tia popped into his head. "Who knows, maybe you'll still get them."

She paused. "Lance Lawrence Kingston, are you seeing someone else?"

"Not really, Mom. I just met someone and I'm excited about where it's headed."

She started firing off questions. "Who is she? Who are her people? When do I get to meet her?"

"Hold your horses, Ma. I just met her myself. If we hit it off, I'll let you know. And I promise, you'll be the first to meet her."

"Well, I don't care, anyway. I want my grandbabies to be with Crystal."

"Then you'd better go adopt you another son and have him get with her because that's not gonna happen on this end." He immediately regretted his words, hoping his quip didn't send her spinning back to memories of Paul.

"Fine," she huffed. "Well, I want to meet this girl."

Lance was grateful he hadn't set her off. "In due time, Ma. We haven't even been out on a date yet."

"What? Then why are we even talking about her? For all you know, she could be a psycho serial killer."

Lance laughed. "Bye, Ma. I gotta get back to work. I'll check on you later. Love you."

Lance hung up before his mother got to rambling some more. He jimmied his mouse to take his computer off sleep mode. The article he'd been reading about Houston's top attorneys popped back on the screen. Lance gazed at the photo of Tia, then picked up the piece of paper he'd written Tia's number on. No, this woman was beautiful, a distinguished attorney and dedicated community servant. The only thing killer about her was her body. And Lance couldn't wait to get to know everything about her.

Chapter 4

Tia's heart broke at the sight of the elderly woman sitting in the conference room, wringing her dingy lace handkerchief as she slowly rocked back and forth. She had been muttering the Lord's Prayer the whole time Tia had been on the phone.

"Mrs. Bailey, I'm sorry, Mr. Wynn still won't budge, so it looks like we're going to trial," Tia solemnly said.

Mrs. Bailey's shoulders sank in defeat. They'd been hoping that Tia's last-ditch efforts to resolve the case prior to today's hearing would be successful.

"Jesus, take the wheel," the woman muttered. She looked every bit of her eighty-three years. Fighting a company bent on taking her home had taken its toll. The sad part was, she was being threatened with eviction because of a $790 tax bill that Mrs. Bailey wasn't even aware she owed. Her husband had taken care of all the bills, and when he died last year, her nephew took over. But a greedy developer paid off her nephew to get him to "overlook" that tax bill, and before Mrs. Bailey knew anything, the house she'd lived in for forty years had been auctioned off. The developer that purchased the home, Jeremy Wynn, had given Mrs. Bailey thirty days to vacate the property. Her church member had told Tia about the case, and she'd taken it pro bono, even though real estate law wasn't her area of expertise, because no other attorney wanted to go against the powerful developer, especially not for free. Tia had tried to reason with Mr. Wynn, but he had major plans for an upscale shopping center and community development in the area, which was undergoing some serious gentrification, so the only thing he wanted to hear was what date Mrs. Bailey would be out so he could demolish the home. Tia had managed to get an injunction, but only for ninety days. The only hope they had left lay with a sympathetic judge.

Tia's buzzing cell phone snapped her out of her thoughts. *Looking forward to tonite. Lance.* She felt a small flutter at the sight of his text. She was looking forward to tonight as well. But right now she had to focus all of her attention on Mrs. Bailey.

"So now what?" the old woman asked.

"So, now we go to court," Tia said, rising from her seat. "But I have to ask again. Won't you please reconsider and allow a trial by jury?" Tia thought a jury would be more sympathetic to Mrs. Bailey, but the elderly woman was horrified at the idea of going to court and "letting the whole world know" her business.

"Absolutely not! My husband would turn over in his grave

six times if I let all them folks know what my nephew Kenny did."

"But—"

"No. You said yourself that a judge can make the decision just like the jury. The less people that know my business, the better. The judge is bound by law not to tell folks my business. All them folks on the jury get to talking, then everybody at my church know what's going on."

Tia sighed heavily. This woman was about to lose the house she loved, and she was worried about what folks would think about her scandalous nephew. Tia immediately thought of her own mother and her desire to keep "family business" private. Just as with Tia's mother, any attempts to convince Mrs. Bailey to change her mind had proved futile.

"Okay, Mrs. Bailey."

Mrs. Bailey nodded in satisfaction, even though her eyes betrayed how worried she was. "Tia, am I gonna lose my house?" Her voice cracked. "I raised all six of my babies in that house. I even raised that no-good nephew of mine." Kenny had tearfully admitted what he'd done, claiming the money was too good to pass up, but now he was long gone, off to California with no way for anyone to get in contact with him, and couldn't therefore back up his confession in court.

Tia walked over and took Mrs. Bailey's hands. "I promise you, I'm going to do everything I can to keep that from happening."

Deep lines filled her client's face. Her stringy gray hair was pulled back into a long plait and tucked underneath a black pillbox hat. She'd donned her Sunday best for this court appearance, an appearance Tia had hoped wouldn't have to happen. Tia had spent many hours on this case, becoming more incensed with everything she dug up. She'd found thousands of homes on sale because of back taxes, a large majority of them seniors'. She'd even found several programs that could provide property tax relief for seniors, but it was too late in this case because the home had already been sold.

"I hate I can't pay you," Mrs. Bailey softly said. "I know you're a busy woman."

"Would you stop with that," Tia admonished. "I told you. What I do at the law firm is to pay the bills. My heart lies with helping people like you who have been wronged."

Mrs. Bailey pursed her lips, showing a row of vertical hashes, as Tia released her hands. "I sure have been wronged. That Mr. Wynn is an evil, evil man."

Tia motioned toward the door. "Let's go to the court and pray that the judge agrees."

Chapter 5

Tia stared at the five-by-seven law school graduation photo of herself behind a large podium. She'd placed it next to her law degree from the University of Texas, her undergraduate degree from Rice University, and her honor's commendation from the president of the United States. The photo appeared to be mocking her.

So, you really think you have a shot with someone like Lance Kingston?

"Yes," she muttered.

How many times have you tried this?

"Shut up," Tia said, trying to quiet the voice that always crept up in moments of doubt. It was trying to convince her that she wasn't capable of maintaining a relationship.

"It's just a freakin' date." She laid the picture flat. She could do this. She could go out with Lance and have a great time.

She'd been given a break in Mrs. Bailey's case because the judge had fallen ill, so the hearing had been rescheduled. That actually gave Tia time to go find something to wear on her date tonight, and she'd been delighted when she found the perfect plum maxidress that accentuated her size 8 frame in all the right places.

Tia made her way into the bathroom and began removing the clips that were holding her hair up in pin curls. Her eye fell on the words written across the top of her bathroom mirror: *I Am Worthy.* She'd written that in lipstick to remind herself whenever her dark angel entered her mind to try to tell her otherwise.

I can do all things through Christ, who strengthens me. Her uncle Leo had written that on her mirror when he'd come to fix her leaky bathroom faucet. She was glad she'd obeyed her first impulse to leave it, because just seeing that some days gave her the strength she needed to get through the day.

"Lord, please let this be the start of something fresh . . . something normal," she muttered.

Tia had just finished applying her makeup and was about to put on her dress when she glanced at the medicine cabinet.

The Lord helps those who help themselves, she thought. She reached into the cabinet and grabbed a small, brown pill bottle. Tia popped it open, bemoaned that only one pill was left, then popped it in her mouth,

Thirty minutes later, she walked into the Brazilian steak house Fogo de Chão. She smiled when Lance waved to her from a corner, took a deep breath, then walked his way.

"Hi," she said, approaching him. He looked even better than she remembered. She took in his smooth complexion, perfectly cut hair, and immaculate caramel linen, button-down shirt and khaki slacks. Everything about this man was on point.

"Hi, beautiful," he replied, standing to greet her. He gently hugged her, sending a bolt of electricity through her body.

It's just a date, she reminded herself as she sat down. That allowed her to relax, and after ordering drinks and their meal, they made small talk about everything from world affairs to his demanding job.

"So how did the case you were telling me about go today?" he asked.

"It was rescheduled." She took a sip of the pomegranate martini the waiter had set in front of her. "The judge suddenly became sick. It's a shame because I know my client is really ready to get some resolution to this case."

"So, you seem like you like fighting for the underdog."

She shrugged as if it were no big deal. "If I don't, who will?"

"So, you do all that, your regular job, *and* you work with Pay It Forward? Man, I thought I was busy."

"I guess I do fill up my day. What makes my life easier is having some great people working with me on the foundation. Unfortunately, one of the biggest challenges we have is getting people to join our mentor program." She gave him a pointed smile.

"Guilty as charged. Honestly, I just didn't think I had time."

"Most people think that. But you'd be amazed at what a difference you could make by just giving an hour to those kids."

"Then, I guess I'll sign up. I admit that it took a minute, but the good news is, I'm ready now."

"That's all we ask."

By that time the waiter had brought out their food, and since the tableside service was continuous, they spent the rest of the evening on lighthearted subjects. They steered clear of any personal issues, such as past relationships. She didn't want to answer the *Why don't you have a man?* question. She respected that Lance kept it strictly friendly. If not for the longing in his eyes, she would've questioned if he was even interested in her that way. But the way he acted, as if she were the loveliest creature on the planet, left little doubt as to his true feelings.

By the end of the evening, they felt like old friends.

"I really do hate to bring this to an end," she began.

"Let me guess, you have to go deliver meals to the homeless in the morning?"

"Are you being funny?" She raised an eyebrow.

"No, I'm kidding," he said apologetically. "It's just that, well, what is there not to like about you?"

Relax, she reminded herself again. "If only you knew." She laughed.

"No, I'm serious, you're ambitious, intelligent, beautiful, and smart. You're like an all-around woman."

"Trust me, I have my issues."

"Let me guess, you like to shop."

"What woman doesn't?" She giggled. "I do like shopping. I could do it every single day. Well, except for Monday nights."

"Why, what's on Monday nights?"

"Monday night football, baby," she said as if that were a no-brainer. "I'm a Pittsburgh fan, but I love watching all the teams, so I don't miss a game."

Lance's mouth dropped open. "Oh my God, I've died and gone to heaven. And you like football? Wait, let me brace myself," he joked as he gripped the edge of the table, "do you like sex?"

She grinned. This was the first time the conversation had gone in that direction. "Nah."

He looked deflated.

"I love it."

He grabbed his heart as if he were feigning a heart attack. "Thank you, Jesus," he mumbled.

"But I like to wait until the time is right," she quickly added.

He put all joking aside. "And I'd be willing to wait for you," he said, erasing all doubt about his interest in her.

They enjoyed more chatter until they looked up and discovered they were the last ones in the restaurant.

"Is it just me or are those busboys over there giving us the evil eye?" Lance said, motioning toward two short men with scowls, standing near the kitchen glaring at them.

"I guess we are preventing them from getting off from work."

Lance signed the check that the waiter had set in front of them an hour and a half ago. They gave apologies as they made their way toward the entrance. They had barely stepped foot outside when the hostess locked the door behind them.

"I guess we were holding everything up," Tia said, fidgeting with her purse. She really didn't want this night to end, but she did have to get up early and work on her copyright case.

"When you're in the midst of stimulating conversation, you lose track of time," Lance said. "I hate to see this evening end, but it is late and I don't like keeping a lady out. How far do you live from here? I mean, I could follow you back home."

She eyed him suspiciously. "No, thank you. I think I can make it," she said, softening her words with a slight smile.

"I didn't mean anything by that. I just wanted to make sure you got home safely."

"How about I call you and let you know I made it home safely?" She leaned in and kissed him on the cheek. "I had a great time, Lance."

"I did, too, and I hope we can do it again."

"Most definitely."

Tia all but floated back to her car. Not only had she shone in this date, she'd opened the door to other possibilities. So far, nothing had gone wrong.

Chapter 6

It was hard to describe the feelings whirling around inside her. Tia hadn't felt this way in years. Not even with Gavin, who, like every other man she'd loved, had run when the going got rough. She'd had a few incidents where her temper got the best of her, and an "episode" at a friend's party had pushed Gavin over the edge. Tia had thought he was flirting with another woman and she'd flipped out, dousing the woman with punch and going ballistic on Gavin. Tia wasn't the jealous type, so the whole incident had been out of character for her. She'd come clean about her issues (although she'd downplayed the problem) in hopes of getting him back, but learning about them had terrified him even more, and he quickly dumped her after that.

"All right, *mamacita,*" Lucinda said. "What are you wearing?"

The Secret She Kept

Tia had almost regretted telling Lucinda about her date because Lucinda was making her anxiety worse. Tia wanted to make a good impression with Lance because she was meeting his best friend, Brian. This would be their fifth date in less than two weeks, and already Lance was introducing her to his friends. Everything was moving too fast. But Lucinda had convinced her to sit back, relax, and enjoy the ride.

"So, are you sure I shouldn't wear this one?" Tia said, holding up a beige peasant blouse. "I mean, I think with my skinny jeans and these heels, that's still sexy."

"Ahhh," Lucinda said, wiggling as she held a chocolate wrap dress up to her body. "This is so much more sexy." She started doing a salsa across the room. "It's cut just low enough in the front to toy with his imagination, but not enough to be considered a loose woman. Although there's nothing wrong with being loose." She winked.

"Gimme that." Tia playfully snatched the dress. "So, you really think I should do this one?" she said, holding the dress up and surveying herself in the mirror.

Lucinda stepped up behind her. "I don't think. I know. You're not trying to turn his friend on or anything, but you want him to say, 'Man, she's hot.' Now, stop trying to procrastinate. You only have thirty minutes before he gets here."

Tia's smile drained away as she turned to face her friend. "Lucinda, you don't think that I should . . . slow down?" Lucinda was a good friend, but she didn't know *everything* about Tia. No one did. At least not outside of the family. Sometimes

Tia wished that she could talk to someone, anyone besides her family. But her mother had been adamant that family business was to stay family business.

"I told you, just relax and see where it goes. Now, tell me more about this *papi,*" Lucinda said, lying down across the bed. She propped her hands up under her chin like a teenager waiting on some good gossip. "From what you've said, Lance sure seems to be taken with you."

"I'm taken with him. We talk on the phone three to four times a day. It's crazy. I mean, I've never been involved with someone where it moved so fast."

"Well, all I know is, I've never seen you smiling this much."

Tia released a happy sigh. "Yeah, it feels good to be wanted."

Lucinda tsked. "Oh, plenty of men wanted you. This is just the first time you wanted someone back."

"Yeah, I've been burned before, and after you've been burned a few times, you tend to stay out of the fire."

"Girl, please. You know you have to sleep with a few frogs to get to your prince."

All the chitchat was starting to wear on Tia. "Okay, and on that note . . ." Tia laughed as she pulled Lucinda off the bed and pushed her toward the door.

"You're putting me out? I don't get to stay and meet him? No fair, you're going to meet his friend. Why can't he meet yours?"

"His friend got us tickets to the Sade concert, so that's why I'm meeting him. Besides, I don't need you embarrassing me."

Lucinda feigned an innocent look. "Who, me?"

"Yes, you. I'll let you know how it works out." Tia pointed to the door. "Now, would you go?"

"Okay, just use me and kick me to the curb," Lucinda said, throwing her purse over her shoulder. "Call me when you get home tonight. I expect a full report. Unless of course, he spends the night. In that case, I'll expect a full report in the morning."

"He is not spending the night," Tia protested.

Lucinda shook her head. "What in the world am I going to do with you? He needs to spend the night. That's what's wrong with you. You need some—"

"Bye, Lucinda." Tia pushed her friend out the door.

Tia laughed as she made her way back to her bedroom. Lucinda was the closest thing to a best friend that she had, but Tia still wasn't 100 percent comfortable sharing everything with her, so she wasn't quite ready to bring Lucinda into her relationship with Lance. Not when she wasn't sure how long the relationship would last.

Tia was putting some finishing touches on her makeup when the doorbell rang. She made her way back to the front, trying to contain her excitement.

"Just what I like, a man who's prompt," Tia said, opening the door.

"Well, dang, look at my cuz."

Tia groaned at the sight of her trampy cousin, Bobbi Jo. Why in the world hadn't she checked the peephole? She hadn't been thinking clearly. Because if she had known Bobbi Jo was on the other side of that door, she definitely wouldn't have opened it.

"Where you going, Cuz, looking all fancy?" Bobbi Jo asked, inviting herself in.

"Out. On a date."

"Oooh, I hope it's with a man."

"Bobbi Jo, what do you want?" Tia said, ignoring her cousin's dig.

Although they were only two years apart in age, they were twenty light-years apart in maturity. Bobbi Jo was footloose and fancy free. Tia had more ambition and intelligence in her left pinkie than Bobbi Jo had in her entire body. Not only that, Bobbi Jo was prone to pushing Tia's buttons. The less she was around her cousin, the better it was for everyone.

"Again, what do you want? I have to go."

"Yeah, on your date." Bobbi Jo plopped down on her sofa. The last thing Tia wanted was Bobbi Jo lounging around when Lance arrived. Lance didn't seem like her type, but Ronald hadn't seemed like her type either, and Tia had come home to find Bobbi Jo straddling him. They'd sworn nothing had happened and it was just the vodka both of them had been drinking. Luckily, Tia and Ronald hadn't been going out for long, so she wasn't completely heartbroken. But it still hurt. That had actually been the second time Bobbi Jo had messed with one of Tia's boyfriends. The first had been back in high school. Tia would've preferred to cut Bobbi Jo loose altogether, but since she lived with Tia's mother, she didn't have much choice.

"Bobbi Jo . . ."

"Chill, Cuz, I was just checking on you. You know, making

sure everything is fine." She looked around the room, then smiled. "I see you don't have any sharp objects around here."

"Shut up, Bobbi Jo."

Her cousin laughed. "I'm just messing with you. I was actually visiting this hot little thang I'm messing around with, and he lives nearby. So I broke him off a little piece and on my way home decided to check in on you."

"Well, you've checked, so now you can go."

"Has anyone ever told you you're rude?"

Tia huffed. Bobbi Jo was going to completely ruin her mood. "Seriously, my date will be here any minute."

"I want to meet him."

"No!"

"Why not? Is there something about him that you don't want me to know about?"

"Because I said no."

"Fine." Bobbi Jo rolled her eyes as if she were really hurt. "But let me hold fifty dollars."

"I don't loan money to people who don't have jobs."

"Girl, haven't you heard? We're in a recession. Nobody has jobs. But I'm supposed to start doing hair at this shop on the north side in two weeks, so I'll pay you back."

Even if Bobbi Jo did start working, Tia doubted that she would ever pay her back. But Tia decided that the sooner she gave her cousin the money, the sooner she'd leave. Besides, if Tia didn't give it to her, she'd just go to Tia's mom, Virginia, taking what little money she had. "Fine, Bobbi Jo," Tia said, stomping over to her purse. "I only have forty dollars cash."

Bobbi Jo held her hand out. "I'll take it. You can just owe me the other ten."

Tia handed her cousin the money and shuttled her to the door. "Bye, Bobbi Jo," she said, swinging the door open.

"Bye, Cuz. Thanks for the dough. I can't wait to meet your . . ." Her words trailed off as Lance walked up.

"Hello," Lance said.

"Helllllloooo to you, too," Bobbi Jo said, slithering toward him.

He immediately looked uneasy, and Tia stepped in between them, took his hand, and pulled him away.

"Hey, Lance. This is my cousin Bobbi Jo. She was just leaving."

"Nice to meet you, Bobbi Jo."

"It could be," Bobbi Jo replied seductively.

"Good-bye, Bobbi Jo," Tia said, pushing her cousin out the door.

"Fine, I can take a hint," Bobbi Jo said.

"It's not a hint. Good-bye."

Bobbi Jo laughed as she headed down the stairs. "He's a hottie, Cuz. Hope he sticks around." Tia wanted to hurl a brick at her cousin when she added, "But he probably won't," and left a trail of laughter in the air.

"What did she mean by that?" Lance asked as he followed Tia inside.

"Just ignore my cousin," Tia said uneasily. "She loves getting under my skin." Tia hoped he didn't ask any more questions. She'd told him a little about her past, but the last thing she wanted was for him to start questioning why her men never stuck around.

Lance pulled her into a tight bear hug. "I'd love to get under your skin, too."

She smiled coyly as she wiggled loose. "And in due time you will." Lance just didn't know. She wanted him so bad, but she didn't want to turn him off by jumping into bed too soon. Lance was the kind of man she'd always dreamed of, so Tia wanted to do everything right—take her time with sex, get her issues under control—anything she could to make him fall head over heels in love with her.

"Let me turn out the lights in my room, then I'll be ready to go," she said.

"I'll be right here, in this very spot, waiting," he joked, pointing at the floor.

Tia smiled again, then pinched herself on the way to her bedroom, just to make sure he was for real. Why should she worry when everything was going so right?

Chapter 7

This could not possibly be happening. Lance groaned as he watched Crystal sashay his way. He'd almost passed on the Sade concert because he knew Crystal loved Sade. But then, Tia had mentioned how she wanted to see the concert and Brian had managed to snag prime tickets. Ultimately, Lance's desire to please Tia overrode his fear of bumping into Crystal. After all, Lance had told himself, the Toyota Center was huge and the chances of his bumping into Crystal were slim. Well, slim had just showed up at his door.

"Hello, Lance." Crystal seemed just as shocked to see him. A nerdy man standing next to her, upon noticing Lance, quickly eased his hand into Crystal's, as if staking his claim. Crystal just as quickly eased her hand away, and Lance couldn't help but smile. Crystal had proclaimed so many times that she had no desire to see anyone else because she was still so in love with him.

"Hi, Crystal," Lance said, gently pulling Tia toward him. He hadn't meant to hug her, but he was staking his claim as well. "Tia, this is Crystal. Crystal, this is my girlfriend, Tia."

Crystal cringed.

Tia glanced at Lance, surprised by the "girlfriend" comment, but she merely said to Crystal, "Hi, nice to meet you," as she extended her hand.

Crystal hesitated a beat too long, but then she shook Tia's hand. "Nice to meet you, too," she said curtly.

"So you decided to come to the concert?" Lance asked.

"Of course," Crystal said, forcing a smile. "You know how much I love Sade, so it's no surprise that I'm here."

Lance nodded and they stood awkwardly for a few long seconds before Crystal's date stepped up.

"Hi, I'm Francis. I'm Crystal's—"

"Friend," Crystal interjected. Francis gave her a sidelong glance, not pleased with her interruption. "But, umm, we gotta get going," she quickly added. "Good to see you, Lance." She pulled Francis away without bothering to say anything else to Tia.

"Well, I'm going to assume that's your ex-girlfriend Crystal," Tia said after they were gone.

"What gave it away?" Lance joked.

"Oh, the daggers she shot at me were a slight indication."

Lance was glad that Tia could take Crystal's rudeness in stride. Yet another reason for him to fall for this woman. She wasn't the jealous type.

"Come on, babe. It's been a long night. Let me get you home," Lance said, taking Tia's hand.

Thirty minutes later, they sat in Tia's living room, sipping Moscato. It was the perfect ending to a perfect evening.

They made small talk while the sounds of Luther Vandross drifted in the background. Tia gave Lance her assessment of Brian—she loved his sense of humor and admired their bond—before finally opening up about her family. She told Lance all about her super-religious mother and uncle and her crazy cousins. He'd sympathized when she talked about their struggles growing up and laughed at some of the shenanigans of her family.

Lance refilled their glasses, then said, "So, you mentioned that your father died when you were a teenager. How did he die?"

Tia grew forlorn as she began playing with the rim of her glass.

"Hey, I'm sorry, if it's something you'd rather not talk about . . ."

"Nah, it's just that, well, I was a daddy's girl for the longest. You see, my dad, well, he just kinda flipped out one day."

"What do you mean, 'flipped out'?"

"He was injured in the Vietnam War before I was born, but my mom says when he came back, he couldn't find work and he got really depressed. When she got pregnant with me, she said things just got worse. He would disappear for days on end, then come back like nothing was wrong. He finally did find work, so everything was good for a while, but then he started abusing drugs." Tia paused, inhaling deeply as if she were trying to gather the strength to continue. "To put it bluntly, those turned him into this abusive monster. My mother finally left him, and he committed suicide when I was sixteen. I think he was just heartbroken and tired of being depressed."

"Wow, I'm sorry to hear that."

A sad smile crossed her face. "Enough about my father. Why don't you tell me about yours? All you ever talk about is your mom and grandmother."

Lance's mood immediately turned sour. He frowned as he sat back on the sofa.

"Whoa, did I hit a sore spot?"

"I'm sorry. It's just that on the list of people I respect the least in this world, my father is at the top." Lance stopped himself. Should he really continue? He hated talking about his father. He hated rehashing the pain he had felt when his father came into his bedroom, declared that this "whole family thing" was more than he bargained for, and left. "My dad abandoned us when I was nine," Lance said, deciding to be open with Tia since she'd just shared her painful past. "He just decided he didn't like being tied down, so he left."

"What do you mean, he left?"

"Just what I said. Disappeared. Vanished. Finito."

"So where is he?"

Lance shrugged. He tried to act nonchalant, but his anger at his father still left him shaking. "I don't know. Don't even know if he's dead or alive. I heard from him when I was nineteen, but haven't heard from him since." Lance didn't like the word *hate,* but he couldn't think of another word to describe the emotion he felt for his father. "My mom's family had money, so it's not like we struggled financially, but my father's abandonment tore at her soul and it messed all us kids up for a long time as well. My sister swore she'd never get married because she'd never give a man a chance to leave her."

Tia gently caressed his arm. "I'm sorry, Lance."

Lance gazed at her fixedly. "Because my father ran out on us, I promised myself I would never do that to the woman I was with. When I'm with a woman, I'm in for the long haul."

Tia hesitated. "Then what happened with Crystal?"

Lance bit down on his bottom lip. "Crystal cheated on me. That's the reason I left her. I found out she slept with an old high school boyfriend. She lied and told me she was going out with her girls, but instead she shacked up in a hotel with him. She actually went to the hotel where Brian's then-girlfriend was working. She told Brian, who immediately called me. I guess I don't have to say how upset I was. I came over and waited all night for Crystal to come downstairs. They did the next morning. Needless to say, she was shocked. He, on the other hand, didn't even know about me." A flash of how wounded Lance was flashed across his face. "That's the reason I could never take Crystal back."

He sighed as if the conversation were draining him, but he didn't stop talking.

"Before my father left, he spent his days seeing how many women he could bed. Oh, my parents tried to keep it from me, but I heard the late-night fights when he came home reeking of another woman's scent. So, I detest a cheater, and when Crystal did that, I saw her in a whole new light. A light that is forever tainted for me."

Tia held up her wineglass.

"What's the toast for?" Lance said, holding his glass up as well.

"To Crystal. Because if she hadn't cheated, I wouldn't be here and there's no place that I'd rather be."

They both smiled as they clinked glasses before leaning in for a long and passionate kiss.

Chapter 8

"We're gonna win this." Tia wished that she felt as confident as she tried to sound. But the truth was, Jeremy Wynn had hired an entire team of lawyers, and they all sat at the defense table, buried under mounds of paperwork. As Tia sat next to a weeping Mrs. Bailey, there was no doubt who was the underdog here.

Still, Tia refused to let them intimidate her. Mr. Wynn hadn't even shown up. This case was of so little importance to him that he didn't bother making time to appear in court. He had left all the dirty work to his attorneys.

Tia reached into her briefcase and gently ran her hand over a rock she kept there. Uncle Leo had given it to her on her last pro bono case, another case of a little guy against a big guy. He'd told her that she was David and the corporation she was battling was Goliath. The comparison was a little clichéd, but she had won the case and she'd decided to hold on to the rock. Now she was hoping for the same results.

"All rise," the bailiff said as the judge walked into the courtroom.

Tia closed her briefcase and stood, helping Mrs. Bailey up as well.

"You may be seated," the judge said as he took his seat on the bench.

After some preliminary questions, the judge said, "Miss Jiles, you may call your first witness."

"Yes, Your Honor, I'd like to call to the stand Mrs. Naomi Bailey."

Mrs. Bailey hoisted herself to her feet and began walking to the bench. Her small frame looked weak and feeble, and she was moving at a snail's pace. She wasn't doing it on purpose, but Tia could only hope that her frailty would work to their benefit. Tia had been hesitant about putting Mrs. Bailey on the stand because she didn't want the defense to eat her alive. The poor old woman had been through enough. But Mrs. Bailey had been adamant that the judge hear her side directly from her.

The bailiff pulled out a Bible, but Mrs. Bailey reached in her purse. "That's okay, I got my own," she said, pulling out a tattered King James version.

The bailiff took her Bible amid a few chuckles in the courtroom. "Please place your right hand on the Bible," he said. "Do you swear to tell the truth, the whole truth, and nothing but the truth, so help you God?"

"I always tell the truth," Mrs. Bailey proclaimed.

"Mrs. Bailey, just answer the question, yes or no," the judge admonished.

"Yes."

Out of the corner of her eye, Tia noticed Lance walk into the courtroom and slide into the back row. She felt good that he'd taken time out of his busy schedule to come support her in the trial. He noticed her looking his way and gave her an inconspicuous thumbs-up.

"Mrs. Bailey," Tia said, turning back to her client. "Let's jump right in and start with your home. When did you move into it?"

"January third, 1972," she said proudly.

"And how did you get the money for it?"

Mrs. Bailey sat up straight, looking Tia directly in the eye. "My husband, God rest his soul, he worked three jobs. And I cleaned. We did what we had to do to raise the money to have a house for our kids."

"How many kids did you have at the time?"

"We had two and we were living with my sister, Betty, till we got up enough money for Senior to buy us a house."

"By *Senior* you are referring to your husband, Walter Bailey, Sr., correct?"

Mrs. Bailey nodded. "That is correct."

Tia questioned Mrs. Bailey about everything from her family to her moving into the house.

"How much does this home mean to you?" Tia asked after an hour of questioning. Surprisingly, the defense hadn't interrupted much.

"It means the world. People say it's just a material possession, but it's not. I birthed six of my eight babies there. My husband died right there. It's where I wanna die."

Tia allowed Mrs. Bailey's words to sink in before saying, "Thank you, Mrs. Bailey. Your Honor, I pass the witness."

"Mrs. Bailey," a tall, red-haired attorney in a tailor-made suit began, "are you aware of what a property tax is?"

"Well, yeah. It's taxes paid to the city for your home."

"Yes, that is correct." He walked around to stand directly in front of her. "Do you understand that every homeowner has a responsibility to pay those taxes?"

"I do, but Senior took on—"

"I didn't ask you all of that," he quickly interrupted. "I simply want to know, were you aware that every homeowner must pay taxes?"

Mrs. Bailey slowly nodded as the attorney continued firing off questions. The defense actually wasn't as hard on Mrs. Bailey as Tia would've thought. Probably because they didn't want to be seen attacking a feeble old lady.

"Mrs. Bailey, my client sympathizes with your situation, but the law is the law. He bought the property fair and square, wouldn't you agree?"

"No, I wouldn't," she said with conviction. "Fair and square is not bribing some poor and struggling young man with more money than he's ever seen, to get him to turn against his own flesh and blood."

"Your Honor, please?" the attorney said, turning to face the judge. Since Kenny wasn't there to testify, the judge had ruled that information couldn't be admitted in court.

"Miss Jiles, you did instruct your client that she cannot talk about an alleged exchange between Mr. Wynn and her nephew?" the judge asked Tia.

"It wasn't alleged," Mrs. Bailey announced.

Tia stood. "I did, Your Honor." She shot Mrs. Bailey a chastising look, while silently praising how she just slid that in there. The remarks would be stricken from the transcript, but the two reporters sitting in the courtroom were scribbling like crazy, so Tia hoped they would investigate that claim more.

"Mr. Vanderbilt, do you have any more questions for this witness?" the judge said.

"We don't, Your Honor."

The judge looked around the courtroom, then down at his notes. "Where is your client? Isn't he supposed to take the stand?"

"Your Honor, as you know, Mr. Wynn is a very busy man—"

"And I'm not?" the judge questioned, his eyebrow raised.

"No, sir, I wasn't suggesting that," the attorney stammered. "It's just that, um, Mr. Wynn's plane from New York was delayed and—"

The judge cut him off. "Mr. Vanderbilt, I have been more than patient with you on this case. I am continuing it for two weeks, at which time I'll make my ruling. If your client can't see fit to make it to testify, then I'll proceed without him. Understand?"

"Yes, Your Honor."

The judge looked over his notes. "This hearing is reset for

two weeks. Both sides please check with the clerk for the exact time and date." The judge banged his gavel, then stood to leave.

Tia walked over to help her client off the stand. "How long before this nightmare is over?" Mrs. Bailey asked.

"Hopefully soon," Tia responded. "You go on home and I'll get back with you on the details of the next hearing."

Mrs. Bailey nodded, weariness etched across her face. Tia gathered her things and they walked out of the courtroom.

Lance met them in the hallway. "Hi," he said.

"I didn't know you were coming," Tia replied. They had a date tomorrow and she hadn't expected to see him until then.

"I just wanted to see a beautiful woman at work." He turned to Mrs. Bailey. "Imagine my surprise when I saw two beautiful women." Mrs. Bailey blushed. "I'm praying that everything works out for you."

Mrs. Bailey patted his hand. "Is this your husband?" she asked Tia.

Tia gently corrected her mistake. "Mrs. Bailey, I told you I'm not married."

The old woman looked at Lance again, her eyes roaming up and down his body. "Well, if he ain't your husband, he should be." She smiled for the first time that day as she wobbled down the hallway and out of the courthouse.

Chapter 9

Tia enthusiastically described the first time she'd ever gone ice-skating.

"What?" she said, stopping as she noticed him staring. She'd been on a euphoric high for the last few weeks—without medication.

"I'm just taking it all in."

"Taking what in?"

"You, your beauty. Your effervescent smile."

"Oh, my *effervescent* smile. Somebody got their word of the day."

He chuckled, for she knew he had it up on his home page. "Seriously, I just love watching you. I love being around you. You make me feel so at ease. I know it's only been a couple of months, but I feel like I've known you forever."

They were leaving the House of Blues in downtown Houston

and walking back to the parking garage. He was going to valet-park, but since it was such a beautiful night, they'd parked four blocks away and walked.

"Did you enjoy yourself?"

"I did," she said, then sighed. "You remember when we were at the Sade concert, umm, you introduced me as your girlfriend."

"Did you have a problem with that?"

She shrugged slightly. "Well, no, but I still remember how beautiful Crystal is. Do you think maybe you'd want to get back with her?"

He adamantly shook his head. "Everything happens for a reason." He stopped to face Tia. "Things didn't work out with Crystal because maybe God was saving me for you."

"Okay, someone has been to mack school," she joked.

"I'm not kidding." He took a small step forward. "And if you think so, maybe this will show you how serious I am." He leaned in and kissed her with such passion. She loved the way he kissed her. It was so intense, as if his soul were trying to jump out and dance with hers. Tia felt her resolve weaken as they used their tongues to explore one other.

"Nice," she said. "Real nice." It had been so long since she'd been kissed by a man like that. Gavin, her last boyfriend, had dropped her nine months into their relationship. The one before that left after only three months.

After Gavin changed his number, Tia had all but given up on dating and immersed herself in her work. She took on extra cases, pro bono work, the Pay It Forward Foundation, anything she could to keep herself busy. That's why the prospect that she and Lance could go anywhere made her a nervous wreck.

"So, you never said anything about me introducing you as my girlfriend. Was that okay?" he asked.

He just didn't know. That's all she had been thinking about. She hadn't brought it up because she didn't want him telling her that he hadn't really meant it.

"It's okay with me, but are you sure . . . well, that we aren't moving too fast? I mean, we really haven't known each other that long. You don't know some things—"

"I don't know what?" he asked, cutting her off. "Everything I don't know, I want to know. I'm not asking for you to marry me. I just want to spend time with you. Get to know you better. That's all I ask."

She fell silent for a moment, then finally said, "I can do that."

"Good." He smiled. "You're officially my girlfriend."

She laughed. "What are we, in the third grade?"

"All we need is a note saying, 'Will you go with me?' Check a box, yes or no."

They laughed some more as he took her hand and continued walking. Tia felt peaceful as she strolled, hand in hand, down the street with Lance. She wished her old psychiatrist, Dr. Stanton, hadn't moved to Florida. Tia would've loved for Dr. Stanton to see her with a man like Lance. Dr. Stanton had referred her to another psychiatrist, Dr. Monroe, but Tia didn't feel the same closeness, so she'd only been twice.

As Lance squeezed her hand, Tia wondered if she even

needed to see a psychiatrist anymore. After all, she'd run out of pills after their first date and the new doctor wanted four sessions before he issued a prescription. Tia had not been taking the pills for weeks, and everything had been going great. So maybe she didn't need the psychiatrist or the pills. Maybe a normal relationship was all she needed. Everything with Lance sure felt normal. So good. So right. Maybe all she needed was the love of a good man.

They had just crossed the street when a scraggly homeless man with a long gray-and-white beard, knotted gray-and-white hair, a dingy T-shirt, and dirty sweatpants approached them.

"Hey, brother, can you spare some change?" the man asked.

Lance was digging into his pocket when the man said, "Baby girl?" He narrowed his eyes at Tia.

Tia's mouth fell open as she realized who he was.

"Looky here," he said, breaking out in a huge, toothless grin. "You sho lookin' good."

Tia was speechless.

"You know him?" Lance asked, looking back and forth between the two of them.

"Sho she do. We family." The man stood tall and brushed his clothes with his fingertips. "Don't let the fine duds fool you." He cackled. "I'm her blood. Uncle Junior. Her mama's baby brother." He held his arms out. "Girl, gimme a hug."

Tia was absolutely mortified as he stepped toward her. Out of all the homeless men in Houston, she would run into *him.* "Umm, yeah, I'm good," she said, stepping back as his stench assaulted her nostrils. Her family had pretty much washed their hands of Uncle Junior. He roamed the streets of Houston. Had been doing that for the last eleven years. It was his way of life.

Uncle Junior sniffed under his arms. "Yeah, guess I am a little tart." He laughed before turning back to Lance, looking him up and down. "Who you is? Her boyfriend?"

"Yep," Lance said without hesitation. Had this been a different situation, Tia would've been moved by his declaration.

"You wearing some nice digs. You a lawyer? I need legal advice."

"Umm, no, I run a magazine."

"Well, you need to do a story on me." Uncle Junior's eyes were darting from side to side, seemingly beyond his control. " 'Cause I need some help." He lowered his voice as he leaned in. "The government has planted a chip in my brain and they tracking me."

Tia thought she would die of embarrassment. What in the world was Lance thinking?

"They're tracking you? Why would the government want to track you?" Lance asked.

" 'Cause I seen the assassination of Abraham Lincoln and Martin Luther the King, and I know who did it," Junior said matter-of-factly.

Lance frowned. "Abraham Lincoln was killed in 1865."

"And?" Uncle Junior said defensively. "I know when he was killed. I was there. Just like I was at the Ramada Inn in Dallas when they stabbed Martin."

Lance looked confused. “Dr. King was *shot* at the Lorraine Motel in Memphis.”

“How you know?” Junior said angrily. “Was you there? No? But I was, so I know! And I know who the real killer is! Now, Michelle Obama done sicced the CIA and the IRS on me!”

Tia wished she could crawl up under a rock and die.

“Everyone knows who killed both of those men,” Lance protested. Tia didn’t understand why he was even engaging her uncle. “And even if they had the wrong person, I imagine the real killer is dead now,” Lance continued.

“You can imagine all you want. I know who the killer is and where he’s living. He’s hiding out in Cuney Homes,” Junior said, referring to some projects in Houston’s Third Ward. “But I won’t give the gov’ment the apartment number.” He tapped his forehead. “That’s why they put this chip in my brain. They think I don’t know, but I know.” He whipped a pocketknife out and pushed it to his temple. “I wanna cut it out, but I don’t know if they put it in the front of my head or the back.” He turned and showed a long scar on the right side of his head. “My friend Scully went looking for it one time, but we couldn’t find it.”

Tia sighed heavily. She remembered that nightmare. Uncle Junior had almost died, and her mother had been devastated. They’d been called to the hospital because her uncle was hemorrhaging from the brain. He was hospitalized for two weeks. Once he was released, Tia’s mother had hoped he would come stay with them and get back on his feet, but he liked to wander.

"Well, Uncle Junior, we have to get going," Tia said.

"Baby girl, it sho was good to see you. Call me sometime!" He slapped his knee. "Just put your hand to your mouth." He cupped his hands over his mouth and yelled, "Juniorrrr!" He laughed as if something were really funny. " 'Cause you know I ain't got no phone."

"Okay, bye." Tia took Lance's hand firmly to lead him away.

"Hey," Junior said, stopping them, "can I borrow twenty-three dollars and fifty-three cents?"

Lance looked nonplussed. "What an odd amount."

"Okay, twenty-two dollars and fifty-four cents."

"Here's a twenty, how's that?" Lance asked.

Junior sighed. "Guess I'll go try to round up the other two dollars and fifty-four cents."

"Is there some bill you're trying to pay?" Lance said.

Junior looked disappointed. "Nah, that's just my goal every day."

"You live off twenty-three dollars and fifty-three cents?"

"Yep," he said, stuffing the twenty in his pocket. "But I gotta go. I can't stay in one place too long." He reached in his basket. "Here." He handed an empty soda can to Lance.

"What am I supposed to do with this?"

"Trade it in at the scrap-metal yard."

"That's okay, I'm good," Lance said, handing the can back to him.

"Your loss." Junior shrugged, then dropped the can back into his cart. "Gotta go; gotta go. The ATF hot on my trail." He darted off before anyone could reply.

Tia stood there, humiliated. She couldn't even look at Lance.

"I'm sorry to subject you to that," she finally said. "I never saw him coming."

"Is that really your uncle?" Lance asked as they resumed walking.

"Unfortunately, it is." She sighed. "My mom has three siblings. One of them, a sister, died when they were teens. My uncle Leo lives with my mom. That's their baby brother, Junior."

"It's obvious he's, um"—Lance was struggling to find the right words—"a little off."

"A *little*?" Tia quipped.

"Has anyone ever tried to help him?"

Tia couldn't endure this line of questioning with Lance. His inquiries cut too close to home. "No offense, but can we please change the subject? Uncle Junior is the family blemish that we don't talk about."

"You don't talk about it?" Lance asked, surprised. "Do you think that's best?" He abruptly stopped himself and grabbed her hand. "No, we're changing the subject. We're talking about us. We're talking about me getting to know my woman even better."

Tia smiled as he led her away. She was just glad he didn't push the issue. What she couldn't tell him was, crazy ran in the family.

Chapter 10

It had been exactly six months and three days since Lance had met Tia, and he was sure about one thing—he wanted to spend the rest of his life with this woman. She was loving, caring, witty, and ambitious, and her intellect, compassion, and ambition seriously turned him on.

Lance knew he was moving fast, but he knew love and happiness didn't come around often, and these past six months had been the happiest of his life. They'd finally broken down and made love a month after they met, and it had been phenomenal. Tia had been right: she was a sensual person, and that only turned him on more.

They'd met each other's family, and while his mother had been standoffish, Tia continued trying to penetrate her cold demeanor. Lance had apologized and explained his mother's affection for Crystal, but Tia simply said, "She'll come around in due time."

Lance knew he was making the right decision. Regardless of what anyone else said, he planned to move forward with securing a future with Tia. That's why he was here—at Virginia Jiles's house. He couldn't help but notice the peeling, once-white paint on the front of the modest house. The screen door was hanging on its hinges, and Lance felt that with one wrong step he could fall through the creaky boards on the porch. No wonder Tia was so ambitious. If he had grown up in a place like this, he'd be determined to never go back, too. His first time visiting the house, he'd tried not to react because he could tell Tia was ashamed of the place and he was determined to make her feel at ease. But now he took in everything and could only shake his head. How much would it really cost to slap a new coat of paint on this place?

Lance shook off his disgust over the dilapidated house and forced a smile as he knocked on the door.

Virginia Jiles swung it open, her eyes dancing at the sight of Lance.

"How are you doing, Mrs. Jiles? May I come in?"

"I'm fine, baby." She stepped to the side and opened the screen door to the small wood-frame home. "Of course, you can come in."

Tia's uncle Leo was sitting in the den, reading the Bible. Leo's two grown children, Bobbi Jo and Curtis, were sitting on the sofa, watching a reality show.

He could tell Virginia adored her daughter. Pictures of Tia at every age lined the walls. She was as beautiful then as she was now. He stopped at a photo of Tia with long, braided pigtails and bright yellow ribbons, sitting on a heavyset man's lap. Even at a young age, the two of them bore a strong resemblance, and Lance assumed that was Tia's father.

"Hello, everyone," Lance said, shaking himself out of his thoughts.

They all grunted hellos. Tia's mother led the way into the kitchen, which overlooked the small den. "I'm just in here cooking some mustard greens," she said, lifting the lid of a huge metal pot. "You hungry?"

"No, thank you, Mrs. Jiles."

She turned to him, frowning. "I told you the last time you were here, just call me Mama."

Leo looked up from his Bible. "But you ain't the boy's mama."

"Shut up, Leo," Virginia snapped.

"I'm just saying. You just met the boy and you already wanting him to call you Mama," Leo grumbled before going back to reading his Bible.

"What's been up, Mr. Leo?" Lance said, stepping in before the two of them started arguing, which they'd done every single time he'd seen them.

"You got the ham and the bone."

"What?" Lance asked.

"He means," Virginia said, "you've got everything and he has nothing. But maybe if he got up off his behind and got a job, he'd have something."

Lance wasn't so sure. Given Leo's scrawny frame, Lance doubted there were too many things that he was good at.

"What part of I'm *disabled* do you not get, the *dis* or the *abled*?" Leo frowned at her. This was obviously a source of contention with them.

Virginia ignored him and motioned for Lance to sit down. As she began removing dishes from the sink, she asked, "You looking for Tia?"

"Actually, I wanted to talk to you."

"Why?" Virginia asked, nervousness spreading across her face.

Lance was perplexed. She almost looked fearful. "It's nothing bad," he quickly put in, causing her shoulders to relax. "But, well, I want to do something, but I wanted to talk to you guys first. Mrs. Jiles—I mean, Mama—I know it hasn't been long." He swallowed a huge lump in his throat. "But I wanted to formally ask you for your daughter's hand in marriage."

Virginia was wiping a plate off and froze midwipe. Her mouth dropped open. Both Bobbi Jo and Curtis spun around in their seats.

"What did you say?" Bobbi Jo asked, incredulous.

Lance laughed. "I said, I want to marry Tia, and I'd like your blessing." He looked intently at Virginia.

"You want to marry my baby girl?" Virginia all but whispered, as if she needed to hear it again just for it to register.

Leo looked at Lance as if he'd sprouted horns. "You sure you know what you doing, boy?"

"Shut up, Leo," Virginia hissed. "If the boy wants to marry my baby, who are we to question him?"

"I'm just saying, you ain't been going out that long," Leo added, shaking his head. Lance expected that reaction from him. Tia had told him that even though he was a religious zealot, Leo's wife had run off with another man, so he was definitely not a proponent of marriage.

"I know, but when someone is right for you, you just know." Lance had already prepared this speech for his own family, so he knew just what to say.

"You know that, huh?" Bobbi Jo said, snickering.

"Bobbi Jo," Virginia said, narrowing her gaze at her niece. "Don't you have something you could be doing?"

"So I guess that means you're giving him your blessing." Bobbi Jo chuckled.

"Well, of course I give my blessing." Virginia turned back to Lance, adoration all over her face. "A fine young man like yourself, I consider my daughter lucky."

"Crazy girl done hit the jackpot," Curtis mumbled as he turned back to the TV.

Lance ignored him and said sincerely, "I'm the lucky one, Mrs. Jiles." Lance had fallen so hard, so fast, and he couldn't wait to make Tia his wife.

"Oh, that just warms my heart," Virginia said, looking as if she was about to cry.

"I'm just honored that you think I'm worthy of your daughter."

"Humph," Leo chortled. "You'd better remember the book of Genesis, boy. It was woman that led man into sin."

"Don't you start with that foolishness, Leo," Virginia snapped.

Lance didn't know what to make of Leo's reaction, but Virginia's enthusiasm didn't give him much time to think about it.

"Tia is going to be overjoyed," Virginia said, beaming.

"You got a ring?" Bobbi Jo asked.

"Actually, I do." Lance smiled as he reached in his pocket and pulled out a blue Tiffany box.

"Dammmmn!" Curtis and Bobbi Jo said at the same time as Lance held the ring up for everyone to see. Lance had been eyeing this Tiffany's ring for years. He thought that he would buy it for Crystal, but looking at it now, he knew that it was meant for Tia.

"Lord Jesus," Virginia said, her voice once again just above a whisper, as she leaned in and studied the ring.

Bobbi Jo raced into the kitchen to get a closer look at the diamond. "How many carats is that?"

"It's three and a half," Lance proudly replied.

Leo leaned back in his chair and tsked. "There's a sucker born every minute," he muttered.

"Leo, would you just hush?" Virginia put her hand on Lance's arm. "Don't pay him any attention. He's just a bitter old man, so he's not the one to talk to about marriage."

"You think she's going to like it?" Lance asked, ignoring Leo.

"Let me try it on," Bobbi Jo excitedly said, sticking her hand out as if Lance had proposed to her.

Virginia intervened. "You ain't trying her ring on."

"Come on, let me see it," Bobbi Jo said, jerking the box her way. The ring tumbled to the floor.

"Look at you, you about to break that diamond!" Curtis yelled.

"Get away from the ring!" Virginia said, scurrying toward it. "Ain't nobody trying on nothing." She picked up the ring with a huge smile on her face. "No, sirree." She blew on the ring and rubbed it against her dress. "This ring is for my baby." She handed it back to Lance, handling it as if it were the Cullinan diamond. "When you gon' give it to her?"

"I'd like to give it to her at dinner next week. She thinks we're going out for my birthday, but I want to surprise her." Lance put the ring back in the box, closed it, then dropped it back into his jacket pocket.

"Where are you taking us?" Bobbi Jo asked.

"He ain't taking *us* nowhere," Virginia said, "specially your scandalous behind."

"There you go with that," Bobbi Jo said, rolling her eyes. "You ain't gon' never let me live down messing with Tia's boyfriend."

"Boyfriends," Virginia snapped, holding up two fingers. "Plural."

"Whatever. I did her a favor anyway, because both of them dudes was trifling. And if she had stayed with them, she wouldn't be with this fine thing." Bobbi Jo motioned toward Lance. "So y'all need to be thanking me."

"Why we can't go to dinner?" Curtis whined. "I wanna go to a fancy-schmancy restaurant and celebrate your birthday and my cousin's engagement."

"You the one don't even want her to get married," Virginia retorted.

"Actually, I do want all of you there," Lance interjected. "I'll tell Tia I just invited everyone to my birthday dinner so our families could meet."

"Sounds like a plan to me," Curtis replied.

"Alrighty then, what time and what place?" Virginia was absolutely thrilled and didn't bother trying to contain her excitement. "I need to iron my good dress."

"Well, I'll get you the details tomorrow after I confirm the restaurant. But promise me you won't say anything to Tia. I want her to be surprised."

"I promise." Virginia stared at him, misty-eyed. "My baby's getting married," she said softly.

Lance returned her smile. He couldn't help but notice how happy everyone was—everyone except Leo.

If Lance didn't know any better, he'd swear that was a warning in Leo's eyes.

Chapter 11

"Hey, Ma." Tia was in a cheerful mood as she walked into the den, where her mother and Uncle Leo were sitting, watching *Let's Make a Deal.*

"How are you, baby?" Virginia said as Tia leaned over and kissed her on the forehead.

"I'm actually doing great today," Tia replied. Lance had sent her some more flowers today at work. Her office was beginning to look like a floral shop and she was loving every minute of it.

"Well, that's just fantastic," Virginia replied.

"Hey, Uncle Leo," Tia said.

"Hey," he grunted, never taking his eyes off the TV.

"So, what's going on?" Tia plopped down on the sofa.

"Oh, nothing much," Virginia said with a guilty grin.

Tia cut her eyes at her mother. She seemed extra-giddy.

"How was work today?" Virginia asked.

"It was okay. Found out today my client Mrs. Bailey is doing much better." The elderly woman had broken her hip, and Tia had got a continuance on her case, but it was only so long that Mr. Wynn would wait, so Tia was glad Mrs. Bailey was on the mend.

"Well, that's wonderful to hear," Virginia said. "I can't imagine being forced out of my home."

"I'm also preparing for another big trial. It's a copyright-infringement case."

"Have I ever told you how proud I am of you?" Virginia was grinning from ear to ear.

"Yes, you have, and that means the world to me." Tia looked from her mom to her uncle: a contrast of glad and glum. "Okay, what's going on?"

Virginia kept smiling. "Oh, I just wanted you to know how proud I am."

"Thanks, Ma." Tia felt that something else had her mother excited, but she let it pass. She didn't have much time, so she needed to get to the real reason she'd dropped in. She had been meaning to tell them about her uncle but she kept forgetting. "Look, I came by because I wanted to talk about Uncle Junior."

Virginia's head snapped toward her daughter. "Why?"

At the mention of his brother's name, Leo shook his head.

"I saw him not too long ago."

"How was he?" Virginia said, losing all trace of a smile.

"The same. He actually came up to me while I was on a date with Lance. It was really embarrassing." Tia fumbled with her belt strap. She had to tread lightly with her next question. It had been bothering her since Lance brought it up. "Mama, why hasn't Uncle Junior ever gotten any real help?"

"The only help he needs is from Jesus," Virginia firmly said. "And as long as he refuses to acknowledge the Father, the Son, and the Holy Spirit, that demon can't be cast from his body." Virginia stood up abruptly and walked into the kitchen. Tia knew that was her mother's way of trying to end the conversation.

"Then why hasn't the Lord helped Junior?" Tia asked, following her.

"Because God helps those who help themselves and Junior ain't trying to help himself. He likes being out there on the streets." Virginia started rearranging the spices in the cabinet. She always busied herself when she didn't want to discuss something.

"How can anyone like being that way, Mama?"

"Well, everyone has tried to help him and he doesn't want our help."

"I'm talking about professional help." Tia had wondered that about herself. She'd had some serious bouts of depression growing up, but her mother had been mortified at the idea of talking to someone professional about it. She lambasted the "stigma that would come with being admitted to a mental hospital." The only reason Tia had started seeing Dr. Stanton, her previous psychiatrist, was because she knew she needed some help controlling her condition. When Virginia found out Tia was seeing Dr. Stanton, she hadn't spoken to Tia for two weeks.

"Tia, I told you"—Virginia wagged her finger at her daughter—"we don't need to let strangers know our business. We don't need to be airing our dirty laundry for the whole world to see."

Tia debated getting into it with her mother, but she knew that was an argument she wouldn't win. "Well, you will be happy to know, I've stopped taking the pills. I ran out, and with Dr. Stanton gone, I haven't gotten any refills."

Virginia stopped, then turned to face her daughter. "Thank God," she finally said, running over to hug Tia. Tia knew that news would be music to her mother's ears. She hated that Tia took medication.

"I haven't been depressed lately; everything's going great. In fact, anytime I find myself about to get worked up, I'm able to calm myself down." Tia smiled in genuine relief to be able to say that. "Mama, I've never been happier. I feel so normal. I haven't had an episode in almost a year, and, well, I think you were right. I just needed to give it some time and everything would work itself out."

Virginia's eyes watered. "That ain't nothin' but Jesus." She patted Tia's cheek. "The power of prayer. Thank you, Jesus."

Tia knew that her mother prayed for her every day, several times a day. She prayed herself. She prayed for a normal life. And for the last six months her prayers had been answered.

"This couldn't come at a better time. Because you and Lance seem to be getting real close." Virginia's eyes were dancing once again.

"We are," Tia said with a nervous laugh.

"You love him?"

"Yeah." Tia nodded, surprising herself because she'd sworn that she would never love another man.

"I'm proud of you, baby. I just want you to be happy."

Tia shifted uneasily. "Mother, do you think I should—"

"No," her mother said, grabbing Tia's arms so hard that she startled Tia. "I know what you're about to say, and you said it yourself, you're doing great." She gave her daughter a slight shake. "Some things are best left in the dark."

Uncle Leo released a loud grunt. "Hmph."

Tia knew how her uncle felt about secrets. He believed in being open and honest, but he'd learned long ago not to fight his stubborn sister on anything.

Virginia exchanged uneasy looks with her brother. He shook his head as if he was giving her some kind of warning.

"Sweet pea, I didn't want to tell you this because I really want you to be surprised," she began, "but I don't want you to be caught off guard. And, well, I need you to know why you simply can't say anything now."

"Virginia, you need to stay out of their business. That boy swore you to secrecy."

"What boy?"

"Hush, Leo. This is my daughter. I know what I'm doing."

He shook his head and resumed watching his show.

"What is Uncle Leo talking about, Mama?"

Virginia slid into a seat at the kitchen table, giddy with excitement. "Lance came by yesterday."

"For what?"

Virginia inhaled, then slowly said, "He came by to ask for your hand in marriage."

Leo groaned.

"What?" Tia was stunned. That was the last thing she expected to hear.

"Had you guys talked about marriage?" Virginia asked.

"Yeah, we discussed it," Tia said slowly, digesting this total surprise. "I know he's ready to settle down. It's something that he longs for. But I had no idea it was something he wanted to do this soon."

Virginia rubbed her daughter's hair. "Well, you're the perfect woman for him to settle down with."

Tia sat back, stunned. Marriage? He was really moving forward with marriage? She thought he had just been talking for the future, like *way* in the future.

"Mama, I can't get married," Tia said solemnly.

Her mother squeezed her hands. "Yes, you can. And you will. It's not often a man like Lance comes along, and . . ."

Tia stared at her mother, her gaze piercing. "Say it, Mama. It's not often a man like Lance wants a woman like me."

"That's nonsense. It's obvious he wants you."

"That's because he doesn't know the real me."

"Oh, hush with that nonsense. He does know the real you, the kind, loving woman that you are."

"But what if—"

"What if nothing. Now, I told you one day you were going to find your Prince Charming, and you found him. He wants to make you his wife and I think that's exactly what you need to do. Give him what he wants and let him give you your lifetime of happiness."

"But . . ."

Virginia put her finger to her daughter's lips. "You gotta stop selling yourself short, baby. Granted, I know you think because your other relationships didn't work out, none of them will. But God does everything for a reason. Maybe those relationships didn't work out because God was getting you ready for this man."

Tia smiled, having a flicker of recognition. "That's the same thing Lance said."

Virginia beamed, as if hearing that was validation. "See, we both know what we're talking about."

Leo huffed, then turned to his sister. "Maybe the girl has a point."

"Maybe you need to mind your own business. You worry about your son making babies all over town and that loose daughter of yours. You let me take care of my daughter."

"You been taking care of her; that's part of the problem. You baby her too much. 'Train up a child in the way they should go and they won't depart from it,' " he quoted. "That should be enough."

"I do not baby her." Virginia turned back to Tia. "Sweetheart, I just want you to be happy, get the happiness you deserve."

Yet Tia had been infected with her uncle's uncertainty. "Do I really deserve it? Will Lance stand by me or will he leave me like everyone else?" Just minutes ago, she'd been ecstatic about where her relationship was heading. But that never stopped doubt from creeping right back.

"Lance is a good man."

"That's the same thing you said about Gavin and Richard."

"Well, that's because I wanted them to be. But this one I feel in my heart," Virginia said with confidence. "There is no doubt about it. He loves you and he'll see you through any firestorms you may encounter."

"I wish it was that easy." Tia sighed.

"It is."

"We'll see how he feels after I sit down and talk to him about everything."

"You'll do no such thing!" Virginia interjected. "You leave well enough alone." She patted her daughter's cheek again. "You've been doing so well. Now you're off the medications. I'm a praying woman. I told you all we had to do was keep praying, and look what happened. God cured you and you're fine."

That was Virginia's answer to everything. Just pray and it'll all work out.

"Doesn't Lance deserve to know?" Tia had been asking herself this question ten times a day, but she was too worried that she'd scare him off.

"All he needs to know is that you love him and he loves you. Don't go stirring up trouble when there ain't none. You and that man love each other and will live happily ever after."

Tia wished she could be as optimistic as her mother about this situation. She wished she could have her mother's faith. And more than anything, she wished that what her mother said was true. Maybe this time she really had turned a corner.

Chapter 12

"Are you insane?"

Lance took a deep breath, reminding himself that this was his mother standing in front of him. As prissy as she could be, she wouldn't hesitate to slap him in the mouth if he disrespected her. So, he chose his words carefully.

"Mama," Lance slowly began, "I'm going to need you and Grandma to respect my decision. I love Tia and we're getting married."

"But you barely know her," Beverly Kingston protested.

"I know enough. I dated Crystal for three years and look how that turned out. I didn't really know her at all." He hated bringing up Crystal, but he had to get his family to see his point. The sooner he let them know his plan to propose, the more time they had to prepare and accept it.

"There you go complaining about Crystal. Everyone makes

mistakes," his grandmother interjected. "Do you know how many times I took your grandfather back after his dalliances with other women? When you commit to someone, it's for the long run."

"Well, that's you, Grandma." Lance wanted to add that unlike his father he didn't have commitment issues. He simply didn't want to be with an unfaithful woman. But since that was still a sore spot with his mother, he left it alone. "Besides, maybe if I had been married to Crystal, things would've been different. Maybe I would've given her another chance because I believe in for better or for worse. But the fact remains, I wasn't married. And I couldn't say 'I do' to her if I didn't trust her." He was tired of going through the same old argument all over again, and he cut himself off short. "Besides, Crystal is the past. Tia is my future and I'm going to need you two to accept that."

Lance's grandmother shook her head in exasperation. "Beverly, you'd better talk some sense into this boy," she muttered as she hobbled over to the cabinet and began making tea.

Beverly sat down at the table and took her son's hands. "Lance, just hear me out, sweetheart. Okay, so you *think* this girl is the one you want to marry. Why don't you just take some time to be sure?"

"I *know* she is, Mother. I know what my heart tells me."

"I don't think he's thinking with his heart. He's thinking with that little Weedwacker," his grandmother said, pointing at his crotch.

"Grandma!"

Beverly shot her mother a chastising look, but kept talking. "Son, why do you have to get married so soon?"

"I thought you liked Tia," Lance protested. When they'd initially met, besides being standoffish, his mother had said Tia seemed "like a low-class woman who came into a little money," and his grandmother had called Tia "shifty-eyed." But over the past few months, Tia had broken down their barriers, and both his mother and grandmother ended up singing her praises.

"I do like Tia," Beverly said. "We just don't know enough about her yet. In fact, we barely know her. And we don't know anything about her people."

Lance knew this was coming, which was why he wanted their families to meet. You would've thought the Kingstons were royalty the way Beverly was always concerned with someone's "people." That was part of the reason she adored Crystal. Crystal's grandmother was one of Beverly's bridge partners and from an affluent family in Galveston.

"I know Tia's people," Lance said. "So, that's all that matters."

Beverly sighed. "Son, we just think you should take some time to get to know her better. What happened to long engagements? There's no need to rush into anything."

"Is she pregnant?" his grandmother blurted out, as if the possibility had just dawned on her.

"No, Tia is not pregnant."

"Then there is no reason for you not to wait," his mother replied. "And how do you know she's not trying to snag her a big-time magazine man? Everybody knows you make all that money."

"Although I ain't seen none of it," his grandmother interjected. "All that money and you won't even buy me a car."

Lance cut his eyes at his grandmother. "Grandma, you don't even have a license and you keep asking me for a Corvette." When his grandmother had first asked for the sports car two years ago, he thought she was kidding, but she talked about that car every chance she got.

"Oh, pooh," she said, waving him off. "What good is it to have a rich grandson if he doesn't buy me nice stuff?"

Lance ignored his grandmother. Truth be told, if she truly wanted a Corvette, she had more than enough money to go buy it herself. "First of all, getting married was my idea. Second, Tia is an attorney. She makes her own money." He was not changing the long, drawn looks on both their faces, and he stood up. "I can't understand why you don't want to see me happy."

"We want to see you happy," Beverly protested.

"Then respect that this is something I want to do and wish me the best," he said firmly.

His mother leaned back in resignation. "Fine. But mark my words, you're moving too fast. You need to tell Tia there is nothing wrong with waiting."

"For your information, it's me who's pushing. Tia actually wants to wait." Tia hadn't said that per se, but every time he mentioned marriage, she tensed up. Lance could tell that was just because she was scared. She'd told him about her failed relationships, so she held a lot of fear about relationships.

"Then you need to listen to her," his grandmother said.

"You know what? I'm done listening—period. I'm leaving. We'll be at Morton's Steakhouse at seven on Friday. If you want to come to the dinner, then fine. If not, that's fine, too." He stomped out of the house without giving them a chance to respond.

Lance didn't care whether his family gave their stamp of approval. He was going to marry Tia. He knew it wouldn't always be easy. But his heart told him they would live happily ever after—despite what anyone had to say.

Chapter 13

"These are the most uncivilized people I ever met in my life," Lance's grandmother leaned in and whispered to her daughter. Well, it wasn't quite a whisper. It was loud enough for Lance to hear. He was just thankful that Tia's family was chatting so loudly, no one else had heard her.

"Grandma," he quietly admonished. "Please?"

"What?" She shook her head as she watched Curtis—who had shown up with a date *and* his best friend—use his fork to flip a pea into his mouth. They were in the private dining room of Morton's. Bobbi Jo was openly flirting with the waiter, and Uncle Leo was preaching about how all sins were based in lust. No one was paying him any attention, but he kept jabbering nonetheless.

"This just doesn't make any sense. Why he got the whole

bread basket sitting in front of him?" Lance's grandmother shook her head in disgust as Curtis reached into the basket and pulled out another piece of bread. "And how many beers has that man had?" She motioned toward Curtis's friend.

The man must've known she was talking about him because he stuck his tongue out and wiggled it in a sexually suggestive manner.

Lance's grandmother gasped.

"He's just playing with you, Grandma," Lance said, though he, too, could have done without the friend.

"Disgusting," she hissed, clutching her pearls.

"Mother is right," Beverly whispered to Lance. "No wonder you didn't want us to know her people. It's amazing Tia turned out so well."

"They're a little unrefined, but that's okay," Lance said. "They really are good people, Mama."

Tia walked over between the two ladies, halting their conversation. "Hi, Mrs. Kingston and Mother Brooks. Is everything okay?"

"It sure is, sugah," Lance's grandmother said, flashing a fake smile. "Just talking about how nice your family seems."

Tia leaned over to the old woman. "Come on, Mother Brooks, you don't have to lie to me," she whispered. "My family is embarrassing the mess out of me."

Lance's grandmother broke out in a huge smile. "I knew there was a reason I liked this girl," she told Lance.

He was glad to hear that because maybe he could salvage this evening yet. He winked at Tia as she took the seat next to him. After she was seated, Lance used his fork to lightly tap his champagne glass. "May I have your attention, please?"

The chatter dimmed down as all eyes focused on Lance. "I'm glad that all of you could join me to celebrate my birthday. Even those of you I don't know," Lance said, nodding in the direction of Curtis's date and friend, who both smiled as if they'd been personally invited. Lance didn't miss a beat as he turned to Tia. "But this celebration is actually twofold, or at least I'm anticipating that it will be twofold."

"What does that mean?" Leo said, seeming agitated. "Can the boy speak English?"

"Leo, shut up. I'm 'bout tired of you," Virginia snapped.

"You don't tell me to shut up," Leo snapped back. "I'm sick of you always trying to boss me around."

"Excuse me," Lance said, interrupting the sibling hostility. "I'd like to finish what I was saying."

"Sorry," Virginia said.

"I'll drink to whatever it is you're about to say," Curtis's friend said, raising his beer. Curtis gave him a high five.

Lance turned his attention back to Tia. "Sweetheart, you satisfy me spiritually, emotionally, and sexually."

"Did the boy say *sexually*?" Leo blurted out.

"That's what it sounded like to me, Pops." Curtis laughed.

Bobbi Jo grinned wickedly. "That's what I'm talking about. My cousin be puttin' it down," she sang. "Go on, Cuz, wit' yo' bad self. You ain't as straightlaced as I thought."

"Would you shut up and let him finish!" Virginia shouted. "Can't take y'all nowhere. Shut your trap 'fore he change his mind." She turned back to Lance, a huge grin on her face. "Go on, baby. Finish what you were sayin'."

"Ay-yi-yi," Lance's grandmother mumbled.

Lance tried to ignore all the chaos as Tia looked on nervously. He took a deep breath. "Tia, I know we're here to celebrate my birthday, and I don't know what you have in that bag"—he pointed to the small gift bag on the floor next to her chair—"but I'm . . . I'm hoping you'll give me the greatest gift of all." Lance knelt on one knee as Tia covered her mouth in shock. "Tia Janelle Jiles, will you marry me?"

"Yes!" Everyone in the room turned to Tia's mother, who had leapt from her seat and was yelling, "Yes! Yes, she'll marry you!"

Lance chuckled, but stayed focused on Tia. Her eyes were wide, but she didn't say a word.

"Wow," Lance said, his grin cracking after she still didn't say anything. "I was kind of hoping that you'd say yes."

"Yes! Yes!" Virginia repeated.

"Virginia, shut up and let the girl answer," Leo snapped. "You telling everybody else to be quiet and you over there cackling like a hen."

"Are . . . are you sure you want to do this?" Tia finally managed to say.

"I've never been more sure of anything."

"Lance, baby, you don't know . . ."

Virginia loudly cleared her throat, causing Tia to stop in midsentence.

Lance seized the opportunity. "Tia, I know that I love you. Do you love me?"

"But . . ."

"Do you love me?" Lance repeated.

"Yes!" Virginia shouted. "I told you, she'll marry you."

This time several people flashed Virginia irritated looks. She shrank back into her seat, embarrassed.

"Lance, I do love you, but—"

"There are no buts," Lance interrupted. "I know you're scared and apprehensive, but what we have is real, sweetheart. And together, there is nothing we can't do."

He held the ring out to her. "So, I'll ask you again, will you marry me?"

Tears streamed down Tia's face as she nodded her head. "Yes, I'll marry you," she softly said.

Lance slipped the ring on her finger, then took her into his arms as the room, waitstaff included, erupted in applause—everyone, that is, except his mother, grandmother, and Uncle Leo.

Chapter 14

Tia stared at the diamond on her hand. It was absolutely gorgeous. Never in a million years did she dream she'd have something like this.

It was even more of a reason for her to feel guilty about not being open with Lance. This man wanted to give her the world, and she couldn't pay him back with a simple thing like honesty. But at this point—after buying her a ring like this—would he be even more angry about her not telling him from jump?

Tia massaged her temples. Life wasn't supposed to be this difficult. And she'd had her share of unhappiness. Wasn't she entitled to some happiness in her life? Wasn't she entitled to the love of a good man?

No, her mother was right, she told herself. She was finally living a normal existence—without medication. There was no need to upset the balance—and risk losing Lance.

Her thoughts were interrupted when her secretary came over her intercom.

"Miss Jiles, Mr. Anderson needs to see you right now." Vicki's voice sounded nervous. It's never a good thing when the boss summons you into the office before 9:00 a.m., so Tia could understand why that would be cause for concern.

"Thank you, Vicki. I'll head over there now."

Tia started replaying in her head any mishaps she may have had on previous cases as she headed down the hall to Mr. Anderson's office. She hoped this demand to come see the president of her law firm wasn't in regard to this copyright-infringement case she'd been working on. She had been devoting a lot of time to Mrs. Bailey's case, but she'd tried to make sure the copyright case didn't suffer. So she didn't know what Mr. Anderson had to complain about. But he was a stickler for business, so Tia's stomach was in knots.

"Hi," Tia said, greeting Mr. Anderson's secretary. "Is the boss in?"

"He is. You can go right in."

Tia tried to read Elizabeth's expression. As his executive administrative assistant, she knew everything. So if trouble was about to erupt, she'd know it. But, of course, what made Elizabeth so good at her job is that her expressions didn't reveal any of her knowledge.

"Mr. Anderson, you wanted to see me?" Tia said, poking her head into his office.

She felt herself relax a little when a big smile crossed his pudgy, pink face. "I did. I did," he said, waving her in. He unbuttoned his tailor-made suit jacket and slid it off. "Come in and have a seat." He pointed at the large wingback chair in front of his desk as he tossed his jacket on the back of his own chair.

"So how are things going?" Mr. Anderson asked after Tia was seated.

Tia was trying to read him as well for signals, and he seemed cheerful this morning. "They're going well. You know we go to trial soon with the Woods copyright-infringement case. I have a good feeling about that one." Tia wanted to let him know up front that she was on top of things.

"You have a good track record, and if that's any indication on how this will turn out, I know you'll do well. How's your pro bono stuff going?"

"The only case I have at the moment is the elderly woman and the developer."

"Ahh, yes." He nodded. The firm had always been supportive of the pro bono work because it was good for the overall image of the company. "How's that going?"

"The client broke her hip, so the case has been on hold. But Mr. Wynn is getting antsy and is ready to move ahead, so I imagine we'll be hearing from the court soon."

"Well, I'm sure you'll emerge victorious."

"So," Tia said, relaxing now that it appeared he wasn't about to rip her to shreds, "what did you want to see me about?"

"Well, as you know," he began, reverting to his business tone, "in the sixty-three-year history at Anderson, Logan, and Smith, we've never had a female partner."

Partner? Tia's heart rate quickened.

"And, the partners and I were thinking that it's about time. I know some guys around here are gonna say it's some affirmative-action crap. But you know all too well how I feel about that. I believe in rewarding hard work based on merit. And, if I can cut to the chase, based on the dedication you have shown this firm, the commitment you have to your cases, no one deserves the partnership more than you."

Tia's mouth dropped open. "Are you saying what I think you're saying?"

"If you think I'm saying that we'd like to promote you to partner, then yes." He flashed a satisfied smile.

"Oh, my God." A wave of panic suddenly crossed over her. Did she really have what it took to be partner? That was an extremely stressful job. Could she take something like that on?

"We don't want you to change a thing," he said. "We're bringing in a new paralegal, a promising young man from Stanford, so he'll help you wrap up your cases. Continue doing what you do, and after the copyright case, we'll move you to more of an oversight position. Of course, your salary will increase greatly. The business office will forward your new contract, but I assure you, you'll be more than pleased with our terms." He winked at her.

"Wow, I'm honored," Tia said, pushing back that nervous feeling in her gut. She was a hard worker and there was no doubt she deserved this. She could do this.

Tia stood and extended her hand. "Thank you so much. I will make you and the other partners proud of your decision."

"We know you won't let us down, Jiles. By the way, congrats on your engagement."

"How'd you hear about that?" She hadn't told anyone but Lucinda, and she'd sworn her to secrecy.

"It's our job to know these things," he casually said. "But you're not planning any babies anytime soon, are you?"

"No, sir. We're getting married fairly quickly just because we don't see a reason to wait, but we want to enjoy several years together before we bring a baby into the fold." She hated lying to Mr. Anderson, but that was information he definitely didn't need to know. Tia and Lance had talked about children, and he'd made it clear that he wanted kids within a year, but Tia didn't even want to get into that. Just the thought of being someone's mother terrified her. Of course, she hadn't shared that thought with Lance. She'd hoped to somehow overcome her fear because she would love to one day give Lance a son or a daughter.

"Good job. We'll make a formal announcement in the morning." He returned to the work on his desk, basically dismissing her.

Tia left his office more tense than when she'd come. Becoming partner meant longer hours. More work. More stress. None of which she needed in her life right now. She caught herself up short. What was the problem? This was the pinnacle of what she'd been working toward. She knew Lance would support her being partner, but was it something she could actually succeed at? Tia shook off her doubts as she approached her office. She could do this. She could handle partner, her pro bono work, and her new life as Mrs. Lance Kingston.

Tia had just settled back at her desk when Lucinda appeared in the doorway. "So, what did the boss want?"

Tia shrugged as if it were nothing. "Umm, he just wanted to let me know they were promoting me to partner."

"Shut the front door!" Lucinda exclaimed, bouncing into the office. "That is so wonderful. Congratulations!" She stopped when she noticed Tia's expression. "Why are you not celebrating? That's fantastic news."

"I don't know. I was just having some reservations, you know, going back and forth on whether I could even do this."

Lucinda waved her off. "Girl, please. If anyone can do it, you can. I am so jealous. You got the man. And now you have the dream job. You are so lucky." Lucinda waved both her hands in a time-out. "Naw, I take that back. You're not lucky. You're blessed, girl."

Tia stared at her friend. *Blessed?* How ironic was that. That was one word she had never used to describe her life. But the more she thought about it, the more she realized Lucinda was right. Tia had prayed to God for a good man, a successful career, and the ability to control her disease. And from the way everything was turning out, it seemed that God had finally answered her prayers.

Chapter 15

"Always working hard."

The sweet, melodic voice filled the air, and Lance looked up from his budget report to see the woman who for years made his heart flutter.

"Sorry to just barge on back," Crystal said. "But Ruby wasn't at her desk, and, well, I knew you wouldn't mind."

She smiled as she settled into the seat in front of his desk. She was beautiful as ever—her sun-kissed skin glowed, and as usual her makeup was flawless. She still wore her hair short and tapered, and Lance had to fight to keep his eyes from roaming over her full, voluptuous figure.

Lance crossed his arms in front of his chest and said a curt "Hello, Crystal. How are you?"

"I've been better." She glanced around the office. "It looks good. You upgraded?"

She wasn't getting anywhere with flattery. "I upgraded a lot of things in my life."

"Ouch."

Lance took a deep breath. He had long ago released his bitterness, or so he thought. Still, there was no need to be ugly. "I'm sorry, that was uncalled for. What can I help you with, Crystal?"

She made sure to cross her legs so that her skirt rode up midthigh. "I can't just drop by to say hello? I mean, it's not like you've returned any of my calls. I know that our relationship ended badly, but I don't understand why we can't be friends."

He stared at her, wondering how she could even fix her lips to say that. After the way that she had hurt him, the idea that he would consider being her friend was ludicrous.

"Crystal, I told you, I have enough friends. I don't need any more. And it seems to me that Francis is doing a pretty good job being your friend."

She waved him off. "Francis is just a guy. I don't want him. I told you, I'm still in love with you."

"Crystal . . ."

Her confident demeanor began to crumble. No words were exchanged until she said, "Please tell me that what I heard is not true."

"What did you hear?"

"I heard you were getting married," she said slowly. The expression on her face begged him to say it wasn't true.

"And where did you hear that from?" he asked, already knowing the answer. He had no doubt that his mother had put in a call to Crystal to come "save" him from Tia and her family.

She was too clever for that. "Just heard it through the grapevine. But I knew that it couldn't possibly be true." She settled a long stare at him, as if she were trying to see through his lies. "Because I know while you may be mad at me, you still love me."

"I'm not mad at you anymore, Crystal. I've forgiven you," he said matter-of-factly.

"Then why can't you forget?" Her eyes started to fill with tears.

"Maybe one day I will. Because now it's irrelevant."

An uneasy pause hung between them, and Lance couldn't help remembering how much he had loved this woman. A love he'd worked too hard to get over.

"How long have you known this girl?"

"This *girl* is a *woman* and her name is Tia." He leaned back in his chair. "I've known her long enough to know that she's someone I want to spend the rest of my life with."

"I thought I was the one who you wanted to spend the rest of your life with," Crystal protested.

"You were. At one point. And we both know just how much that meant to you." He couldn't help the icy glare that filled his eyes.

"I made a horrible, horrible mistake. You know I had trust issues," she said apologetically.

"Because of you, I did, too—until I found someone whom I trust. I hope that one day you can find that, too."

Crystal scooted to the edge of the chair. "But I don't want to find anyone else. I want you," she said bluntly.

Lance rose to his feet. He needed to end this conversation.

It wasn't going anywhere, and now, more than ever, he knew what he had had with Crystal was over.

"Crystal, I can appreciate that you want me, but what we had is finished. I care about you. I always will. And honestly, I will probably always love you."

"Then—"

He held up his hand to cut her off. "No, let me finish." He paused. "I finally closed that chapter of my life and I'm starting a new one with Tia."

Exasperation filled Crystal's face. "Who is she? Where did she come from? Were you messing with her while we were together?"

He bristled at her insinuation. "No, there was only one cheater in our relationship."

She lowered her gaze, ashamed. "I'm sorry."

"If you must know, I met her a little over six months ago."

"So you just meet someone and in six months you want to marry her?"

"You've known where my heart was all along. I'm a one-woman type of man and I've finally found a one-man type of woman."

Crystal sniffled, not bothering to wipe the tears that had found their way down her cheeks. "So, there's nothing I can do to change your mind?"

Lance stood, headed over to his office door, and held it open.

"All you can do for me, Crystal, is wish me well on my new life and stop letting my mother fill your head with these ludicrous ideas of us being together."

Crystal looked as if she wanted to protest, but she didn't say anything as she made her way to the door.

"I'm sorry, I'm not giving up." She leaned over and kissed his cheek. "I can't give up on us—marriage or not. I'm not gonna rest until I get you back."

While her visit had tugged at his heart, he knew Crystal's efforts would be futile. The only person he wanted was the woman he was about to marry, and nothing anyone could say or do would change that.

Chapter 16

Tia put the last of the pin curls into her hair. This time tomorrow, she'd be a married woman. She'd had this dream since she was a little girl. One she'd thought would never come true.

Tia ran her hand over the picture of her sitting on her father's lap when she was seven years old. She wished he were here to give her away tomorrow. Or at least she wished the man in that picture were here. Not the man her father had turned into.

"Knock, knock."

Tia looked up from the photo. She was in her old bedroom—now Bobbi Jo's room. Even though the room was old and dilapidated, it was home, and Tia wanted to spend her last night as a single woman at home.

"Come in," she said, pulling her robe tight around her waist.

Her uncle Leo stuck his head in the door. "Hey, baby girl."

She smiled at the sight of her uncle standing in the doorway in some blue-jean overalls and a plaid shirt, both of which swallowed his frail frame. His salt-and-pepper hair was balding on top, but his skin remained as smooth as silk.

"Hey, Unc. How are you?"

"Fair to middling." He eased into the room and glanced around. "I just wanted to stop in and see how you were doing."

"I'm excited. A little nervous." She plopped down on the bed. The wooden headboard creaked as she sat down. "Where's Mama?"

"Asleep, rattling the hallways with her snoring."

Tia laughed, but her uncle didn't. It struck her that he must have come in for a reason. "What's wrong?"

He released a heavy sigh. "So, are you sure you know what you're doing?"

"What do you mean?" she asked, confused. She knew her uncle wasn't a proponent of marriage, but he had a look of genuine concern on his face. "Are you talking about marrying Lance?"

Uncle Leo shook his head. "Nah, I think he's good for you. But you know how I feel about lies." He narrowed his eyes at her. "Deuteronomy 25:15: 'You must have accurate and honest weights and measures, so that you may live long in the land the Lord your God is giving you. For God detests anyone who does these things, anyone who deals dishonestly.' "

She should've known he was going to come in spouting Bible verses. Growing up, Uncle Leo was known to find a Bible verse for everything. If you scraped your knee, there was a verse for that. If your boyfriend dumped you, there was a verse for that, too.

"Unc, you know I want to be honest with Lance, but Mama—"

"I know what your mama said. But your mama is wrong," he said with conviction. "What's done in the dark will always come to light."

He was stirring up the voice of her conscience. "So what are you saying, Uncle Leo?"

"You know exactly what I'm saying, and I don't have to say it. Deception is a horrible way to start a marriage. Remember, Proverbs 10:9: 'The man of integrity walks securely, but he who takes crooked paths will be found out.' Just think about that." He glared at her one last time before leaving the room.

Tia fell back on the bed and mulled over his words. Her uncle was right. She needed to tell Lance the truth. She couldn't start this marriage by deceiving him. But then images of her telling Gavin the truth came rushing back. The look of shock on his face, followed by disgust, as if she had just told him she'd contracted some horrible communicable disease.

He had shown his disdain when he said, "So you mean if you really were pregnant, something could've been wrong with my kid," referring to the false-pregnancy scare they'd had.

"But I wasn't," she'd replied.

He said nothing else, then suddenly excused himself. That was the last time she'd ever seen him. He left a message about how this "wasn't working out," then changed his number.

Tia snapped out of her thoughts when her cell phone rang.

She glanced at the caller ID, then smiled. "Hi, Mr. Kingston," she answered.

"Hi, Mrs. Soon-to-Be Kingston. I just wanted to hear your voice."

"How was your night?" Lance had passed on having a full-scale bachelor party, but a few close friends had taken him out for a night on the town.

"It was cool. But you know the whole party scene isn't really my thing, so I just wanted to get home. Get ready for tomorrow. I'm on my way home now."

What's done in the dark . . . Tia sighed. She really needed to go through with this, no matter what the consequences were. "Lance, I need to talk to you. There's something I need to tell you. Can you come by here?"

"What's wrong? You're not getting cold feet, are you?" He sounded alarmed.

"No, of course not."

"Then what is it?"

"Ummm . . ."

"Okay, Tia, you're scaring me."

She gave a brittle laugh. "No, it's nothing like that. I just have something I need to tell you. Can you come over to my mom's?"

"I'm on my way."

Fifteen minutes later, Tia tiptoed out the front door. Uncle Leo was sitting in the den watching a late-night TV show. "Where are you going this late?"

"I'll be outside. Talking to Lance."

Uncle Leo nodded approvingly. "I think that's best." He smiled. "And that man loves you. So everything will work out."

"I hope so, Uncle Leo." She took a deep breath. "I really hope so."

Tia walked out on the porch. She wanted to jump into Lance's arms at the sight of him. "Hey, baby," she said, hugging him.

He hugged her, then immediately pulled back. "So, what's going on?"

Tell him before you lose your nerve.

Tell him and you'll lose him.

"Umm, I just wanted to tell you I love you."

He looked at her skeptically. "I hope you love me, since you're marrying me tomorrow. But I know that's not why you had me race over here."

Tell him.

Tell him good-bye if you do.

Tia closed her eyes to drown out the voices warring in her head. Finally, she opened her eyes and said, "Are you sure you want to do this?"

"I've never been more sure of anything. Why, you're not?"

"No, I am. I . . . I just want to make sure. I mean, what . . . if you get with me and things aren't everything that they seem?" She knew she was losing her nerve. She was being a coward.

"Oh, I'm expecting that. I know you women change when you get married," he joked, finally smiling.

"I'm serious, Lance. What if you get with me and things aren't everything that they seem?"

"I'm in it for the long haul, baby. I'm not going anywhere."

I'm in it for the long haul. Those were the exact words Gavin said . . . right before she told him. But she also knew what they all said when they realized her aura of perfection was just an illusion.

No, she thought frantically. *I'm getting married tomorrow. I love him. I'll make him a good wife.* She knew that was right. She had this disease under control. It would never even come up.

Tia smiled widely, feeling relieved at last. "Then, I can't wait until tomorrow so we can begin our happily ever after."

Lance pulled her close. "Babe, you just don't know. That is music to my ears."

Tia hugged her future husband tightly and said one more prayer for her happily ever after.

Chapter 17

Lance was just hours away from being a married man. He'd heard horror stories about grooms-to-be and their last-minute jitters, but he felt surprisingly calm.

Lance adjusted his silver bow tie, gave himself a once-over, admiring the simple black tux, before going to check to make sure his mother was okay. Lance knew the whole idea of his getting married so quickly—and without all the pomp and circumstance—was eating her alive.

He'd just reached for the doorknob when it swung open.

"Whoa," Lance said, jumping back as the door just missed his nose. "I don't need a black eye on my wedding day."

"Sorry, man," Brian said, stepping into the room. He glanced around the small bathroom. "Good thing you got dressed at home. This place is awful." He turned his nose up at the bare walls, rusted sink, and the door falling off the raggedy stall.

"Well, I just stepped in to check and make sure I was looking my best," Lance replied.

"Please. You look good, man. No homo," he quickly added. They shared a laugh before Brian's expression turned serious. "But, um, I was looking for you because . . ."

Lance wasn't sure what to make of his friend's confusion. Nervousness was etched all over Brian's face. "Because what?"

Brian looked to be weighing his words carefully. Finally he said, "There's someone here to see you."

"Who?" It's not like they'd invited a bunch of people. This was strictly family and their closest friends.

Brian continued to shift uncomfortably. "Ummm . . ."

"Would you just spit it out? Who's here to see me?"

"Ummm, he, well, he says he's your father."

Lance stared at his friend in stunned disbelief. He'd shared his hatred for his father with Brian a number of times, so Brian knew this would be unwelcome news.

"I mean, I started to tell him to beat it," Brian continued, "but I didn't know if you, you know, you wanted to see him."

Lance didn't give Brian a chance to finish as he brushed past him and stomped out into the foyer.

He rounded the corner and stopped in his tracks. It was as if Lance were looking in a mirror twenty years later. The man standing in front of him was his spitting image, minus the gray hair. They had the same muscular build, the same broad shoulders, and the same chiseled features.

Keith Kingston grinned at the sight of his son. "Well, look at you."

"What the hell are you doing here?" Lance hissed, stepping closer.

"I just wanted to see you."

"That's the joke of the century. See me since *when*?" The sound of female laughter coming down the hall jolted Lance out of his astonishment. He grabbed his father's arm and pushed him out a side door. The last thing he needed was his mother seeing her ex. It would ruin the whole day.

"Hey, so you're into manhandling your old man now?" Keith said, stumbling as Lance pushed him out the door.

Lance wasn't amused. "I'm gonna ask you again. What are you doing here?"

Acting offended, Keith brushed imaginary lint off his jacket. "I heard you were getting married and I wanted to be here."

Lance stared at his father as if waiting for some sick joke to be revealed. "Are you serious?" he finally said. "Are you freaking serious?" Lance ran his hand over his forehead as he paced back and forth in the small alley. "I haven't seen you in years and you just show back up on the most important day of my life like you have an invitation?"

Keith stepped toward Lance and extended his hand. "Look, Son—"

Lance slapped his father's hand away as if it were contaminated. Lance took a step back. "Don't. Don't *Son* me." He shook his head in disbelief. "I can't believe your nerve. What in that warped mind of yours made you think this was a good idea?"

Regret filled Keith's face. "Lance, I know I haven't done

right by you." He inhaled deeply. "But I . . . I miss you and I just wanted to see you. I've been following you for a while," he quickly added. "You're doing great things at that magazine. You don't know how many times I've bragged to my friends about what a success you've become."

"Are. You. Freakin'. Kidding. Me?" Lance yelled.

The side door swung open and Brian stuck his head out. "Lance, are you okay?"

Lance took a deep breath to compose himself. He was not going to let this man mess up his day. "Yeah, Brian. Give me a minute. Just make sure my mom doesn't come out here."

Brian flashed an unsure glance between Lance and his father, then eased the door closed.

"How is your mom?" Keith asked.

"You don't get to ask about her," Lance snapped.

Keith actually looked hurt. "Lance, I know you hate me—"

"You think?"

"And rightfully so. But you have to understand, I never wanted to be tied down."

"That's funny," Lance replied sarcastically, "I thought when you married someone, you knew you were being tied down."

"Man wasn't meant to be monogamous." Keith let out a small chuckle, then caught himself. "I'm sorry, it's just that I always have been a rolling-stone type of guy." He shrugged and flashed a small smile. "I mean, the Temptations could've written that song 'Papa Was a Rolling Stone' after me."

Lance couldn't believe what he was hearing. "And you're

proud of this?" he asked, astonished. "You're proud of marrying my mama, then leaving her with three kids?"

Keith lost his smile. "Of course I'm not proud of abandoning you guys. But your mom made it clear that I couldn't pop in and out of your lives, and, well, to be honest, I just thought it was best if I just let you go."

It was Lance's turn to laugh. He had to laugh to keep from crying. "Then why the hell are you here?"

"Lance," Keith said, his voice softening, "believe it or not, I love you. I love all you kids and I even love your mother."

"You don't abandon people you love," Lance said through gritted teeth.

"Son, you're still young. And I know you're about to get married, but trust me, that marriage crap is for the birds. I don't know a man around that's happily married. It's just a matter of time before you realize that what I'm saying is true and you'll leave just like I did. Trust me, sooner or later, you'll leave. It's our nature."

Keith had the nerve to smile proudly, making Lance feel sick in the pit of his stomach. He knew one thing, though. He was going to impart some words of wisdom to his father, seeing that it wasn't going to happen the other way around.

"First of all, I'm pledging my eternal love to that woman in there." Lance pointed at the courthouse. "Eternal. For better or for worse. Not 'until I get tired.' "

"So young and naive," Keith said, shaking his head as if Lance just didn't get it.

He was infuriating Lance. Not only did he have the audacity

to show up on Lance's wedding day, but then he was actually trying to convince Lance that he was making a big mistake by getting married.

"If you came here to talk me out of my marriage, you're wasting your time. I don't know you like that."

"Ouch," Keith said, his hand covering his heart.

"Furthermore, what you don't understand is, I'm not you." Lance stepped closer to his father. "I will never be you. I will never turn my back on my family. I will never run out on someone I claim to love."

Keith shook his head in pity. "So you mean to tell me you honestly believe that once you marry her and she changes into a nagging, overbearing slob who lets herself go after she starts popping out kids, you're gonna be okay with that?"

Lance was dumbfounded. "Are you trying to say that's why you left my mama?" Lance wasn't buying that. For as long as he remembered, his mother took immaculate care of herself.

"I'm speaking hypothetically. I'm just saying that you're judging me and one day you're gonna be me. So, try to understand what I'm saying to you."

"For the last time, I will never be you. I will never understand you. And there is nothing on God's green earth that you can say to me to get me to ever forgive you." Lance adjusted his jacket and stood erect. "Now, I'm going to ask you to go back to whatever hole you crawled out of. Go back to your wonderful, carefree, rolling-stone life and don't ever try to contact me again, or, I promise you, blood or not, you will regret it."

Keith ignored the threat. "So I can't be here when you get married?"

Lance snorted. "First of all, you don't believe in marriage. Second, the only people here are people who love and care about me."

"I told you, I love you."

Lance glared at him. "And people *I* love and care about. And, Mr. Kingston, that would not be you." Lance spun around and left his father standing in the alley.

Once back inside, Lance leaned against the door and fought back the tears that were threatening to overcome him. He always wondered how he would react if he saw his father again. He never knew it would hurt so much.

"Hey, sweetheart, are you okay?"

Lance jumped at the sound of his mother's voice. Brian came racing around the corner as Lance tried to compose himself.

"I'm sorry, man, I didn't—"

Lance held up his hand to cut Brian off. "It's okay." Brian nodded and retreated back around the corner.

Beverly stepped closer to her son. "Baby, are . . . are those tears in your eyes?"

Lance quickly wiped his eyes, then forced a smile. "No, Mama. I'm fine."

She gently touched his cheek. "Are you sure? Because if you're having second thoughts, it's not too late," she said wishfully. "I was just about to go check on Tia, I can let her know."

He chuckled. "No second thoughts, Mama." He took her hands. "But can I ask you something?"

She nodded.

"Do you think I have what it takes to make a marriage work?"

She smiled lovingly. "Boy, you have more willpower than anyone I've ever seen. When you set your mind to something, you're going to see it through." She patted his hands like a fond mother. "No matter what anyone else has to say."

"I do, don't I?"

A new look entered her face. "Baby, you know I would rather you wait on this marriage, get to know her a little better—"

"Mama—"

She held up her hand to cut him off. "But that's what I love about you, you are your own man. And at the end of the day, if you like it, I can't do anything but love it. And the one thing I do know, you've never failed at anything. You won't fail at your marriage."

Those were just the words he needed to hear. Lance pushed away all thoughts of his father. One day he'd tell his mother about the visit. But today, he wanted to erase all memories of Keith Kingston and focus on one shining prospect—marrying the woman of his dreams.

Chapter 18

Tia stared at her reflection in the mirror as Lucinda placed the flowered bobby pin in her hair.

"Te ves magnífica!"

"We speak English round here," Lance's grandmother said.

"Mrs. Brooks, that simply means 'Tia looks magnificent,'" Lucinda said.

Mrs. Brooks examined Tia for herself. "You do look lovely," she said with a genuine smile.

Tia noticed her future mother-in-law standing by the door to the small, converted dressing room. Her eyes were puffy and red.

"Mrs. Kingston, what's wrong?" Tia asked.

Beverly Kingston tried to fake a smile, but she wasn't convincing.

"What's wrong?" Tia asked again.

"Nothing, nothing," Beverly finally said.

"Oh, just tell her. No sense walking around here acting like everything's fine when it's not," Lance's grandmother said.

"Oh, no, is it Lance?" Tia jumped from her chair. "Did he change his mind about marrying me?"

Beverly shook her head. "No, it's not that." She sighed heavily. "It's just that, Lance is my only son and I can't believe he's getting married . . . at a courthouse."

Tia's shoulders sank in relief. Lance had already told her that his mother would probably have a meltdown once she learned they weren't having a fancy church wedding. That's what she had dreamed of for her son. Yet Tia and Lance had decided against a big wedding. He didn't have a whole lot of friends, and she had even fewer. In fact, Lucinda, who was Tia's maid of honor, was the first and last name on her friendship roster.

"I know that you wanted a much more elaborate occasion," Tia said. "But we just wanted to come before the JP for a simple ceremony."

"Yeah," Virginia interjected. She was dressed in her absolute Sunday best—a cream suit that looked like something a first lady would wear to a church anniversary, complete with the matching feathered hat. "This day is about Lance and Tia. All that matters is that they're happy. And we should support them. Just because they're not in a church doesn't mean the Lord isn't right there with them."

Tia knew her mother would support her. She'd convinced Tia

that she didn't need to spend all that time or money planning a wedding. She had wanted Tia to get married at her church, but when the minister insisted that Tia and Lance go through six months of premarital counseling, Virginia quickly changed her tune.

"I know," Lance's mother sniffed. "But not only that, you didn't even have an engagement party."

"They weren't engaged long enough to have a party," Lance's grandmother pointed out. "What was it, a month?"

"They didn't want or need a long engagement," Virginia piped in.

"I just never dreamed Lance would be getting married here." Beverly motioned around the room as if it were where they locked up the town drunks.

"Well, at his next wedding, he can have a big shindig," Mrs. Brooks mumbled.

Everyone in the room turned to her in shock.

"I'm kidding. I'm kidding. Gosh, you all don't have any sense of humor."

"You ladies ready?" Lucinda said, breaking the tension. "It's time to get this show on the road."

"Yeah, because I'm sure the judge has to deal with some parking tickets after he gets done marrying you," Mrs. Brooks joked.

"Mama, don't be rude," Beverly said.

Mrs. Brooks shrugged as she headed to the door. "A joke, a joke. Remember what I said about a sense of humor?"

After they left, Tia was left alone in the room with her mother. "Why are you looking at me like that?"

"I'm just so proud of you, sweetheart. I told you, all your

life, you'd be successful. You did things the right way. You got a career; now you got a good man. Next up, you'll give me some grandbabies."

"One step at a time," Tia nervously said. She checked her reflection in the mirror, then said, "Mama, are you sure about this?"

Virginia stepped up behind her daughter and hugged her. "I'm more sure of this than of anything else in my life."

"I hate starting my marriage off deceiving him." Tia had told her mother how she'd tried to tell Lance the truth. Virginia had been adamant that Lance's interrupting her proved "God wanted that secret to stay buried."

Virginia spun her daughter around. "You're not deceiving him. Do you think you know everything about him? Does cancer run in his family? Does he have a history of diabetes?"

"I don't know."

"Exactly. You don't know everything about him, either. But that's what a good marriage is. You learn over the years. You learn and you grow." Virginia brushed down the skirt of Tia's simple white, floor-length dress. "You're starting fresh, sweetie. Everything is going so wonderfully for you. The Lord worked it all out. And I'm glad you stopped taking those pills. I need some grandbabies and we don't want them coming out with three legs."

"You really think it's okay that I stopped?"

"I know it is. You're covered by the blood of Jesus. Look how well you've been doing so far. Now, come on. We don't want to keep my son-in-law waiting."

Tia hugged her mother. "Let's go get me married."

Chapter 19

They'd just returned from a fantastic honeymoon in Antigua, and Lance knew Tia had been impressed with the five-star week they'd had. But his surprises weren't over yet. This was the gift to outdo all gifts. Judging from the look on her face, she was definitely shocked.

"So, you actually want to give me a house as a wedding present?" Tia asked, standing in the foyer of the spacious four-bedroom, five-thousand-square-foot home. "I mean, you actually bought a house?"

"Well, it's not ours yet," Lance replied. "I had to get your stamp of approval. But I have the down payment in escrow, and if you say yes, we just have to turn in the paperwork and it's ours. What do you think?"

"I love it. But you don't think it's a little too big?"

"No, it's perfect for us"—he pulled her closer—"and the family I hope to have one day."

Tia flashed an uneasy smile. They'd talked about kids again on their honeymoon, and she had promised Lance they could start trying in a year.

The house was a dream, with two spiral, wrought-iron staircases, two fireplaces, four oversize bedrooms, and a master closet to die for.

"So, like I said, this is a steal," Brian, Lance's friend and their realtor, said, walking back into the room. "This is a foreclosure property, but as you can see, the owners kept it in top-notch shape. However, at this price, it isn't going to be on the market long."

"Isn't that what you're supposed to say?" Tia asked, smiling.

"Yeah, it is, but I'm being honest on this one." Brian hit Lance on the back. "I wouldn't run game on my boy."

Lance squeezed his wife tighter from behind. "Trust me, babe, he's right, because for this price, I don't see how it can last long."

"Exactly," Brian said. "So go home, think about it, and let me know as soon as possible what you want to do."

Lance looked at Tia. "Do we even need to go home and talk about it? If you say the word, we can move forward now."

She was still feeling overwhelmed. "I do like it." She glanced out on the patio with the gazebo overlooking the pool. She imagined herself relaxing in a hammock underneath the large oak tree. "No, I love it," she whispered. She'd moved her stuff into Lance's house about two weeks after he'd proposed, but she'd told him from jump that she wanted a place they could call theirs. "I really love it."

"Okay, then." Lance beamed, turning back to Brian. "We'll take it!"

"Great! I already have your paperwork." He opened his briefcase and pulled out several legal-size papers. "Tia, you just have to sign at the places where I have the yellow sticky notes. Lance has already filled out everything and signed."

Tia was getting in deeper and deeper. "Oh, I thought you were just getting the house in your name, Lance."

"Why would I just get it in my name?" Lance asked, confused. "This is our house. We're a team, baby."

Tia bit her bottom lip. Lance knew she rented her place and liked it that way, so signing to buy a house was a major step.

Brian held the paper and pen out toward her. Tia hesitantly took it.

"Great," he said after she finally signed.

Two hours later, they were back at home. Tia was fast asleep upstairs and Lance was busy taking care of some paperwork from his job. His cell phone rang, jarring the silence in the house.

"Hey, Lance, it's Brian." He sounded distressed. "It looks like we have an issue here."

"What's wrong?" Lance hoped someone else hadn't placed a bid on the home.

"We might just have to get the house in only your name."

"Why?"

"Well . . ." Brian seemed unsure of how to go on. "Honestly, your wife's credit is shot."

"What are you talking about?" They'd talked about credit and Tia had told Lance that her credit was fairly decent. Granted, he'd never seen her credit report himself, but he had trusted her word.

"Well, I . . ." Brian sounded exasperated. "It's partly my fault. I shouldn't have moved forward and gotten you all excited. I mean, I just assumed that it wouldn't be a problem."

Lance slid open the patio door and stepped out. "Okay, so she's had a few credit issues," he said, sitting down at the patio table, "but it can't really be that bad, can it? I mean, factor in both of our salaries, and I just don't see how it could be bad enough to keep us from getting a house."

Brian blew a heavy breath. "No, man. I couldn't get a lender to touch you with a ten-foot pole with this credit report of hers."

"Okay, Brian, stop beating around the bush. What's Tia's score?"

"It's four hundred twenty."

"Four-twenty!" Lance almost screamed. He didn't even know scores went that low. "How the hell does she have a four-twenty?"

"Umm, let's see, there are three bankruptcies, numerous charge-offs, and"—Brian paused—"several high balances on a number of credit cards."

"What kind of balances?" Lance asked as he grabbed a pen and a napkin and started jotting down what Brian was telling him.

"Okay, there's nine thousand at Macy's, six thousand at Victoria's Secret, fifteen thousand at Nordstrom's." Brian stopped briefly. "Wow, there are credit cards here to almost every major department store that exists. She even has one to Old Navy. I didn't even know Old Navy had credit cards. And each of them are maxed out. A few have been closed, but on the rest, it looks like she makes the minimum payment. Then there are two judgments against her from creditors. According to this, Tia pays roughly eight thousand dollars a month in minimum payments. No way will a lender touch this."

Lance was stunned. This didn't sound like Tia in the slightest. She said she liked to shop—what woman didn't—but this was ridiculous. "It has to be some kind of mistake."

"Maybe so. Hopefully so," Brian replied. "But this is what the report says, and it's what the lender will pull. You can dispute this stuff or try to get it cleared up, but that's gonna take some time. Since the mortgage crisis, lenders have been real strict, so they're gonna want your spouse listed, especially since Texas is a community-property state. Unless of course, you're willing to lie about being married."

Lance couldn't believe what he was hearing. He held the phone against his ear, not responding, trying to analyze everything his friend was saying.

"Lance, you there, man?"

"Yeah," Lance said, shaking himself out of his trance, "I'm here. Just a little shocked, that's all."

"Yeah, I was, too. But, man, I'm sorry. Unless you got the cash to pay for the house free and clear, I can tell you it's going to be a serious challenge to get you financed. Or I could try to get you with a B or C lender who might be willing to just do it in your name, but I can tell you, your interest rate will be higher."

Lance shook his head. "No, no, Brian. We want the house, but if what you're saying is true, we need to stay right here in my house that's already paid for."

"Yo, I get that, man. So just let me know what you want me to do."

"Okay."

Brian allowed a few beats to pass. "Lance, I'm sure this has to be a mistake. I see it all the time. People aren't even aware that someone is racking up debt in their name."

"Thanks, man." Lance hung up the phone, praying that Brian was right. He took a deep breath, then went inside to confront his wife.

Chapter 20

Lance hated waking Tia. She'd been out of it all day. Since they'd gotten back from their honeymoon, she'd been a little sluggish. He assumed that she hadn't quite recovered from jet lag.

"Tia," he said, sitting on the edge of the bed and tapping her lightly on the leg. She stirred, then turned over on her side.

"Tia," he repeated, shaking her a little harder.

Tia's eyes slowly opened. "Huh?"

"Wake up, babe. We need to talk."

She slowly pulled herself up on the headboard, still groggy. "What's going on? I was knocked out."

"I'm sorry to wake you up."

"This couldn't wait till later? I'm worn-out."

"No, really, it can't wait."

The tone of his voice grabbed her attention because she completely woke up. "What's wrong?"

"I just got off the phone with Brian."

"And?"

"And I see why you wanted to get the house in my name."

"What does that mean?"

"It means, your credit score is so low that nobody would give you a woodshed, let alone a house." Lance didn't give her time to respond before he continued. "Now, I told Brian that this has to be some type of mistake because you did tell me that you had good credit."

"I said it was decent and I hadn't looked at it in a long time," she said defensively.

"Okay," Lance said slowly. He was trying not to get upset, but if he prided himself on one thing, it was good credit. So this revelation was definitely unsettling. "But there still has to be some type of mistake because you have numerous charge cards that carry large balances—unbelievable balances, I might add."

"Yeah, I've heard people say there are always mistakes on credit reports." She tried to appear casual, but he could tell he'd hit a nerve.

"That's why I would think you'd check it more regularly. But let me ask you," he said, pulling out the napkin he'd been writing on earlier. "Do you have a credit card with Nordstrom's?" Her silence answered his question. "What about Macy's, Dillard's, Old Navy?"

"So? I like to shop."

"Tia, these credit cards have ridiculous balances. Who spends five thousand dollars at Old Navy?"

"I bought summer stuff."

He massaged his temples. "Okay, Tia, this isn't making sense to me. Why would you run up your credit cards like that? And I distinctly recall asking you about credit cards during one of our discussions. You said you had a Visa and a couple of department store cards that you use."

"I do have a couple that I *use.*" She stopped and looked as if she was debating whether to continue. "I can't use the others," she finally said.

"Because they're maxed out?"

Again, her silence answered his question. "Whatever. I was only talking about the ones I use."

"So now we're lying by omission?"

She was starting to become more animated. "Don't start with me. It's my credit."

"Tia, there's no such thing as *your* credit anymore. We're married. We're a partnership now."

"Well, I like to shop. All I do is freaking work from sunup to sundown. And the only outlet I've had over the years is to go shopping. So sue me if there is something wrong with that."

He glanced down at his notes. "Yeah, it looks like someone has already sued you."

She started quickly patting her leg, rocking back and forth. Lance wasn't sure, but it almost seemed that she was trying to keep herself from getting angry. Why the hell would *she* be the one who was mad?

"Tia, this is a real problem," Lance said, waving the napkin.

"Look, don't come in here judging me," she snapped.

"I'm not judging you, but how are we supposed to buy a new home?"

"You're the one who wanted the stupid house. What's wrong with this home?"

He looked at her, confused. "You were the one who was adamant that we move because you wanted to 'start fresh with something that belonged to both of us.' "

She rolled her eyes as if he was really agitating her. "Just get it in your name like I said in the first place."

"We can't, but that's not the point. Your credit is so messed up that we need to do everything we can to dig ourselves out of that hole."

"So, now I guess you wish you'd never married me. I knew it," she said, throwing back the cover and pulling herself out of the bed.

He grabbed her arm gently. "What? Why are you being so extreme? I'm upset, yes. But nobody said anything about wishing I hadn't married you. I just wish you'd been honest with me."

She folded her arms. "So, I guess we're gonna have to wait to move now?"

Lance couldn't believe her attitude. "Yeah, I guess so. Right now we need to get this mess you created cleaned up."

"So exactly what is it you want me to do?"

Lance wondered how this issue had gotten turned around so he was to blame.

"We can fix this," he finally said. She was getting worked up and Lance didn't want the conversation to get any worse than it already had. He didn't want their first real fight to escalate out of control. "Just promise me that you'll be honest with me from now on." He lifted her chin. "No more secrets, okay?"

She shrugged. "Fine."

"And there's nothing else you need to tell me, right?"

She looked him in the eye, then casually said, "What else is there to tell?"

Chapter 21

The stress of everything she had been doing had taken its toll—the wedding, the copyright case, Mrs. Bailey's case, the promotion, and now, fighting with Lance. A part of her wished she had just lied and told him someone had stolen her identity. But she didn't want to dig herself into a hole deeper than the one she was already in.

Tia felt she desperately needed to take a couple of days off, especially because she hadn't been feeling well lately. Maybe the traveling to Antigua—as relaxing as it had been—had created too much stress. Maybe the wedding had created this awful feeling of pressure. Even pulling together a small ceremony had been a headache, given that she still had to handle her increased caseload. She knew stress could be a trigger for her disease, so she had to do something to truly relax her mind.

Tia was feeling wired as she pulled open the Home Depot bag and took out the bag of soil and gardening gloves. She wanted to lose herself in the feel of the dirt. She'd bought roses, tulips, and baby's breath and was looking forward to watching them bloom. She had always had a green thumb. Ever since her first science project in the third grade, when she was responsible for babysitting the eucalyptus plant her class was growing. She didn't get to indulge in gardening much these days, so she was really hoping it would relax her.

But first she needed to get comfortable, so she changed into some old jogging pants and a big, green, floppy hat. Tia grabbed her iPod and headed outside. She lost herself in her Vivian Green album as she worked in the flowerbed. This was absolutely the right idea, she thought. She felt euphoric.

She didn't look up until she felt a tap on her shoulder. "Hey, Mama," she said, removing the earphones from her ears.

Her mother looked uneasy. "Hi, sweetheart." Virginia studied the plants. "Ummm, what are you doing?"

Tia pulled herself up off the ground. "What does it look like?" she said, chuckling. "I'm gardening. You like?"

"Ummm, yeah . . . I think they're beautiful," her mother said with a tight smile.

"I do, too." Tia wiped her hands on her pants. "I was just wrapping up. Come on in. I fixed chicken salad."

Virginia glanced at the flowers one last time and walked inside.

"So, Ma, what's up?" Tia asked as she grabbed a bottled water out of the refrigerator.

"I just stopped by to check on you. See how things were going." Her mother shifted uncomfortably.

"I'm good, Ma. I really am." Yet her mother had a worried expression on her face. "I'm happy and I never thought I would be."

Finally, Virginia relaxed and smiled, patting her daughter's cheek. "I knew he would make you happy, baby. And that's all I've ever wanted."

They hugged, then sat down and chatted some more as her mom filled her in on Uncle Leo and Curtis's latest fight. They'd been talking for about twenty minutes when the front door opened.

"There's my Prince Charming now," Tia said, looking up at her husband. He hadn't brought up the credit issue in the past three days, so Tia promised herself that she would adjust her attitude as well.

Lance stood in the entrance to the kitchen, looking baffled.

"Hey, honey," Tia said, rising to greet him.

"Hey," he said, before glancing over at his mother-in-law. "Hi, Mrs. Virginia."

"I told you, it's *Mama*."

"Okay, Mama." He forced a smile. "But, um . . ." He held up his hand, which was clutched tightly around one of the flowers Tia had just planted. "Tia, what's this?"

She gasped. "Why did you pick my tulips? I just planted those!"

Lance looked at her, then at the flowers in his hand, then over at Virginia, who was sitting there with a crazy smile on her face.

He turned his attention back to his wife and shook the flowers. "Tia, these are plastic. All of them are plastic."

"And?"

"And, why would you plant plastic flowers?"

Tia snatched the tulips. She was distraught that he had destroyed her hard work. She had barely planted them. "Give me my flowers!" She started crying. "I try to do something nice to beautify this house and this is how you show your thanks? You just mess everything up." She stomped out of the room.

"Tia"—Lance took off after her—"I wasn't trying to upset you. I just don't understand why you would plant plastic flowers."

She stopped at the bottom of the stairway and spun toward him. A wave of uncontrollable rage filled her body.

"*And?* What's wrong with plastic flowers?!" she screamed. Suddenly, the surge of rage gave way to confusion, and Tia felt her mind jumbling up. Were these flowers really plastic? She couldn't remember. She remembered being in the store and seeing one batch of flowers and deciding the other batch looked so much better.

"Tia . . ."

"No, don't worry about it!" She snapped out of her trance as she stomped back outside. "All I wanted to do was make this house beautiful," she cried as she began ripping the flowers from the dirt. She viciously flung them across the yard. As she touched them, she had no doubt they were plastic. By this point, though, her mind had moved beyond that point. Lance shouldn't have touched them, period.

"Hey, stop, stop!" Lance said, coming up behind her and wrapping his arms around her. "I'm sorry."

He held her as she broke down crying. How the hell could she have planted plastic flowers?

She saw the stunned disbelief across his face. "Babe, I'm so sorry. I wasn't trying to upset you, really I wasn't," he said. "It was just *different*. I haven't ever seen plastic flowers planted in a garden. But they're nice, so we'll leave them as they are. And if our neighbors don't like it, too bad. Okay?"

Tia was still in a daze. What had just happened? She shook her head trying to gather her bearings. Lance wiped the tears away.

Her mother was standing in the doorway, watching the scene unfold. Why hadn't her mom said anything about the flowers being plastic?

But then Tia quickly knew the answer to that question. Her mom never said anything when she had her manic attacks.

"I just put on a fresh pot of tea, so come on in," Virginia said, smiling at her son-in-law. "Lance, I need to tell you how that fight with Curtis and Leo turned out. You won't believe those two fools."

She laughed lightly as she turned and walked into the kitchen as if nothing had even happened. Tia, on the other hand, knew that this was a bad sign. The mood swings always started like this. Some obsessive, irrational behavior. She felt her eyes tear up. *No, no, no,* she thought to herself. First thing tomorrow, she was calling Dr. Monroe. She had to nip her problem in the bud before it snuck up on her again. She couldn't let that happen because this time she had too much to lose.

Chapter 22

Tia closed her eyes and inhaled. This was not a good sign. She had called Dr. Monroe first thing this morning, only to be told he was on vacation for the rest of the week. That meant that if Tia was backsliding, she couldn't do a thing about it.

She'd tried to sleep yesterday after the flower fiasco, but she was so worked up that all she could do was clean. She'd scrubbed the house from top to bottom. At 2:00 a.m. Lance had begged her to come to bed, but Tia was still worked up. She blamed her nervousness on her pending case, and he'd left her alone. At four in the morning she finally lay down, only to get up two hours later.

Tia was sure Lance had pressed her mother for some answers when he'd walked her to the car yesterday, but Tia knew how that had turned out. Virginia had probably downplayed everything and said Tia was just stressed.

That was the same lie she'd reiterated to Lance this morning. Despite her lack of sleep, she wasn't tired as they got dressed this morning. She did feel anxious, though, as if a hot wire were vibrating all through her, which usually was a bad sign.

"Dear Lord, please let everything be okay," Tia said, mumbling a small prayer.

"Tia, what are you doing?"

Tia snapped her eyes open to see Lucinda standing in her office doorway. "Huh?"

"Court!" Lucinda jabbed at her watch. "You have court in ten minutes. And it's before Judge Gilmore. You know she doesn't play."

"Oh, no!" Tia said, jumping up. She didn't know what had happened. She remembered getting to work early, calling the doctor, then fixing her coffee and sitting down to go over the briefs before her 9:00 a.m. court date. How in the world had two hours passed by just like that?

"What were you doing?" Lucinda asked as Tia frantically began gathering her things.

"I don't know." Tia didn't want to admit that she'd literally zoned out.

"You are not going to have time to find a parking space at the courthouse. Let me drop you off," Lucinda offered as they hurried toward the elevator. "You can get Clive to drop you back at the office after court," she said, referring to the second-chair attorney working on this case with Tia.

"Thank you, girl. You're a lifesaver," Tia said as they stepped on the elevator.

On the ride over, Tia kept reviewing the briefs. Lucinda didn't say much, probably because she was worried as well. This was completely unlike Tia to be late for court, especially in Judge Gilmore's court. She would hold an attorney in contempt of court in a minute.

As Tia continued reading, she started to freak out. None of the words on the brief were making any sense. But it was her work; she'd prepared it. She had to figure it out.

"What in the world is going on with you?" Lucinda asked after they'd been riding for a few minutes.

Tia leaned back in the seat and rubbed her temples. Now, on top of everything else, her head was throbbing.

"Girl, I don't know. I guess I'm stressing behind all the stuff going on in my life."

"Okay, well, you need to let the stuff go for now. You'll be just a few minutes late. Tell the judge something came up."

Tia cut her eyes at Lucinda. Both of them knew that excuse wouldn't fly. Judge Gilmore would be livid. On top of that, the client was going to be pissed.

"Come on, you'll be okay," Lucinda said reassuringly as she pulled up to the curb at the federal courthouse.

"Let's hope so," Tia mumbled as she climbed out of the car. "Thanks. I'll call you later."

Inside the courtroom, all the parties were sitting at their respective tables. This was a multimillion-dollar copyright-infringement suit, and Tia was representing a noted writer who was suing. He shot her daggers as she strode swiftly to the table.

"Nice of you to join us, Miss Jiles," Judge Gilmore coldly said.

"It's Kingston now," Tia replied. "Jiles-Kingston."

The judge looked at her as if she were crazy. "Miss *Jiles,* I am really not up for debating the merits of your last name. This trial was scheduled to start at nine. If I could be here, the jurors could be here, the defense, even your client, why is it you could not be here?"

"I . . . I'm sorry, Your Honor. If we can just go ahead and get started, I'm ready."

The client mean-mugged Tia as she tried to get situated. Agitated, she opened her briefcase, only to have papers fall out everywhere.

"Is everything okay?" Clive Lewis whispered. Clive was fresh out of law school, and this was his first real case.

"Yeah, yeah, I'm fine." Tia knew everyone was astounded because usually she was together, thorough. This scatterbrained behavior was totally out of character, and she had no idea where it was coming from.

Judge Gilmore shot Tia one last, angry look, then ordered the jurors in. After all twelve of them had been seated, she turned to Tia. "Miss Jiles, you may call your first witness."

"Yes, Your Honor." Tia studied her scattered papers blindly. Who was her first witness? The courtroom was silent as she tried to remember. Luckily, the name finally came to her. "Um, the plaintiffs call film director Colin Woods."

A tall, stocky man entered the courtroom, walked to the front, and held his hand up to be sworn in. After he was seated, Tia began with the basic questions—name, age, qualifications, experience, etc.

A few minutes into questioning, the director had given no more than curt answers. He'd made it clear that he was a "busy man" and didn't have time for "this foolishness." His hostile demeanor started to frustrate Tia.

"Look, Mr. Woods," she said, slamming her folder down onto the podium, "let's stop with the games. You know you stole my client's screenplay and sold it to this studio, so let's cut this bull. Just admit that you lied, you dirtbag!"

The courtroom erupted in alarmed chatter.

"Your Honor!" Two of the defense attorneys shot to their feet and objected at the same time. Colin's eyes grew wide in shock.

"Miss Jiles!" Judge Gilmore said, banging her gavel. "Have you lost your mind?"

Tia didn't take her eyes off Colin. "No, Your Honor. I'm just fed up with crooked snakes like Mr. Woods here trying to get over on innocent people. Liars like him make me sick."

As the attorneys stood to object again, Tia picked up her notepad and hurled it in Colin's direction. He ducked, but not before the corner of the pad clipped him in the forehead.

Once again, the courtroom erupted in chaos.

"Bailiff, get Miss Jiles out of here!" Judge Gilmore demanded, banging her gavel several times.

The bailiff rushed over to Tia. She didn't try to resist as he grabbed her by the arm.

"What are you doing?" Tia asked as the bailiff stepped toward her. She paused to catch her bearings. She was way off-kilter. Could it be another "episode"? That's what her mother called it whenever Tia's mind got jumbled up.

"I'm sorry, you have to come with me," the bailiff said. He looked just as bewildered as she did.

Her moment of clarity passed as quickly as it had come, and she asked, "Oh, are we going to lunch already?" A smile spread across her face. She could definitely use some lunch. She was starving.

The judge studied Tia. "Miss Jiles, are you okay?"

Tia answered serenely, "I'm fine. What is everyone getting so worked up about?"

"Miss Jiles, you just hit the defendant in the head with your notepad."

Tia noticed that Colin was still staring at her in utter disbelief.

She shrugged. "He deserved it, Your Honor. His head is so thick, he probably didn't even feel it."

The judge continued to study her. Tia had been in her courtroom many times, which was probably the only reason Judge Gilmore said, "Miss Jiles, I need to see you in my chambers immediately. Court stands in a fifteen-minute recess." She banged the gavel, stood, and headed out of the side door.

Tia followed, smiling at Colin as she passed. "Cute tie," she told him as she sauntered out of the courtroom.

Someone knocked on the door to the judge's chambers just as Tia took her seat.

"Yes?" Judge Gilmore said, irritated.

Clive poked his head in the door. "Your Honor, I'm sorry to disturb you, but may I come in as well? I'm a little worried about Tia."

Judge Gilmore waved him in. "As well you should be." The judge sat behind her desk. "Miss Jiles—"

"Kingston," Tia said, cutting her off. "You know I got married." She held out her hand and waggled her fingers, displaying her ring. "He is sooo fine and rich, intelligent, and he adores me."

Judge Gilmore ignored her. "Are you on any type of medication?"

Tia shook her head. "No." Nope, she hadn't had any medication in months now.

"What about illegal substances?" the judge asked more pointedly.

"Of course not."

The judge shook her head, trying to make sense of what had just occurred. "Miss Jiles, you'd better be glad I respect your work and think very highly of you. Otherwise, you would be sitting *under* the jail. Can you please explain to me what just happened in there?"

Once again Tia shrugged nonchalantly. "He was lying."

"Okay," Judge Gilmore said slowly, "but that is up to the jury to decide. You are to present your case, and that's it."

Tia looked at her watch. "How long is this going to take? Girl, I'm hungry."

Judge Gilmore's mouth dropped open. Finally, she turned to Clive. "Mr. Lewis, I am going to adjourn court for today. I suggest that you take Miss Jiles home and figure out what in the hell is wrong with her. And I want to see you here tomorrow as the lead attorney on this case."

"What?" Tia said, jumping up from her chair. "I'm the lead attorney on this! He can't take my case."

"He can when I'm banning you from my courtroom."

"Banning me?" Tia was set back on her heels for a moment, but she recovered. With a sly grin she said, "Oh, you must've forgotten, I know what happened at the mayor's Christmas party in 2008." Tia smirked. "Unless you want everyone else to know, I suggest you lift that stupid ban."

Judge Gilmore's eyes burned with fury. "Miss Jiles, since it is obvious there is something terribly wrong with you, I'm going to pretend that you did not just say that."

"You want me to say it again?" Tia asked defiantly.

Judge Gilmore pounded her desk. "I'm going to pretend that you are not blackmailing me, or threatening me, or acting a damn fool in my courtroom!" She took a deep breath before turning to Clive. "Get her out of my chambers."

"Come on, Tia, let's go call your husband," Clive gently said, taking Tia's arm.

"Call him for what?" Tia asked as he led her out. She stopped at the door and gave the judge a flirty wave. "Bye, girl. I'll talk to you later."

Halfway down the hall, Clive stopped and turned Tia around so that they were face-to-face. "Tia, what in the world is going on? First, you assault the defendant, then you try to blackmail the judge. I know this is my first case, but . . ." His words trailed off as he was too dumbfounded to say anything else.

Tia paused. Her mind was swirling again. *Assault? Who was assaulted?* she wanted to ask. But everything was jumbling together, so instead she simply said, "I don't feel well. Can you please take me home?"

Chapter 23

This had been the day from hell. The superstar singer who was supposed to appear on the cover of next month's issue had just been arrested for domestic abuse, and since it was an issue featuring women's empowerment, they'd been scrambling to find a replacement. Lance didn't like being caught off guard like that and had given his staff a good tongue-lashing. He'd come home to retrieve his personal Rolodex. He'd have to call in some favors to get a major celebrity to fill the void.

When Lance pressed the button to open the garage, he was surprised to see his wife's BMW. By the time he'd gotten home yesterday, she was already in bed and Lance didn't want to disturb her, since he knew she had to be exhausted after staying up the whole night before. He'd left before she woke up this morning, but since he knew she was in the middle of a trial, he just assumed she'd be at work.

"Tia," he called out as he made his way inside.

"In the den," she answered.

Lance found her sitting on the sofa watching *Law & Order*. Her hair was wet, as if she'd just washed it, and she was wearing some comfortable sweatpants and a T-shirt.

"Hey, there," he said, dropping his keys on the bar with a metallic click. "You didn't have to work today?"

"Nah, they canceled court for today," she said, not taking her eyes off the TV. She looked worn-out.

"How are you today?" Lance asked, leaning down and kissing her on the cheek.

"Okay," she replied tensely.

"Are you sure?" She didn't look okay. The flower incident had disturbed him, but both Virginia and Tia had played it down. He had reasoned with himself later that maybe in her neighborhood, people thought differently about plastic flowers.

"Just a little stressed." She flashed a tired smile. "Since I was off today, I cooked. I have your favorite, shrimp enchiladas. So go get changed and meet me back here for dinner."

Lance kissed her again, then made his way to the back of the house to their master bedroom. He walked inside and froze.

"Tia!" he shouted.

She came racing in. "What's wrong?"

"What in the world is this?"

She grinned and folded her arms across her chest. "Oh, the room. You like it?"

"It's purple!"

"I know. I just wanted to change things up." She said that as if she'd simply added a plant or something.

"When did you do this? Better yet, *why* did you do this?" This was unbelievable. Their entire bedroom was a putrid shade of purple.

"Since I got off work early, I decided to paint. I just wanted to do something different. I was tired of the same old stuff."

"Tired? What was wrong with the color it was?"

"The beige was boring. I wanted to spruce it up."

"Then you buy a plant, a picture, a new comforter. You don't paint the whole bedroom purple!" he bellowed.

Tia's expression instantly changed and a scowl crossed her face. "I was trying to surprise you," she hissed.

"Yeah, this is a surprise, all right." He was stunned as he looked around the room. Purple paint was splashed all over the ceiling and the carpet. She'd missed some spots altogether, and beige peeked through gaps all over the place. It looked as if a three-year-old had painted the room in ten minutes.

"You really painted this yourself?"

She folded her arms defiantly. "Yes, I sure did, and I think I did a pretty good job."

"Are you freaking kidding me?" He walked around the room in shock. She'd even gotten paint on the leather love seat in the corner.

In even worse shape was the Berber carpet, an upgrade that Tia "just had to have." The carpet that hadn't been there three weeks. "Why didn't you put something down to cover the carpet and the furniture?"

"There is just no pleasing you!" she shouted. "I've been in this stressful court case, and I finally take some time off and try to surprise you with dinner and a little something different, and instead of saying thank you, your ungrateful ass wants to start bitching about a little paint on the carpet!"

Lance was shocked by her outburst. They hadn't had a real argument the entire time they had been dating. Now, in two days, they were having their second major blowout. She was even cursing at him. He'd never heard her curse.

Lance softened his tone. He had to lower the temperature so they could discuss the matter logically. "I just thought it was a bit . . . purple."

"*And?* Purple is your favorite color."

"Yeah, my favorite color for a T-shirt or a pair of shorts," he said, his anger flaring again. "Not for my bedroom."

"You know what? Forget I painted it!" She turned around and stomped out.

"Tia!" he called out as he took off after her. This wasn't making any sense. "Where are you going?"

She didn't answer as she flung open the garage door. She pushed everything off the worktable in the garage, then grabbed a paintbrush and a can of paint.

"Tia, what are you doing?"

She pushed past him. "You hate purple," she said sarcastically, "so we're going to change it. We'll change it back to the boring-ass beige walls. Boring, just like you!"

"Tia . . ."

"No! Who cares what I want?" She continued stomping

toward the bedroom. "It is, after all, your house. I'm just a nobody in this stupid marriage. It's all about what Lance wants!"

Lance kept trying to reason with her as he followed her to the bedroom. She plopped the can of paint down, then used a pair of keys to flip the top off. She was moving so fast that the top popped off and onto the carpet, adding another stain.

"Tia, we don't have to do this, babe." Lance was dumbfounded. He didn't know who this woman in his bedroom was.

Tia took the brush and slammed it against the wall, right over their prized John Biggers portrait.

Lance reached out to grab her hand and stop her, but that sent her into even more of an out-of-control spiral.

"Don't touch me!" she screamed. "Don't ever put your disgusting hands on me again. You're a demon!" With that, Tia ran from the room. Lance stood with paint dripping from his custom-made suit—onto their Berber carpet. All he could think was *What in the hell just happened?*

Chapter 24

Tia sat in the plush Victorian chair, nervously wringing her hands. She hated that she had called, but since she'd come to her senses, she knew that she *had* to make this appointment.

"Mrs. Kingston," Dr. Monroe began, "I am so glad you took the initiative to come see me."

"I'm sorry to make you cut your vacation short." She was grateful that Dr. Monroe's secretary had put Tia's call through to him and he'd agreed to meet her today. As it turned out, he was only taking a staycation.

"I only had a couple of days left, and trust me, I'll make up for it." He grinned. "Now, tell me, what's going on?"

Tia didn't know where to begin. Between the flowers, the outburst in court, the painting, and the homicidal thoughts she had been having this past week, she knew she was in trouble. And Lance knew something was wrong, too. Tia had apologized for the paint incident this morning and told Lance that she was just extremely upset about her cases. She said she was going to her family practitioner for migraines because she believed that's why she'd been so over the top.

Lance had wanted to come, but she'd purposely told him her doctor's appointment was at the same time as a crucial business meeting he had. He'd even tried to reschedule the meeting, but Tia had convinced him that wasn't necessary. He'd finally acquiesced, but Tia knew it was just a matter of time before Lance stopped buying her excuses. That's why she'd broken down and called Dr. Monroe. She had to get things back under control.

"I . . . I wish that I weren't here, to be honest, Dr. Monroe. But, well, things have been pretty bad for me lately." She had hired professional painters to clean up the mess she'd made in the bedroom. They should be finished by the time Lance got home today.

"Yes, that's what you said over the phone. Tell me what's been going on." The doctor pushed RECORD on his little digital recorder. "I know you've gotten married since the last time we spoke. Congratulations." When she didn't respond, he asked, "How is your husband coping with your illness?"

Tia continued wringing her hands and she kept her eyes diverted.

Dr. Monroe leaned forward. "Tia, please tell me you've told your husband about your illness."

She mumbled almost inaudibly, "No, he doesn't know."

The doctor looked extremely disappointed in her.

"I was fine until recently," she protested. "For months. But

I've had a couple of episodes this past week, so he definitely knows something is wrong now. I thought I was over it, so I never told him about the . . . ummm . . . ummm, the . . ."

"Bipolar disorder?"

She sighed. "Yes, I've never told him I suffer from my condition. I thought I had it under control."

"You've got to be honest with him, Tia."

Dr. Monroe didn't know how badly Tia wanted to come clean with Lance, but she simply couldn't risk it. Tia had no doubt Lance genuinely loved her, and she didn't need him questioning his decision. She couldn't bear thinking he would start hating that he'd married her.

"You know the last man I told, left. I love Lance, I really do. I couldn't take it if he abandoned me as well."

"Tia, the only way your husband can help you deal with this is to know what's going on. What does he say when he sees you taking the medication?" He eyed her curiously when she once again looked away. "You are taking your medicine, right? I know I haven't renewed your prescription, but the last time you were here, you told me you had three refills from your prescription from Dr. Stanton."

Tia lowered her eyes in shame. Her first inclination was to lie. But she also knew that lying to her doctor would help no one.

"Dr. Monroe, if I may be honest—"

"It's the only way to be."

"I ran out of the medication about nine months ago. And, well, I never refilled the prescription. I just felt like everything was fine. I was starting a new life."

"Which is even more reason for you to take it." His eyes were chastising, and Tia knew this was exactly why she hadn't wanted to see a doctor in the first place. She didn't want anyone standing in judgment of her. Unlike Dr. Stanton, she had always felt that Dr. Monroe disapproved of her.

"Tia, we talked about this in our first session. If you want to live a normal, happy life, you can't get off the medication. It just seems that things are okay and you can handle it. But you can't. You're bipolar, and pretending nothing is wrong isn't going to make it go away."

The words made her cringe.

"You also know stress and change can be a trigger," he continued. "And from what you've told me, you've had changes in your job as well as your marital status. Those are major stressors. So you need your medication more than ever."

Tia lowered her head like a child being scolded. The stress she was feeling had escalated to a whole different level. Mr. Anderson had personally called her yesterday, livid about what had happened in court. He was out of town but demanded that they meet when he returned in two days so that they could "reevaluate" everything.

Tia was devastated, which is why she'd painted the room—to take her mind off the mess she'd made with the copyright case. But all that had done was make an even bigger mess. Now her personal life was in shambles, too. All Tia knew was that she wanted a sane and normal life. Not one shadowed with medications. Her mother swore the medicine was the reason Tia couldn't get better. Tia believed her mother when she said that if Tia prayed hard enough, she'd lead a normal life without the medication. Lord knew, she prayed every day and every night to get rid of the spells. She'd actually thought her prayers had been answered—until recently.

"Tia, are you listening to me?" Dr. Monroe asked, leaning over his desk. "There is no other way to live the life you want. You've got to get back on your medication."

"But, Doc—"

He would not permit any objections. "Tia, there simply isn't any room for discussion about the issue. You're no good to anyone if you're not sane."

"I wish you would stop saying that. I'm not insane."

"Tia, you know I don't dance around. It is what it is. You're bipolar." He tried to soften his words. "Look, you're not alone. Two out of every twenty people suffer from bipolar disorder. I assure you, there are people in your job, your community, your church, going through the same swings. Did you hear about Catherine Zeta-Jones?"

Tia had read an article about that and was shocked because Catherine was one of her favorite actresses.

"You never see them in their manic stage because they take their medicine," he continued. "You can live fine the rest of your life if you take your medicine."

"But I hate the way the drugs make me feel. Besides, my mother said—"

The doctor smiled wearily. "I told you, your mother means well, but she is not the voice of reason you should be listening to. Now, if you don't believe me, I encourage you to get a second, third, fourth opinion. But from a professional." He stood and grabbed a small white pad off his shelf. "First and foremost, we need to get you back on some medication." He scribbled on his pad. "Here, I want you to try a different medication. It's a milder version. I'm going to go ahead and write you a prescription now." He stopped. "No, on second thought, I'm going to have my nurse call it in. Do we have your pharmacy information on file?" Tia nodded slowly. "I'll have the nurse call this in immediately. Are you going to use the pills?"

She blew out a frustrated breath. "Yes, but—"

"Tia, I can't stress enough how much you need to take it," he interrupted before she could start giving excuses. "It's hard enough trying to deal with episodes, but you can't expect your new husband to tolerate them."

She hated when Dr. Monroe used words such as *manic* and *insane*. Those words made her feel that she was really crazy and she wasn't. Her mother called them spells or episodes, or even "that place you go to." Those were the words Tia preferred.

"Tia, I need you to go, pick up your medicine, then go home and talk to your husband. Then you need to get rid of some of the stresses in your life. You know that's the main factor that triggers sixty percent of the episodes in people with bipolar disorder. You just got married. Maybe now isn't the time for a promotion or extra responsibilities at work. Maybe now isn't the time to take on stressful cases. Maybe now isn't the time to move. You've got to cut some of those stresses out or it could have disastrous effects. Do you understand? But before you do anything, you need to talk to your husband."

Tia nodded slowly, even though she knew that conversation

would be so much harder now. She bid the doctor good-bye, then made her way back out to her car. On the drive home, Tia tried to craft the right words to come clean with Lance. But nothing sounded right. The lingering question was always there: *Why are you just now telling me?*

Tia parked and made her way into the CVS pharmacy. At least she was picking up her prescription. She felt like a failure, having to go back on medication after doing so well for so long.

Tia waited behind a young man with curly, red hair, wearing baggy shorts and a plaid, button-down shirt. He looked like a surfer, minus the surfboard.

"What's up?" he said to Tia as he gathered his purchase and left the counter.

She nodded a hello, then stepped to the register. "Hi, I'm picking up a prescription for Tia Kingston."

The pharmacist tapped some keys on the computer, then said, "Oh, Ms. Kingston, we just left a message for you at home. We are out of this medicine, but I can have it sent overnight and you can pick it up tomorrow."

Tia's mouth fell open. She finally got up the nerve to come pick up her medication and they were out?

"I am so sorry," the man apologized.

She released a long sigh. "Okay, fine. I'll come back tomorrow." She turned to leave.

"It should be here after six," he called out after her.

Tia nodded, frustrated as she made her way back out to the car. She'd just opened her door when she heard someone say, "Excuse me."

Tia turned toward the young man from inside. He looked harmless; still, Tia's hand went to the Mace on her key chain.

"Yeah, I, umm, I heard they were out of your prescription in there. Was it for pain?"

Tia looked at the young man as if he were crazy. "I'm sorry?"

"No, I mean, I wasn't trying to get all up in your business," he said quickly. "It's just that if you needed some oxycodone or Valiums, I got some."

Tia looked at him in disbelief. Was he dealing drugs in her exclusive neighborhood? "Wow, no, I'm not looking for painkillers, and if I were, I wouldn't buy them from some stranger on the street," she said, going to unlock her door.

He shrugged. "Just asking."

Suddenly, Tia stopped in her tracks as a memory flashed of the only other way she had been able to help reduce her anxiety in the past. "Hey," she said, stopping the boy as he walked off. He turned back toward her. "Ummm, well . . ." She almost stopped herself, then she thought about the last few days and knew she had to do something. She'd tried to get her medication and it hadn't worked out. She still needed something to take the edge off—help her take her anxiety down a notch.

The young man was waiting. "Yeah?"

"Well, I don't need painkillers, but, umm, maybe there is something else you can help me with."

He looked around the parking lot. "You say the word, and I got whatever you need to fix what ails you." He chuckled, a huge grin spreading across his face.

Chapter 25

It had been another long day. Between putting out fires at work and his SUV's transmission slipping a few times—a bad sign—Lance was worn-out. He was looking forward to getting home and relaxing. He'd tried to call and find out how Tia's doctor's appointment went, but she wasn't answering her phone. He hoped that meant the doctor had given her a sedative for her migraines and she was at home fast asleep.

As soon as Lance walked in the door, the smell hit him in the face. "Is that what I think it is?" he mumbled while sniffing the cloying odor.

He followed the scent into the kitchen, where he saw Tia standing over the stove, wearing nothing but a pair of stilettos.

"Tia?" His wife slowly turned toward him, revealing all of her naked glory. "Do I smell . . ."

His words trailed off as Tia lifted a joint to her mouth, took a long huff, held it, then blew the smoke out.

"Do you smell what? Dinner?" she said coyly. "Yep, I got the Italian spaghetti going like a world-class chef."

He stared at the rolled-up cigarette in her hand. "Is that marijuana?" Surely he was seeing things. Lance was hardly a prude; he'd tried a joint or two in his college days. But he dang sure never thought he'd come home and see his wife smoking weed in his kitchen.

"Yep, want a hit?"

"No, I don't! And since when did you start smoking joints?"

She looked as if bliss had come to pay her a visit. "I don't see what the problem is. I just wanted to relax a bit."

"With dope? Are you serious?"

"Oh, good grief." She took a long whiff of the joint. Then she smashed it out on the kitchen counter. "Damn, I thought my daddy died fifteen years ago."

Something wasn't right here. She'd just gone to see the doctor. Was this some sort of medical-marijuana cure? Lance tossed his keys and iPhone onto the kitchen counter and approached his wife. "Tia, what did the doctor say?"

She rolled her eyes. "He said I have a case of nagitis. I'm being nagged to death," she snapped, as she grabbed her robe and slipped it on.

Lance gritted his teeth, trying his best not to get upset. The doctor's visit obviously hadn't helped whatever was seriously wrong with his wife. He would go upstairs, find her family practitioner's number, and call the man himself. "Fine, Tia. I'm going to take a shower and change my clothes. When I come back down, you are going to tell me what the hell is going on with you."

Lance stormed out of the kitchen.

"You sure you don't need me to lay out your clothes, massa?" Tia called out after him.

Lance stopped, spun around, and glared at her. He debated firing off a response, but decided he needed to calm down first so they could talk rationally. "Whatever, Tia," he said, turning and walking away.

"Well, your good little slave will stay here and get your meal ready to serve you, massa!" she yelled.

Lance sighed heavily as he made his way into the bedroom. At least the walls were back to their normal color. The rug had been pulled up, and he decided the bare floor looked pretty good. The smell of the paint was nearly overpowering, though.

He was starting to hunt around for her doctor's information when he realized it was after five. That meant, even if he did find it, he would only get an answering service. No, if he wanted answers, he was going to have to make Tia talk to him.

But first, he needed to shower and get out of his suit. Lance undressed, then stepped into the shower and savored the hot-water pellets against his skin. He tried to make sense of everything that had been going on since he and Tia had gotten married. No way could this educated, beautiful, successful woman be acting like this. Erratic, crazed, temperamental. And now she was smoking dope?

Lance had stepped out of the shower, dried off, and changed into a pair of shorts when Tia came busting into the room.

"Why is Crystal texting you?" she screamed at the top of her lungs.

"What are you talking about?" He slipped a T-shirt over his head.

"Your phone," she said, shaking it at him. "I just saw a text from Crystal." She started reading the message on the screen: " 'Trying to be respectful but I meant what I said in your office. I can't give up. Love, forever, Crystal.' "

Lance groaned. He hadn't told Tia about Crystal stopping by his office—he didn't see the need to—but now he wished he had because he knew how this had to look.

"What the hell does she mean *love, forever*? So are you sneaking off and seeing her?"

Lance held out his hand for her to calm down. "It's nothing. She came by the office a few months ago. Before we got married."

"For what? What did she need to see you for? And what does she mean she's not giving up?"

"Whoa, Tia. Since when did you become the jealous type?"

"Since I found out my husband was a cheating dog."

His eyes bucked in astonishment. "Are you serious?"

"Oh, it's right here in black and white," she said, violently shaking the phone in his face. "You can try and deny it all you want, but I'm not stupid. *Love, forever, Crystal.* Oh, she loves you *forever*? Y'all gonna be together *forever*?"

Lance had to shake his head to make sure this was actually happening. "Tia, you are being completely irrational."

"Why, because I'm not okay with you sleeping around?"

"I'm not sleeping around, Tia," he cried. "Crystal stopped by the office just to say hello. I told her I was getting married and I haven't talked to her since."

"Why would she say she's not giving up and sign it *love, forever*?"

Lance blew a frustrated breath. "I don't know, Tia. We were together for three years. Maybe that's why she said it. I don't know. You'll have to ask her."

Tia glared at her husband. "You know what? Maybe I will." She pulled the phone to her chest, then stormed into the bathroom. She locked the bathroom door just as Lance made it to the door.

"Tia!" he said, pounding on the door.

"Is this Crystal?" Lance heard her say through the door.

"Tia!" he yelled. "I know you are not calling her!"

"Yeah, tramp, this is Lance's wife. I saw your text. You need to give it up, you fat pig. He told me he dumped you because you're a fat, ugly, cheating whore. He's not going to be with you, so you can give it up!"

"Tia, come out of there!"

She ignored him as she kept yelling into the phone. "If you come near my man again, I'll kill you, do you hear me?"

Lance stepped back from the door. This had to be a nightmare. This could not possibly be happening. He would consider the situation ludicrous if not for the consequences. Lance wasn't worried about Crystal getting mad, but he knew his mother would hear about this before the night was over.

Defeated, Lance sat down on the bed and waited until the bathroom door opened.

"Do you feel better now?" he asked as Tia walked out of the bathroom.

Lance couldn't make it out, but he saw something different in her eyes. Not the blissful expression he'd seen earlier. Now, her eyes seemed hollow and crazed.

"I sure do," she said casually, tossing the phone onto the bed. "Maybe you'll think twice before you cheat on me the next time."

Tia had turned into someone he didn't even know. Lance no longer had the strength to argue with his wife. What good would it do when she was high? Disgusted with the whole mess, he grabbed the remote, turned on ESPN, and tried his best to lose himself in the wide world of sports.

Chapter 26

Tia grabbed her head and massaged her temples. Her head was throbbing and she wasn't sure if it was a pot hangover or the stress of her fight with Lance. The pain in her head caused her mind to race back to last night. Lance hadn't even bothered to come back down to eat and hadn't said two words to her the rest of the evening. Tia knew he was furious because each time she'd tried to talk to him, he ignored her. He had slept in the guest room last night. She'd stayed up all night, rearranging the shoes in her closet because she had so much anxious energy and couldn't sleep. She'd finally dozed off around 4:00 a.m., and when she awoke, Lance was once again already gone. He didn't even say good-bye. Tia hadn't apologized because she didn't feel that she was in the wrong. But now, her rational self was trying to get her to see Lance's point. How would she have reacted had she come home and Lance was in the living room doing drugs? How would she have felt if he had embarrassed her by calling up one of her exes?

Had she really called Crystal? That woman probably thought she was a certified fool. Why had she overreacted so? It was a stupid text. She trusted Lance, so why in the world had she let irrational fears make her doubt him?

"Knock, knock," Lucinda said, poking her head in Tia's office door. Tia immediately regretted coming in to work today. She wasn't in the mood to chitchat, but she had to try to clean up the mess she'd made with the copyright case before Mr. Anderson returned.

"Hey, *chica*. Are you okay?" Lucinda asked, entering without waiting for a greeting.

"Yeah," Tia replied, even though she knew her expression belied her emotions.

Lucinda paused, studied her friend. "Nah, *mami,* you're not doing well. Come on," she said, walking over and pulling Tia from behind her desk.

"Wha— Where are we going?" Tia asked, almost stumbling as Lucinda dragged her.

"We're going to Starbucks across the street and you're going to tell me what's really going on."

Tia pulled away, stopped, and rubbed her temples. She had to do something about these migraines. They were killing her. This was more than just a pot hangover. "I need some aspirin," Tia muttered.

"I have Aleve in my purse. Come on."

Tia grabbed her purse and reluctantly followed Lucinda out

of the building and across the street to Starbucks. Once they were seated at their table, their mochas positioned right in front of them, Lucinda passed the Aleve to Tia, waited for her to pop two in her mouth, and said, "Now, what's really going on? Everyone is talking about what happened in court." She looked genuinely concerned. "So, what's up? When I dropped you off, I know you were a little frazzled, but did you really hit a witness?"

"I . . . I . . ." Tia couldn't finish her sentence because she burst out crying.

"Oh, my God. Don't cry, it's not that bad. It's just a stupid court case. You're probably just stressed." Lucinda handed Tia a napkin.

Tia tried to compose herself as she dabbed at her eyes. She noticed several people staring so she tried to stifle her cries. But the pain of everything was so intense and Tia felt that she needed to release the load that had been weighing her down. She hesitated, debated whether to continue, then finally said, "Lucinda, I . . . I'm not well. I'm s— I'm sick."

Shock blanketed Lucinda's face. "Oh my God. What is it? Cancer? A brain tumor?" She reached across the table and took Tia's hand.

Tia shook her head, then sniffed. "No, nothing like that."

"What do you mean you're not well, then?"

"I'm sick, but it's a different kind of sickness." Tia took a deep breath and summoned the strength to continue. She'd never admitted her illness to anyone but her family, Gavin, and her doctors. "I have a mental illness," she finally said.

Lucinda frowned, cocked her head. “What?”

“I’m bipolar,” Tia continued, a huge relief passing through her. “I don’t talk about it and Lance doesn’t even know. I want to come clean with him but I’m scared.”

Lucinda continued to look confused. “Bipolar? Like one of those crazy people that wander the streets?”

Tia inhaled sharply. Those words always set her off, but she was doing something she’d been wanting to do for so long, share her pain, so she tried to push back the anger building inside. “I’m not like that. It’s just that sometimes, stuff gets jumbled up in my head.”

Tia couldn’t help but notice Lucinda draw her hand back, and it sent a sharp pang through her heart.

“It’s not contagious,” Tia said defensively.

Lucinda blinked, studied Tia again. “You’re bipolar? Are you serious?”

“I wouldn’t joke about something like this.”

“So is that why you flipped out in court?”

“I don’t know. It’s just the stress of everything. It makes me get out of control. I just don’t know what to do.”

“Wow,” Lucinda said, falling back in her seat. “Workaholic? Yeah. Uptight? Yeah. But crazy, for real? I never would’ve thought that.”

Tia’s fingers drummed the table as she blew short breaths to try to contain her building anger.

Lucinda didn’t seem to notice because she continued, “My old neighbor was crazy and he killed his whole family. Are you that kind of crazy?”

Breathe, Tia, breathe, she told herself.

"I'm bipolar, but I'm no murderer," Tia said.

"Yet," Lucinda mumbled. She shook her head again and stared at Tia. "So you've been lying all this time?"

"I haven't been lying. What was I supposed to say?"

Lucinda shrugged. "I don't know. Maybe, 'Hey, Lucinda. You know when I act kind of crazy? It's because I am.' "

Tia slammed her palms on the table so hard their coffee cups shook. "Stop saying that," she hissed. "I'm not crazy."

Lucinda looked taken aback. "Wow, you know what? Umm"—she looked at her watch—"would you look at the time. I forgot I have a meeting." Lucinda stood and started gathering her things. "I'll just talk to you later."

Tia's mouth fell open. She couldn't believe this. Was Lucinda bailing on her? Tia's mother had always been adamantly opposed to Tia's sharing her issues. This would be why. As she watched Lucinda bolt out the door, Tia realized what she should do. The only two people outside of her family that she'd been honest with bailed on her. Why in the world did she think things would be any different with Lance?

Instead of going back to work, Tia had headed to the parking garage, hopped in her car, sent a message to her assistant that she wouldn't be returning, and headed home. She fought back the tears and the pain as she thought about the mess she'd made of her life. She was a good person, with a good heart. Why would God curse her with a life like this?

Tia had just merged into another lane when a car came out

of nowhere and nearly sideswiped her. She had to swerve to the right to keep from being hit. Luckily, no cars were in the right lane.

"Have you lost your freakin' mind?" she yelled, blaring on the horn. Before she knew it, she set into a tirade of curses. She'd even sped up, trying to catch up to the driver. For what, she didn't know. It was as if she were teetering on the edge and that driver had come along and pushed her all the way off.

Tia continued swerving in and out of traffic as she tried to catch up with the driver. Her ringing cell phone snapped her out of her road rage.

"What are you doing?" she mumbled to herself as she slowed her vehicle down. She pulled off the freeway and into the parking lot of Home Depot. "Get it together, get it together," she said, taking small, deep breaths. She eased her phone out to look at it, and her heart raced when she noticed the missed call was from the pharmacy. She immediately pressed redial.

"CVS pharmacy."

"Yes, this is Tia Kingston. I just missed a call from you guys."

"Yes, Mrs. Kingston," the pharmacy tech said, "we just wanted to let you know that your prescription is ready."

A sense of relief filled her. Maybe God was on her side after all because right now Tia desperately wanted her medication.

"I'm on my way," Tia said, making a U-turn out of the parking lot. In minutes she was walking into the drugstore, her heart racing. She'd never wanted her medication so bad. She'd never *needed* it so bad.

Tia was grateful that there was no wait at the counter. "Picking up for Tia Kingston."

"Oh, yes, right here," the pharmacist said, reaching into a bin and pulling out a white bag. "My apologies on the delay." He handed her the package.

"No problem," Tia said, cutting him off.

"Do you need a consultation?"

"No, I've taken this before." She thrust her credit card at him. "Can you just ring me up?"

She didn't mean to be rude, but she needed something to help her pull it all together before it was too late. In the car, Tia immediately took out two pills, then popped them in her mouth and took a swallow from the bottle of water sitting in her cup holder. The prescription called for just one pill, but since she was so far behind, she needed this to work fast. She wanted Lance to see a different woman when he came home. She wanted to explain to him that while things had been crazy lately, she was anything but crazy. Yes, she had to get this under control, before her biggest fear materialized and she lost her husband for good.

Chapter 27

Tia breathed a sigh of relief when she didn't see Lance's truck in the garage. She wanted some time for the medicine to take effect. While Lucinda's reaction had quelled any thoughts she had of coming clean, Tia still wanted Lance to come home to a sense of normalcy. She wanted to make right all the wrong she'd done these last few days.

Tia made smothered pork chops, one of Lance's favorite indulgences. She chilled a bottle of his favorite wine and even unthawed his favorite strawberry cheesecake. Yet, an hour later, she still felt on edge.

"Two more pills won't hurt," she mumbled. She wanted to be completely relaxed and stress-free, and while she wasn't as high-strung as earlier, she was nowhere near as calm as she would've liked to have been. A flash of the euphoric feeling she had from the marijuana passed through her mind, but she knew she didn't want to go back down that road. She wanted to return to normal without the drugs, at least the illegal ones.

Tia popped two more pills in her mouth, and twenty minutes later, just as she turned the pork chops off, she felt the medication starting to go to work, to the point that she didn't even feel like finishing dinner.

Tia sat down on the sofa and began watching *The Real Housewives of Atlanta*. She hated the garbage that was reality TV. But maybe seeing people whose lives were more jacked up than hers could make her feel better.

Real Housewives was just going off when Lance eased into the house. He looked at her pensively, as if not sure whom he was coming home to. Tia hated that and it brought tears to her eyes. But she quickly composed herself.

"Baby, I'm so sorry," she said, jumping up.

Lance dropped his keys and briefcase. "Tia, I can't keep doing this."

"I know," she said, then struggled to find her balance.

"Are you okay?" he asked, trying to catch her.

She nodded. "Yeah. Think I just jumped up too fast. Felt a little dizzy. I threw up earlier, so I'm probably just dehydrated." She shook off her daze. The pills had made her lethargic, but she tried to pull it together. "About last night, I'm sorry. I was stressed, everything at work, Mrs. Bailey's court date is tomorrow." She pointed at her cell phone. "And I just got an e-mail that my boss will be back tomorrow and wants to meet with me about the troubles with my copyright case. It's just all too much."

"I understand being stressed, but we need to do something if it's causing you to act like this."

She shook off the grogginess, inhaled, then forced a smile. "You're right. I'm going to put in a vacation request for some time off. I probably just need to rest."

Lance looked at her, unsure.

"And if you don't mind, I'd really like to call Crystal and apologize." Tia was on the fence about apologizing, but she knew she needed to clean up this mess, and if that meant humbling herself to her husband's ex, she would.

Lance shook his head. "Nah, let's just leave it alone." They stood in an uncomfortable silence before he added, "I'm gonna go and change. It was a long day."

"Are you still mad at me?"

"Nah, I'm okay."

"I cooked for you," she said, motioning toward the kitchen.

"I'm not hungry," he said, walking away.

Tia watched him leave, and the emptiness felt overwhelming. She could see it in his eyes, Lance was far from okay. He was tired and she had no one to blame but herself.

Tia's BlackBerry buzzed and she picked it up to read the incoming e-mail. She smiled when she saw whom it was from. One of her clients had secured the tickets she'd requested. That brought a real smile to her face. Lance had been dying to go to the Texans play-off game, but the game was sold out. He didn't believe in using his clout for personal stuff, so he hadn't been able to snare any tickets. But Tia had come through. Four suite tickets should be enough of a peace offering.

Tia was just about to set her phone down when she noticed Lucinda's name. Tia quickly dialed her number, not expecting her to answer. When she didn't, Tia left a quick message. "Lu, I am so, so sorry about today. Being irrational is, umm, just part of what I have to deal with. Hope you understand. Call me. Bye."

Tia tossed the phone, went into the kitchen, grabbed a Red Bull to try to get some energy, then headed to her bedroom.

Lance was lying across the bed, watching ESPN. Tia pulled herself together, managed a big smile, and stepped in front of the TV.

"Tia, what are you doing?" Lance said, waving for her to move.

"I interrupt your regularly scheduled program for this message."

He sighed, sat up, and looked at her as if mentally preparing himself for some more foolishness.

"I know I've been testing your patience." She paused for him to protest. When he didn't, she continued, "But I bring you a peace offering." She held out her hands.

He looked at her. "A hug?"

She smiled. "Well, I don't technically have the peace offering." She scooted to the end of the bed, sitting in front of him. "We have to pick it up."

"Tia, what are you talking about. I'm tired and I can't play 'guess what's going on today.'"

She hated the exasperated sound in his voice. She prayed that the medication could help her get back on track because the look on her husband's face said he couldn't take much more.

Tia climbed on Lance's lap and straddled him. She felt encouraged when his hands immediately went around her waist. "Your wife wants to make things up to you."

"Tia . . ."

She kissed him on the forehead—"How"—then the cheek—"would you"—then the other cheek—"like suite tickets"—then the lips—"to the Texans play-off game?"

He pushed her back, astonished. "What?"

Tia giggled. "That's right. If you forgive me, I have four suite tickets to the game you wanted to go to."

He looked at her skeptically. "Seriously?"

"Seriously. A client got them for me."

He let out a small yelp. "Brian is gonna lose his mind. That game is sold out. He wanted me to pretend I was doing a story so we could go."

"Well, I know you'd never do that. And now, you don't have to."

He hugged her tightly. "Thank you, babe!"

His excitement filled her, made her feel hopeful about their marriage.

"One other condition," she said, turning serious.

He lost his smile, worry lines immediately creasing his face. "What?"

"You have to make mad, passionate love to your wife."

He flashed a wicked grin. "Now that, I can do—with pleasure." He leaned in, kissed her intensely, then made love to her as if it were their first time.

Chapter 28

Making love had only given her a temporary reprieve. This morning, the stress was back and Tia felt more anxious than ever. She'd taken two more pills and wanted to pop a couple more right before the hearing, but she didn't want to chance being lethargic.

"Where's your client?" The judge's booming voice snapped Tia out of her thoughts.

Mr. Wynn's attorney stood and nervously said, "Your Honor, we requested a continuance as Mr. Wynn—"

The judge glared at him over his wire-rimmed glasses. "Mr. Waters, I am so tired of you and your client."

Tia took her cue and jumped in. "Your Honor, Mr. Wynn is inconsiderate of the court's time and my client's time, so we request that you go ahead and rule."

"Are you serious?" the defense attorney shot back. "We've been waiting months because your client couldn't make it."

"My client couldn't make it because she was in the hospital. Not because she couldn't find the time!"

The judge pounded his gavel. "I know the two of you are not standing in my courtroom arguing!" he admonished.

Both of them mumbled apologies.

The judge shook his head in frustration. "I am inclined to agree with Mrs. Kingston." He frowned, disgust across his face. "However, I see you did request a continuance prior to the court hearing." He paused and gave his clerk the evil eye. She quickly looked down in shame. "So this isn't entirely your fault." He studied the papers in front of him for a minute. Finally he said, "I will reset the case for Thursday. But this is my last time resetting. This case has gone on long enough. Court is adjourned." He slammed his gavel down.

"This just isn't fair," Mrs. Bailey cried. She was sitting next to Tia in a wheelchair. "I can't even walk but I managed to come down to this courthouse? Why won't they just give me my house?"

Tia put her fingers to her lips to silence Mrs. Bailey.

"Mrs. Bailey," Tia said, taking her hand after the judge had left the courtroom, "I understand your frustration. Just know that I am working tirelessly to see this through."

"Well, you can't be half as tired as I am." Mrs. Bailey snatched her arm away and motioned for her daughter to come wheel her out of the courtroom.

Tia debated going after her, but there was nothing she could really say. Truthfully, she had her own set of problems to deal with right now. Mr. Anderson was back from vacation and had summoned her to his office right after her hearing. She wasn't looking forward to the meeting. And as she glanced at her watch, Tia knew if she didn't get moving right now, it would be a meeting she wouldn't make.

Twenty minutes later, Tia had dropped her stuff off at her desk and was heading to Mr. Anderson's office when she spotted Lucinda talking with one of the gossiping women from accounting. Tension filled Tia's body. She couldn't help but wonder what the two of them were talking about huddled together by the watercooler. The knots in Tia's stomach tightened when she approached them and they suddenly stopped talking.

"Hey, Lucinda. Hey, Tammy," Tia managed to say.

Lucinda, who had lost her smile, barely nodded. Tammy, on the other hand, appeared to be struggling to contain her smile.

"What are you guys talking about?"

"A little bit of this. A little bit of that." Tammy giggled.

Tia couldn't believe Lucinda would betray her, but judging from the conspiratorial grin on Tammy's face, that's exactly what her friend had done.

"How are you feeling today?" Tammy asked. Tia could've sworn she had a condescending smirk across her face.

Tia glared at her, then spun toward Lucinda. "You lying, dirty whore."

Both Lucinda and Tammy gasped, but Tia didn't care. "I trusted you," Tia cried. "I thought you were my friend. But you're nothing but a filthy piece of Mexican trash!"

A slow rage filled Lucinda's eyes, but Tia didn't care. If anything, she had the right to be upset. How dare Lucinda share something so personal—and with the company gossip of all people.

"Because I know what you're going through, I'm going to let that slide," Lucinda slowly began. Her chest was heaving as she took a step toward Tia. For a minute, Tia thought Lucinda was going to punch her. "But if you ever—"

"Oh, shut up," Tia said, not backing down. She was the one who needed to be pissed. "I share a deep, dark secret with you and you turn around and start talking about me to the president of the friggin' rumor mill."

"Hey!" Tammy said. "And we—"

Lucinda held up her hand to stop Tammy before she finished. "You know what?" Lucinda glared at Tia. "You *do* have some serious problems. Number one, we weren't talking about you."

Tia turned up her lip. So now Lucinda was just going to stand here and lie to her? "Whatever," Tia snapped.

Finally, Tammy stepped in. "I don't know what's going on, but Lucinda is right. We were talking about the cute new paralegal you had working for you." She looked back and forth between the two of them, as if she couldn't understand where the friction was coming from.

"B-but I saw you looking at me," Tia stammered.

"That's because I had just told Lucinda I was going to approach you about hooking us up." Again, Tammy's eyes darted back and forth between the two. "What's going on? I thought you two were friends. And what deep, dark secret did you think she was telling me?"

Tia couldn't believe what had just happened. She'd overreacted, and the look on Lucinda's face told her that her friend would be hard-pressed to forgive her.

"Lu, I'm sorry," Tia said.

Again, Lucinda held up her hand. "Save it," she snapped. "I'm going to take my *filthy Mexican ass* back to my office," she said, her voice dripping with disdain.

"Lu, it's not me," Tia tried to explain as Lucinda pushed past her. Lucinda ignored her as she continued down the hallway. Tia was about to go after her when she noticed her assistant, Vicki, across the room, tapping her watch to let Tia know she needed to get to Mr. Anderson's office.

Tia let out a sigh. She'd have to go apologize to Lucinda later. She smiled haphazardly at Tammy, who was still standing there as if she was waiting on some juicy gossip. Sadly, Tia knew the entire office would know about it before she got out of her meeting with Mr. Anderson.

"Excuse me. I have to go," Tia said, walking past a confused Tammy.

Five minutes later, Tia sat across from her boss trying to put out of her mind the whole scene that had just unfolded. Judging from the expression on Mr. Anderson's face, she had bigger problems to worry about. The man sitting in front of her was completely different from the man who had, just a few short months ago, excitedly talked about her being a partner. Now he bore a scowl that Tia knew meant he was beyond angry.

"Mrs. Kingston," he said, getting straight to the point, "I've heard about what happened in court, and truthfully, I am hoping that it is nothing more than grapevine exaggeration. But before I go into my spiel, I needed to hear from you exactly what happened. I wanted to call immediately, but it was my daughter's wedding and I promised her my undivided attention. Well, now, my attention is turned back to my business, and if what I heard is true, you almost destroyed my business."

"Mr. Anderson, I . . ." Tia started fidgeting with the belt buckle on her dress. How in the world was she supposed to explain what had happened? She knew she had messed up. The client had been livid about her behavior and they'd almost lost the account. What if Mr. Anderson fired her? Tia was actually being honored at a banquet in a few days for her legal work. What would be the irony in accepting the award just days after she was fired?

"Well, I don't know," she continued. "I just lost it. But, Mr. Anderson, you know me," she said, her voice reeking of desperation. "I would never do anything to jeopardize this firm. I just, I don't know . . ."

Tia braced herself for Mr. Anderson's next words, which she was sure would be *Pack your stuff and get out.*

"Mrs. Kingston," he said, shaking his head in disgust, "I do know you. And you know I have the utmost respect for you, but my company's reputation is on the line, and quite honestly,

I thought I could trust you, but I simply don't know anymore if you're cut out for this job." He exhaled slowly. "You're completely off the copyright case," he bluntly added.

Tia fought back her tears. It's not as if she hadn't seen that coming, after all, she'd been banned from Judge Gilmore's courtroom, but it hurt nonetheless.

"Now I know you have that eviction case with your foundation and I've tended to stay out of your charitable work, so I won't intrude now. But personally, if I were you, I'd let someone else handle that as well."

"I-I can't. We have a hearing in a couple of days," she managed to say.

Mr. Anderson shrugged as if he couldn't care less. "Bottom line, I'm thoroughly disappointed in you. But I don't believe in rash decisions, so you take some time off, get it together, meditate, relax, whatever you need. Your behavior was unacceptable, and whatever is going on in your life, you need to get it together before it's too late."

So he wasn't firing her? That was good, but Tia wanted to ask what that meant for her recent promotion—would she get to keep it? But she knew. She would definitely be demoted. Hell, she'd be lucky if she even had a job after she got back. But at this point, Tia didn't even know if she wanted her job back since she was now making a mess of that as well.

Chapter 29

Lance was glad to see his wife finally getting some sleep. She'd come home from work looking sad and dejected, and he'd readied himself for her mood swings. But she'd gone to bed, claiming exhaustion, and had slept all evening and through the night. Since that had been a rarity lately, he relished the sight of her knocked out. Lance walked over to the sofa, where Tia was sleeping soundly, pulled the afghan up on her, and gently kissed her forehead. Lance headed back to his bedroom, where he changed into workout clothes. Before he left, he scribbled a note to let Tia know he was going to the gym. Part of him was leery about leaving her at home, but he'd been so stressed lately that he'd been skipping his workouts and he needed to burn off some steam.

Thirty minutes later, Lance stood over his friend Brian, spotting him as he lifted weights.

"So, explain this to me again." Brian placed the barbell back on the stand. "Why has all of this been going on and you haven't told me?"

Lance shrugged. "Man, it's just wild. Everything caught me off guard and I'm trying to figure out how to deal with it. I'm trying to be understanding, but this erratic behavior is going to make me lose my mind." He switched places on the bench and began hoisting the barbell straight upward.

After several repetitions, Brian spoke up. "I know you guys think it's the migraines, but that wouldn't cause her to act all crazy, would it?"

Lance shrugged. He really had no idea.

"Maybe she has some kind of hormonal imbalance," Brian said, then snapped his fingers as if an idea had just hit him. "Or better yet, maybe she's pregnant."

Lance stopped just as he was about to start another set. They'd talked about trying to start a family, but they hadn't been trying for a pregnancy. Then again, they hadn't been *not* trying for a pregnancy, either. Lance sat up with this startling realization.

Brian nodded as if he'd figured it all out. "I'm telling you, dude, women flip out when they get pregnant. It's like their hormones go into overdrive."

Lance slowly nodded. That had to be it. That had to be the explanation for these wild mood swings and nutty behavior.

"So is this how Keri acted?" Lance asked, referring to Brian's first wife.

"Keri and Chandra," Brian replied, referring to his second

wife. "They both lost their ever-loving minds when they were pregnant."

"Now that I think about it, Tia did throw up the other day," Lance said.

Brian slapped his knee. "See, I'm a freaking genius. Your wife is pregnant, dude. That's why she's acting all crazy."

A small smile crept up on Lance's face. Could he soon be a father? Could that really be what was wrong with Tia?

Lance couldn't wait to get home. But first, he had to stop by a CVS pharmacy and pick up a pregnancy test. Hopefully, he'd soon have the answer as to exactly what was wrong with his wife.

Lance tiptoed into the front room, not sure if Tia was still asleep.

"Hey," she softly said, sitting up on the sofa.

"How are you?"

"Better. Guess I was just really tired."

He smiled as he slid next to her. "I'm sorry I stepped out. I just needed to go to the gym." He took a deep breath. "Tia, you know I've been really worried about you."

She nodded her understanding and was about to say something when he added, "I think I may know what the problem is." He reached into the CVS bag he'd brought inside, pulled out a little pink box, and set it on the table.

"A pregnancy test?" she asked, an eyebrow raised.

He nodded. "I think you may be pregnant. The mood swings, the nauseousness. It all points toward pregnancy. It doesn't hurt anything to check."

Tia picked up the box. *Pregnant?* That thought had never crossed her mind.

"Come on, babe, just take it and see. I mean, maybe you are pregnant. It would explain so much." Lance seemed so happy. Tia didn't know if he was thrilled about the prospect of being a father or just relieved to have figured out why she'd been acting the way she had.

Tia began to read the back of the box. Even though she'd had a scare or two before, she'd never been pregnant. Still, it seemed as if she would be able to tell if she was.

Tia knew why she was having mood swings. Or at least she thought she did. She'd been fine for months, then everything changed. So maybe this new vicious cycle had been caused by pregnancy.

"I'll go do it now." She made her way into the bathroom, where she peed onto the stick. After she flushed the toilet, she washed her hands, then headed back into the living room, stick in hand. Lance waited with bated breath.

"Well?"

"Well, it's only been a minute. The directions say wait two minutes." They sat next to each other and watched the window on the stick.

"It'll have a minus if I'm not pregnant and a plus if I am."

Silence filled the room until Lance softly said, "It's a plus."

Tears slowly filled Tia's eyes. "I'm pregnant," she whispered. "That's what's been wrong." She threw her hands around her husband's neck in gratitude. This was the best news she'd heard in a long time.

Chapter 30

It felt like old times. Finally.

Lance and Tia had sat up talking, making plans for the baby, last night. She seemed genuinely happy, relieved almost. Lance hoped that meant their lives could now return to normal.

Lance eased out of bed, leaving Tia asleep. He had decided to take the day off and go with her to the doctor to confirm her pregnancy. He just finished dressing when his cell phone rang. He picked it up and smiled when he saw his sister's number.

"Hey, Patricia."

"Hey, Big Bro, what's going on?" As usual, his younger sister sounded as if she were sitting on top of the world.

"The usual."

"That means your wife is doing something else outlandish," he heard his mother chime in.

Lance groaned. His sister loved talking to them on the

three-way, so he should've known his mother would be on the line.

"Hello, Mother."

"Hello, Son."

"How's married life?" Patricia asked. She hadn't been able to come home for the wedding since she'd had such short notice, but she had talked to Tia several times on the phone and given Lance her long-distance stamp of approval.

"It's, umm, a little more work than I thought. But it's good."

"A little more work, huh?" his mother mumbled.

"You know, for someone who's honoring Tia, you sure do give her a hard time," Lance said. His mother was part of a charity that was honoring Tia for her pro bono legal work.

"Well, I don't deny that she's a good attorney. But I just wonder sometimes if she's a good enough wife for my son."

"Patricia, ignore your mother," he said, sighing heavily. "My wife has been under a lot of stress. But I know everything will work out." He debated whether to reveal the pregnancy. Tia wanted to confirm the home test with the doctor before they started spreading the word, but Lance wanted to let his mother know there was an explanation behind the madness.

Lance walked downstairs and took a seat at the kitchen table. "We think Tia is pregnant," he said, deciding to come clean.

Silence filled the phone.

Finally his sister said, "Already?"

"Is that why you got married so quickly?" his mother asked.

"No," Lance said with conviction. "I told you, I married Tia because I wanted to. We just found out she's pregnant. We haven't even been to the doctor to officially confirm it. We just took a home pregnancy test."

"Well, you know those things are always wrong," his mother quickly said. He could hear the wishfulness in her voice, and that saddened him.

"I thought you would be ecstatic at the idea of having grandchildren," he said. "I guess you wanted them from Patricia."

"Hey, don't put me in this," Patricia said defensively. "I've made it very clear, there ain't nothing about motherhood that's appealing to me."

"That is just insane. What woman doesn't want to be a mother?" Beverly said in a familiar complaint.

"This one," Patricia replied with no shame.

"That's because you're over there in London living it up. What's going to happen when you're old and need someone to take care of you?"

"I'll cross that bridge when I get to it." Patricia quickly changed the subject. "Did I tell you I got a gig performing at KOKO, one of the legendary clubs in Camden?" She caught herself before she started rambling. "But I'll tell you about it later. Right now, tell me more about my soon-to-be niece or nephew."

"Well, we don't have any details yet. We'll know more later today—that's if we can get in to see the doctor."

"Well, you'll have to let me know details so I can get a ticket over there to come see my niece or nephew."

Lance was glad to hear his sister give a vote of confidence. "All right. I'll do that."

They made idle chatter, with Patricia filling them in on all that was going on with her. Lance was grateful to talk about someone else for a change.

By the time he got off the phone, Lance was even more hopeful that things were about to turn around. He was about to be a father, Tia seemed happy, and he could only hope that this euphoria would last.

Chapter 31

The news should've made her happy. She was about to be a mother. The doctor had just confirmed that she was three and a half months pregnant. She must've gotten pregnant on her wedding night. Hearing the words, though, had made her stomach churn with anxiety. In her heart, Tia really wanted to be a mother. But in her head, she knew that wasn't a good idea.

Tia couldn't explain the way that she was feeling. She should've been overjoyed at the idea of being a mother. Lance sure was. He'd wanted to tell everyone. She'd urged him to wait—at least until their doctor's appointment today. She wanted him to wait for several months, but she knew he wouldn't be able to do that. In fact, he'd already told his family, which was why she'd had to break down and tell her mother this morning. And of course, Virginia had been thrilled.

"Why do you have that look on your face?" he asked as they

pulled into their driveway. They'd left the doctor's office twenty minutes ago and he'd been giddy the entire ride home.

"What look?" Tia had no idea what he was talking about. She'd been a little preoccupied. Mrs. Bailey's case was this afternoon, so she needed to pull herself together for that. Even though the medication had made her groggy, she could still tell a difference. But there was no way she would take the pills now that she was pregnant. That decision was causing her tremendous worry.

"That look," Lance said, pointing at her face. "Like you're disgusted or irritated."

"Dang, am I supposed to be in a happy-go-lucky mood all the time?" she snapped. She hadn't even realized she had any sort of "look" on her face. All she did know was that she was sick and tired of everyone always telling her how she should be acting.

"Calm down," he said gently, reaching over to pat her arm. "I wasn't trying to upset you."

She snatched her arm away. "I'm just sick of everyone always analyzing me."

"No one is analyzing you, Tia," Lance said uneasily. "I was just . . ." He paused. "You know what? Never mind. Let's just go inside and you can rest while I make us some lunch."

She stuck her lips out like a pouty child. "I don't want to rest. I need to get out of here," she said, jumping out of his truck and heading toward her car.

"Where are you going?" Lance said, following her.

"I have a court appearance this afternoon," she snapped. "That pro bono case about the old lady."

"You didn't tell me. I thought we had all day together."

He sounded genuinely disappointed that they wouldn't be spending time together, and she was touched. "I shouldn't be gone long," she said softly. "We're just hearing the verdict today."

He eyed her skeptically, as if he didn't want to let her out of his sight.

"Baby, I'm okay," she said gently. "I really am happy about the baby, just scared."

He hugged her, and she actually sank into his touch. Every time he held her, he made her feel the one thing she needed most—hope.

The good mood that she'd been feeling on the drive over to the courthouse changed on a dime once she heard the awful decision the judge had made. Tia felt like crying. This had to be some kind of nightmare. This judge did not just pound his gavel and dismiss this case.

"Tia, do you hear me? What does that mean?" Mrs. Bailey's face was wrinkled with fear. "What does he mean 'case dismissed'?" she asked again, panicked.

Tia tried to get her bearings about her, then jumped up. "Your Honor. I'm sorry, I don't understand."

"What's not to understand, Mrs. Kingston? You presented the merits of your case. The defense presented theirs. I reviewed both and decided there is no case. Unless you can get me Mrs. Bailey's nephew to corroborate your allegations, that is strictly hearsay and you really have no grounds."

"But, Your Honor—"

The judge looked exasperated as he cut her off. "Mrs. Kingston. You've been an attorney long enough to know how this works. You are welcome to file an appeal, but my ruling stands." He turned his focus to Mrs. Bailey. "Ma'am, I feel your pain. I really do. But the law is the law. Mr. Wynn bought the property legally. I'm not here to determine any ethical or moral obligations. Only the legalities of the case. I do understand your dilemma, so I'll give you ninety days to vacate the property."

"Vacate? So, I have to leave?" Mrs. Bailey looked up at Tia. "But you said we were gonna win this."

Tia's heart broke at the sight of the woman near hysteria. Tia's mind raced back over the trial. Had her illness made her less effective? She was pretty sure she had done everything right. "Your Honor," she started to protest, "you know—"

The judge shot her a disapproving look, then banged his gavel. "Case dismissed," he firmly repeated.

The defense released celebratory claps as everyone stood. Mr. Wynn, who had shown up now that he no longer had a choice, seemed as if he'd known he'd win all along. Tia couldn't even remember what questions she'd asked when he took the stand.

Tia groaned when Mrs. Bailey's daughter stomped her way. The heavyset woman looked furious, flinging her braids from side to side. "What kind of attorney are you? You just let them take my mama's house," the woman barked.

"What happened? You didn't even do anything today," Mrs. Bailey said, tears streaming down her cheeks.

"So what now?" Mrs. Bailey's daughter asked.

The lead attorney from the other side approached them. He motioned to his client, standing there with a smug grin on his face. "So now, Mr. Wynn would like to know how long will it take you to get out of his house."

"How can you do this to me, you horrible man?" Mrs. Bailey hissed.

Mr. Wynn stepped forward. "Just to show you I have no hard feelings, here." He held out a blue sheet of paper.

"What is that?" Tia asked.

"It's a twenty-percent-off coupon for the grand opening of the new mall I'm going to build where your house is." He winked, dropped the paper in Mrs. Bailey's lap, then walked out of the courtroom.

Mrs. Bailey buried her face in her hands and sobbed. "My house, everything we worked for, we're about to lose it all."

Tia's heart sank. How could Mr. Wynn be so cruel? How could she have messed up so badly?

"I am sorry. So, so sorry," Tia said, her voice hoarse.

"Come on, Mama," Mrs. Bailey's daughter said, grabbing the back of her mother's wheelchair. "I told you we should've went with someone who knew what they were doing." She rolled her sobbing mother out of the courtroom.

Tia forlornly started gathering her things. Losing a case for her real job at the firm was one thing, but losing a case in something that was so near and dear to her heart was devastating.

Tia made her way to the parking garage. Once inside her car, she tossed her briefcase on the seat, closed the door, and burst into tears.

Chapter 32

This seesaw of a marriage was about to drive him insane. One minute Tia was upbeat, smiling, being the woman he fell in love with. The next, she was a raving lunatic. Every day when he woke up, Lance never knew which he was going to see.

"Hey," Tia said, appearing in the doorway.

Lance looked at her skeptically. He didn't know how to respond because he didn't want to set her off. "Hey," he softly replied. "You okay?"

When she'd come home from the courthouse yesterday, her face bore all the traces of someone who had been crying. He tried to comfort her, but she pushed him away. All she would say, over and over, was "I failed her. I thought I did my best, but obviously I did something wrong. Thanks to me, she lost her house."

Now she nodded. "Better," she said, looking up at him.

Her face was still full of weariness, but her eyes were no longer puffy. "I stayed home today to try and pull myself together so I could be halfway decent tonight."

He took a seat next to her on the sofa. "You're gonna be fine."

"I just wanted to say . . ." She paused. "Well, I'm so glad you're coming tonight."

"You know I wouldn't miss this night."

"No, I didn't know that," she said, her words laced in defeat. "After the way I've been acting lately I didn't know if you felt shut out."

The look on his face betrayed his true feelings: yes, he had felt shut out.

"Okay." She nodded as if she was grateful that he was here. "Are you ready to go?"

Lance nodded. He'd gotten dressed in the office and had shown up just in time to pick Tia up and take her to the awards ceremony. He had sent her a text this morning letting her know he'd be here. Tia needed something uplifting in her life right now, and being honored for her pro bono work was just the thing to do it. Besides, since Lance's mother was on the board of the organization, Children First, that was putting on tonight's event, Beverly would've had a stroke if Lance canceled.

"You sure you're up for this?" he asked.

She stepped closer and managed a faint grin. "I know I've been a handful, sweetheart, and I'm sorry, but now that the case is over . . ." She lost her smile.

"Hey," he said, lifting her chin, "you said you were going to appeal, so it's not over."

Tia closed her eyes, and he could feel her calming down. "Okay, I'm not thinking about that tonight. Tonight will be a nice night."

Lance forced a smile, even though he had an uneasy feeling fluttering in his stomach. "All right, let's get a move on."

The two of them made small talk as they drove to the hotel where the awards dinner was taking place. Inside, they mixed and mingled before taking their seats at their reserved table. No sooner were they seated than Tia's mother and Uncle Leo started bickering. As they went at it, Lance could see Tia becoming more and more agitated. Her eyes took on that strange glazed look he was starting to know too well. She finally snapped at them, and they instantly shut up. Lance felt a sinking feeling in his stomach. So they knew how to read the signs, too.

"May I have your attention, please?"

All eyes turned to the stage. Lance's mother had stepped up to the podium. As she delivered her short speech, Lance found himself grateful that, whatever her private misgivings, she was heaping on the praise on Tia's special night.

". . . And so, it gives me great pleasure to present this award," Beverly Kingston said, "to not only a dedicated legal servant who works tirelessly to serve the needs of the disenfranchised, but a young woman who is near and dear to my heart, because she married my heart, my daughter-in-law, Tia Jiles-Kingston."

Tia stood and kissed her husband as the crowd applauded. Lance was proud as he watched her glide to the front. She looked gorgeous in a long, plum Vera Wang gown with her hair pinned up and ringlets framing her face. Tia hugged and kissed her mother-in-law before stepping up to the mic.

"Thank you so much," she said as she approached the podium. "To say I am honored to receive this award is an understatement. When I began working in the legal field . . ." Tia paused and lost her smile, and for a moment Lance felt a flutter of nervousness at the expression on her face. He waited, feeling himself grow as tight as a stretched wire, for what was going to happen next. Then she squinted, shook off whatever had entered her mind, and her smile quickly returned. "I've tried to be a humble servant and not only work for the haves but the have-nots as well." She paused again, oddly, and Lance's heart skipped a beat. Tia looked around the room as if she didn't know where she was, but once again composed herself. "I'm sorry . . . as I was saying, my faith is what has guided me throughout these years." She looked out at the audience with a manic smile. "And my faith is what will guide me in the next chapter of my life."

Lance was confused. *The next chapter?*

"I know that you all are honoring me for my work in the legal profession. That's why it pains me to announce that I'm leaving the field of law."

Gasps resonated throughout the ballroom, particularly from Lance. He made more than enough money for her to quit her job, but still, Tia should've talked it over with him before she just up and quit her job.

Lance's grandmother leaned over toward him. "Why didn't you tell me she was quitting?" she whispered.

Lance didn't want to tell his grandmother that he didn't know, so he just put his fingers to his lips to get her to be quiet. Surely, losing Mrs. Bailey's case hadn't prompted Tia to want to give up on law altogether.

"But no need to fret," Tia continued, "I'm venturing into another line of work. Next month, I'm opening a dog-grooming business."

The room grew utterly still, as if the crowd was waiting on the punch line of a bad joke.

"I know this catches many of you by surprise, including my lovely husband," Tia continued, "but it's something that I've wanted to do for a very long time."

Lance had to place his hands on the table to keep from falling over. Tia didn't even like dogs. What the hell was going on?

"Tia's Fancy Pet Spa is the name, and I've already gotten commitments from several Hollywood actors to bring their pets so that I can personally groom them." She leaned in and in a conspiratorial whisper added, "Don't tell anyone, but Denzel Washington, Angelina Jolie, and John Travolta have all agreed to bring their pets to my spa!"

This dumbfounding announcement was getting worse and worse. Since when did Tia talk to people like that? And why in the world would they fly all the way to Houston to bring Tia their pets? Lance exchanged glances with Tia's mother, who looked just as confused as he did. Uncle Leo, though, had hung his head and was shaking it mournfully from side to side.

"So I hope you will join me in my new venture," Tia continued, holding up the glass statue that they'd given her.

"And again, let me say, thank you for honoring my work."

Tia stepped down from the podium. The applause was light at first, then others joined in, but one look around told Lance that everyone else in the room was just as shocked as he was.

"Tia, what do you mean you're quitting your job?" Lance whispered once she was seated back at the table.

"Sweetheart, didn't you just hear me speak?" She showed him the glass statue. "Isn't this a lovely award?"

Before Lance could answer, his grandmother leaned over and said, "Are you on drugs?"

"Excuse me?" Tia said.

"Grandma!" Lance quietly admonished.

"She's got to be on drugs; maybe she's smoking them funny cigarettes. Why else would she quit a lawyer job to be a dog groomer?"

Several people at their table were watching the exchange, but Lance's grandmother didn't seem to care. His mother looked horrified as she slid back into her seat.

"Grandma, please," Lance said.

His grandmother shook her head. "That's the craziest thing I've ever heard."

"I'm sorry you don't agree, Mother Brooks. But this is my calling." Tia shrugged nonchalantly.

"Since when?" Lance interjected.

Beverly, noticing everyone staring at them, hit Lance's leg with her knee. "Can we talk about this later? Everyone is looking over here," she whispered.

Lance glanced around the room. The emcee was trying to

move the program along, but everyone's attention was focused on Tia. Lance couldn't wait for the ceremony to be over.

Afterward, Lance wanted more than anything else to pull Tia away so they could talk, but she was bombarded with people coming up to chat. They acted as if they were congratulating her, but he could tell they were really trying to get the lowdown on her bizarre decision.

Much to Lance's dismay, the whole family followed them up to the hotel suite he had rented for the two of them. As usual, Tia's mother sat off to the side, silent. Lance's grandmother and mother sat on the sofa. Lance really wished everyone would just leave so he could talk to his wife alone.

"Tia, please explain to me what's going on," he said.

"What's to explain? I'm tired of law," Tia said, fixing herself a glass of cranberry juice. "Obviously, I'm not very good at it anyway, since I lost Mrs. Bailey's case and got kicked off the Woods case."

Kicked off? He didn't know anything about her getting kicked off a case, but he didn't bother addressing it right now. "You graduated at the top of your class; you were just promoted to partner at your firm," Lance pleaded.

Tia raised her glass to him. "I doubt they'll let me work in the file room now," she said, then took a sip.

"Tia, you're a good attorney, and now you want to quit your job to start a dog-grooming business?" Lance asked, incredulous. "Just because you lost one case?"

"Maybe she's going through a midlife crisis," his grandmother threw in.

"Mama, be quiet," Beverly said.

"Or maybe she's just crazy," Mother Brooks mumbled.

"Grandma!"

Tia was exasperated by all the comments. "It's my life. What's the big deal?"

"Actually, it's *our* life and I can't believe you would make a decision like this without talking to me."

"I'm sorry, okay?" Tia chugged down her drink.

"Maybe you can get Denzel to hook you up with the Dog Whisperer," Lance's grandmother said, chuckling.

"Okay, that's it!" Lance angrily stomped toward the door. "This is ridiculous. Everyone, I'm sorry, but I need you to leave."

"Come on, Leo," Virginia said, standing up. "Let's give these kids some privacy." She walked over to her daughter. "Tia, you know I support whatever it is you want to do."

"Thank you, Mama." Tia eyed Lance. "At least *somebody* is supporting me."

Lance debated firing back a response, but he wanted to clear the room. Once he had bundled everyone out the door, he and Tia stood alone in the middle of the hotel room. He tried to keep his tone even-keeled so he didn't set her off.

"Tia," he said slowly, "what's going on? I know you're saying it's the pregnancy and the migraines and the stress, but all of this isn't making sense."

She folded her arms defiantly. "I want to be a dog groomer." She sounded like a toddler on the verge of a temper tantrum.

He took a deep breath. "But, baby, you don't even like dogs."

"So?" She seemed irritated by the whole line of questioning.

"So, why would you leave a lucrative career to open a dog-grooming business?" He couldn't understand her rationale, nor why she couldn't see how crazy this whole idea was.

She huffed as she rolled her eyes.

Lance decided to take another tack. He'd act as if he really wanted to support her, then maybe she'd let down her guard. "Okay, you want to do something different? Let's sit down and talk about it." He tried to take her hand.

She snatched her hand away. "There's nothing to talk about, Lance. I know what I want to do."

Lance inhaled deeply, keeping himself in check. "Okay. Have you done any research on dog grooming? I mean, the economy isn't exactly thriving. Is that really a viable business to be getting into right now?"

"It's what I want to do. Why can't you understand that?"

"It just doesn't make sense."

"I'm sorry you don't approve," she said firmly. "But it's what I'm doing, and if you don't like it, too bad." She stomped into the bedroom and slammed the door, letting him know this conversation was finished.

Lance plopped down on the sofa. He was getting really fed up with this craziness. He'd known pregnant women before, and none had ever pulled a crazy stunt like this. He needed to talk to someone who understood how a woman's hormones worked. Unfortunately, there was only one place to turn to get the answers he needed.

* * *

Thirty minutes later, Lance sat at the kitchen table with his mother and his grandmother. Both of them had no doubt been sitting up talking about Tia.

"I told you something wasn't right with that girl," his grandmother said, shaking her head in disbelief.

"She's pregnant, maybe it's her hormones," Lance said, though he was no longer buying that rationale himself.

His grandmother wasn't buying it either. "Uh-uh, I've birthed five babies and I ain't never acted no fool like that."

"I just don't believe this," his mother added.

"You?" Lance replied. "Imagine how I felt living through it."

"Maybe Tia has a chemical imbalance," his grandmother said. "They were talking about it on *Dr. Phil* the other day."

Lance shrugged. "I don't know, Gram. It's like I don't even know what sets her off, so how do I keep it from happening again?"

"Son," his mother hesitantly began, "I was going to talk to you about Tia anyway. Crystal . . . well, Crystal told us about Tia calling and cursing her out."

Lance groaned. He was surprised his mother hadn't said anything about that sooner. "She did not curse her out."

"Okay, whatever she said, it really upset Crystal," Beverly replied.

Lance knew Crystal wasn't that upset, but she would've played everything up just to get sympathy from his mother. "Tia was just a little jealous," Lance said, now regretting his decision to come over.

"Extreme, unwarranted jealousy, erratic behavior, mood swings—those are not the signs of a stable woman."

"I bet you wouldn't have had these problems with Crystal," his grandmother muttered.

"I would've had a whole set of other problems with Crystal, like her being faithful," Lance snapped. He couldn't believe his family would go there at a time like this. "You know what? Just forget it." He stood up. He was stressed enough. He didn't need his family adding to that.

His mother stopped him just as he was about to walk out. "Sweetheart, your grandmother didn't mean it. You know how she is."

"Yeah, she gets a pass to say whatever she wants because she's old," Lance cried. "But when my wife does something outlandish, she's crazy."

"Hey, you said it, I didn't," his grandmother quipped.

Lance wasn't going to disrespect his grandmother, but he was on the edge of going off. "Grandma," he said, holding up a finger in warning.

"Sit down, boy, before I break that nub off," his grandmother commanded. "I want you to consider this idea. You hire all these people to come work for you at that big fancy magazine. Do you do a background check on them?"

He frowned. "What does that have to do with anything?"

"Answer the question," she demanded.

"Of course I do a background check."

"So, you'll do a background check on someone that you just hire to come work for a company that you don't own, but you don't do a background check on the woman that you plan on spending the rest of your life with, having babies with. Seems like before you jump into a commitment like that—so fast, I might add—that you'd want to make sure you knew all there was to know about someone."

When she put this issue like that, she actually made sense. Lance had to admit that he hadn't thought to do that.

"Well, I did check her out. I mean, I met her family."

"And that should've been your sign," his grandmother said pointedly.

"Mother . . ." Beverly warned.

His grandmother shrugged. "Sorry, I don't have a filter, remember? Those people are crazy, all of them. But that wife of yours is bona fide crazy. I think you need to try and get some answers from her family. Because these problems that she's having, I guarantee you they run deeper than some pregnant woman's hormonal imbalance. If you go digging in that family's backyard, I'd bet my left ovary—if I still had it—that you'd find out they know more than they're letting on."

Lance weighed her words. She was right. If he wanted to know what was really going on with his wife, he needed to go to the people who knew her best.

Chapter 33

Tia needed to figure out a way to shake off this depression. She'd been sinking deeper and deeper into a painful abyss. It was beyond frustrating. It had been a way of life for her since she was a teenager. But usually when she sank into these "spells," she was usually by herself or with family and everyone left her alone. Now Lance was constantly nagging her, constantly asking her questions. His pressure was adding another layer of stress, becoming more than she could handle. Thank God he'd gone ahead and gone to the Texans game, because she finally had some peace and quiet.

Lance.

The man she thought was her knight in shining armor. The man she thought could rescue her from the depths of despair. The man who'd turned into the devil in disguise.

But you love him.

That little voice seemed to be trying to rationalize with her. But the other voice, the short-tempered one, was moving to the forefront.

Tia didn't understand it. She'd been doing so well. She was hesitant to call Dr. Monroe because he would immediately blame it on her not taking her medication, but she was pregnant—what was she supposed to do?

"I need to get out of this house," she mumbled. When Lance had dropped her off at home this morning from the hotel, he'd left without saying a word. She wasn't sure if he was still going to the game, but he'd finally sent a text that simply said, *At the game.* Tia didn't bother calling him. How many times could she keep saying "I'm sorry" and expect him to be okay with it?

Tia debated calling Mrs. Bailey, but for what? To say, "Sorry, I couldn't save your house. Want me to help you pack?" She did plan to appeal, but honestly, Tia had lost faith that she would be able to pull it off.

Tia inhaled deeply and fell back in the reclining chair. *Just come clean. Completely clean,* she told herself. That would be one major level of stress removed. She wished she had enough faith to know Lance would stand by her.

Her mind raced back to Lucinda's reaction.

Lucinda. Maybe she was no longer mad at Tia. Lucinda was her only friend, and at this point Tia felt that she had no choice. She needed to talk to someone before she lost her mind completely.

Tia picked up the house phone to call Lucinda and, at the last moment, decided to punch in *67 and block her number since Lucinda hadn't answered the last few times she'd called. Lucinda answered on the second ring.

"Hey," Tia said.

Lucinda paused as if Tia were the last person she'd expected to hear from. Finally she said, "Hey."

"Look, I'm really sorry about the other day." Lucinda was quiet, so Tia continued, "I'm just going through some things."

"Obviously."

"Well, you've probably heard that I quit the firm."

"Yeah, everyone's kinda talking about it at work."

Tia sighed. "I probably should call Mr. Anderson and let him know."

"You probably should."

Tia hated how cold and distant Lucinda sounded. "Look, are you busy? I really need to talk to you. Maybe you could come by."

"Tia—"

"Come on, Lu. I'm going through some things and I just need to talk to someone." Tia hated feeling that she was begging, but she truly felt at her wit's end, and maybe Lucinda could help her make sense of the nightmare that had become her life.

"Fine," Lucinda huffed, "let me get my friend off the other line." She clicked over, or at least she *thought* she clicked over, because the next thing Tia heard was, "Deb, let me call you back, girl. I got this crazy bitch from work I was telling you about on the other line."

Tia felt as if someone had punched her in the gut.

"Deb?" Lucinda said.

Tia paused, then said, "No, it's the *crazy bitch.* You didn't click over."

Lucinda gasped. "Tia, I didn't mean it."

Tia didn't know what came over her, but she snapped. "Oh, you ain't seen crazy. Crazy is gonna be when your husband finds out what you *really* did in Miami. Crazy is gonna be when Mr. Anderson finds out you've been padding your expense account and when the IRS finds out your husband has been paying people under the table and your mama is in this country illegally!" Tia shouted.

"Tia, don't go there," Lucinda warned.

"Or what? I thought you were my friend! You're evil just like all the rest of them." A flash passed over Tia. "I know you're working for the devil and you're out to get me!"

"Wow," Lucinda said, stunned, "and on that note, I'm gonna let your crazy ass go."

Tia started screaming into the phone, "I'm not crazy! I'm not crazy!"

"Yeah, because sane people scream into the phone that they're not crazy. Psycho." With that, Lucinda slammed the phone down.

Tia went ballistic. She dialed Lucinda's number again, not bothering to block her number this time. Of course, Lucinda didn't answer. Nor did she answer the following thirty-two times that Tia called her phone.

Finally, Tia flung the phone against the wall, more stressed out than ever.

Chapter 34

Lance was tired of the lies. Tia wasn't being straight with him. No rational person has such highs and lows. No one with any sense ups and quits a lucrative job to groom dogs. He'd hoped the game would help him temporarily forget his troubles. But he'd been unable to concentrate and had bailed out early. The last few days had been some of the worst ever. Tia seemed almost catatonic. His grandmother was right, he needed to ask some long-overdue questions. Obviously, Tia wasn't being open and honest, and he was sure Virginia or Leo wouldn't be much help, either. That's why Lance was here—outside the Hair Hook-Up beauty shop, debating whether he really wanted to go inside.

Lance didn't know Bobbi Jo's phone number and decided this was a conversation best had in person anyway. He'd driven to the north side, gone to three beauty shops in the vicinity (all he knew was that she worked at a beauty shop off Tidwell), and at the third one they knew Bobbi Jo and directed him to the right place.

But now that he was here, he found himself wondering if he really wanted to drag Bobbi Jo into this mess.

How else are you going to get any answers? he told himself right before pushing the door open and walking in.

The loud chatter in the beauty shop stopped as he walked in. Half-weaved women, ghetto-fabulous stylists, and a flaming gay man all stared his way.

"Well, call me a clown and slap me silly," the gay man said as his eyes roamed up and down Lance's body.

"Lord, have mercy, my prayers have been answered," some woman muttered.

Finally, a woman at the back sewing blond hair into a client with solid black hair said, "May I help you?"

"Ummm, I'm looking for Bobbi Jo," Lance muttered. All of the attention was making him uneasy.

"Dang," another hairstylist muttered, "how she always get the good-looking ones?"

The gay stylist flashed a smile. "You sure you want Bobbi Jo," he said seductively, " 'cause once you go Mack, you'll never go back."

Several people in the shop burst out laughing. Lance just wanted to cringe.

"Mack, leave that man alone. He is not interested in you," the stylist in the back said. "Bobbi Jo!" she called out. "Somebody's here to see you!"

"Who is it? I'm on my break, dang!" Bobbi Jo said, coming

from the back of the shop. She stopped in her tracks when she saw Lance. "Hey," she said, a perplexed look across her face.

"Hey," Lance replied. "Sorry to just drop by, but I was wondering if I could talk to you."

Bobbi Jo looked around at everyone staring at them. These people didn't even try to hide their nosiness. "Yeah, we can step outside."

"Ummm, Miss Bobbi, you ain't gon' introduce us to your man?" Mack said.

Lance smiled. "Oh, I'm not—"

"No," Bobbi Jo interrupted, as she pushed Lance out the door.

"Why didn't you tell them who I was?" Lance said after they were outside.

"Because it ain't none of their business." She whipped a cigarette out of the pocket of her smock. "What's up? Why you all the way on the north side? At my job at that. You ain't never had two words to say to me."

Lance exhaled. "Look, Bobbi Jo, I know I haven't taken the time to get to know you well, but"—he shrugged—"it's something about you that makes my wife crazy, so I had to keep my distance."

Bobbi Jo laughed as she lit her cigarette. "Shoot, it ain't me that makes your wife crazy." She took a long puff on the cigarette.

"That's actually what I came to talk to you about." He swallowed hard. "I think there's something wrong with Tia."

She smirked. "You *think*?"

"But I can't get any answers—from her, from her mother."

"That's because they're all in denial." Bobbi Jo casually blew a ring of smoke.

"Denial about what?"

"What's it worth to you?"

Lance immediately went to his pocket. He'd been right on the money about Bobbi Jo, which is exactly why he'd stopped at an ATM before coming over here.

"All I have is two hundred dollars." He held the money out to her.

Bobbi Jo actually looked as if she was contemplating if she should say any more, but then she snatched the money. "Your wife ain't right."

"What?"

She stuffed the money in her bra. "In the head."

"What does that mean?"

"It means just what I said. My cousin is cuckoo for Cocoa Puffs."

"Can you speak English?" he said, exasperated.

"She's cra-zy," Bobbi Jo said, twirling her finger at her temple. "We all just pretend nothing's wrong. Guess they didn't let you in on the little game."

Lance was dumbfounded. "You mean Tia is mentally ill?"

"Yep, like I said, cuckoo." Bobbi Jo leaned against the concrete wall and took another puff.

A part of Lance wanted to believe that Bobbi Jo was just jealous. That this revelation was part of the bad blood between the two of them. But another part knew that explained everything.

"Look, Lance, I like you. Shoooot, I wish I had met you first. And believe it or not, I love my cousin. But I'm sick of coddling her all these years. I felt bad that you were hooking up with my cousin and didn't have a clue what was really going on. I wanted to say something before y'all got married, but everybody warned me to stay out of it. Then she went and got pregnant with Aetna."

Lance looked confused. "Aetna?"

"Yeah, her insurance." Bobbi Jo chuckled. "She got her a baby to insure that you stuck around, so I left it alone. But now that you know, you're right. Something is definitely wrong with my cousin. She's one straw short of a bird's nest."

"I don't understand." Lance didn't know what he expected coming here. But he knew what he didn't expect. And that was to find out his wife was—had been—mentally ill.

Bobbi Jo shrugged. "It's the big family secret. She got some kind of mental disease—schizophrenia, bipolar, one of them crazy diseases."

"She is a freakin' attorney. How can she have a mental illness?" he exclaimed.

Bobbi Jo chuckled. "She *was* an attorney. Now, she's a dog groomer." She nodded matter-of-factly.

Lance tried to process everything Bobbi Jo was saying. To say he was stunned was an understatement. "How long have you guys known this?"

She shrugged again. "I guess since she was about seventeen."

"Seventeen! So how did she go to law school?"

Bobbi Jo shook her head. "Your guess is as good as mine. I guess she ain't crazy all the time. I know when she takes her medication, she does all right."

"Medication? What kind of medication?"

Bobbi took another drag on her cigarette, exhaled a ring of smoke, then shrugged. "I have no idea what drugs she was on."

"H-has your family ever tried to get her help?"

Bobbi Jo busted out laughing. "Are you kidding me? Aunt V. would die before she admitted to anyone that her precious daughter was crazy. So she just acts like nothing's wrong, then when Tia flips out, she locks herself in her room and prays. She said it ain't nothing but the devil getting hold of Tia, and when God is ready, he'll cast that devil from her. She keeps holy water and dashes it on Tia from time to time, and when Tia was nineteen, Aunt V. even brought in someone to do an exorcism. That mess was creepy, but obviously, it didn't work."

Lance was absolutely speechless.

Bobbi Jo narrowed her eyes and studied Lance. "So, really, you mean to tell me you didn't think it was strange that someone as pretty as my cousin didn't have a man? That my aunt dang near turned backflips when she found out you wanted to marry Tia? She wanted a quickie wedding before you saw the real Tia and changed your mind. None of that raised red flags for you?"

When Bobbi Jo said it like that, Lance couldn't help but wonder what he'd been thinking. "No, I just . . ." Lance didn't know what to say. Had Tia and her family intentionally deceived him?

"Look, I know this may be a bit much, but my cuz is good people—when she's thinking straight. So, just enjoy those moments." Bobbi Jo let out a small laugh. "And do like my Aunt V. during the rest of the times and hide when Tia flips out."

This was no laughing matter to Lance. What in the world had he gotten himself into? And now that Tia was carrying his child, what did that mean for their baby?

Chapter 35

Lance felt deceived, conned. He felt that he'd been played for a fool. And Tia was about to come clean with him, whether she wanted to or not. But as angry as he was, Lance wanted to give her one more chance to come clean. He *needed* her to come clean. He *wanted* her to tell him that everything Bobbi Jo had said had been a lie.

"Tia!" he called out as soon as he walked into the house.

"What's going on? Why are you screaming like that?" she said, walking in from the kitchen. She had a baby-furniture catalog in her hand. As usual, she looked weary.

Lance took a moment to compose himself. Everything inside him wanted to immediately hurl Bobbi Jo's revelation at his wife.

"Ummm, just wondering if you are okay," he managed to say.

She glanced down at the catalog, then back up at him. “Yeah.” She hesitated, swallowed, and fought back the tears welling in her eyes. “No.”

She plopped down on the sofa and Lance sat down next to her, his heart racing. “Tia, what is wrong?”

As he readied himself for yet another lie, she said, “Lucinda and I just had a huge fight.”

Lance inhaled sharply. With all the issues they had, the last thing he wanted to hear about was some trivial fight between his wife and her best friend.

Even still, he asked, “About what?” He didn’t really care, but he was trying to figure out a way to broach what Bobbi Jo had told him.

Tia fiddled with the catalog, then looked her husband in the eye and said, “She called me crazy.”

Lance was still waiting, hoping, praying that she would continue.

She did. “I flew off the handle because she’s right,” Tia softly said.

Lance remained quiet as Tia turned to face him. “Lance, I need to tell you something. Something I should have told you before we got married.”

His heart raced as he waited. Was he finally about to get the truth he had been seeking?

Tia wiped away a tear. “Lance, I . . . I have a mental illness.” She looked away as if she couldn’t bear to look him in the eye. “I’m bipolar,” she all but whispered.

So Bobbi Jo hadn’t been lying. Lance knew something was

going on, but hearing this from his wife's mouth was something he had never been prepared for.

"How long?" he mumbled.

"How long what?"

"How long have you known?" he snapped, his anger rising. He thought having his wife come clean without being forced was what he wanted. But hearing her admission had only angered him more. This woman had married him, had made his life a living hell the last few months, and she *knew* she was mentally ill? Lance didn't know how he would ever be able to forgive that.

"I just didn't know how to tell you."

"Tia, how could you do that? You don't think that's something I needed to know? That's a major problem."

Tia sank back onto the sofa. "What do you want me to say, Lance? I'm sorry."

"*You're sorry?* Is that all you have to say?"

She started crying hard. "What would've happened if I had told you? Would you have done like every other man and ran out of my life? Would you have married me? Would you have even given me the freakin' time of day?"

"I don't know," he shot back. "But you should've at least given me the chance to decide, to know what I was dealing with." He jumped up and began pacing. "I didn't know what was wrong with you. I've been worried sick and you knew what was wrong all along. You lied about what was wrong. Our whole marriage is based on a lie!"

"You would've left. Just like everybody else," she said, her voice barely above a whisper.

"Tia, I'm not everybody else," he yelled. He took a deep breath to calm himself down. "Is that why your family was so anxious for you to get married?"

Her voice remained at a monotone. "You pursued me, remember? Didn't I tell you over and over again that we were going too fast?"

"Yeah, but somewhere along the way, maybe after you planted the flowers, or painted our bedroom, you could've said, 'By the way, Lance, I have an illness.' "

She glared at him, then simply said, "You don't have to be so nasty. You don't know how much I've agonized over whether to tell you."

"Oh, I see. I'm being nasty. Meanwhile, I'm being lied to by the whole family. The Mafia. The code of silence and all that. Just tell me, is that why they wanted to marry you off to the nearest sucker?"

She jumped to her feet. "Oh, so now you're a sucker for marrying me?" She stomped toward the door, then stopped, her shoulders slumped in defeat. "What difference does it make anyway?"

Lance wasn't letting go of his anger. "It makes a lot of difference," he shouted. "You're pregnant and you're carrying my child."

"And let me guess, you don't want your child to be crazy like me?"

Finally, he seemed to realize that he had gone too far. "Tia, you're not even hearing me."

She rubbed her temples like she was trying to get rid of a bad headache. "No, I hear you loud and clear. The wonderful Lance Kingston can't be married to the crazy lady. Oh, and what if they have a crazy baby? Heaven forbid! You want out? Fine, get out." She spun off and stomped down the hallway toward their bedroom. "You probably want out so you can go be with that Crystal tramp anyway!" She walked into the closet and began tearing his clothes off the hangers and tossing them onto the floor. "Just leave! Just go right now. You're gonna leave anyway. Save us both the expense—"

"Tia, calm the hell down!" he said, following her. "This is what I'm talking about right here. You've been acting insane for months, and I had no idea why."

"I'm not insane!" she screamed, pushing past him. "Stop saying that!"

"What is your problem with that word?" he asked, following her out of the walk-in closet.

"I'm not insane! I'm not insane! You just want to leave to go be with that Crystal slut. Don't make this about me!"

"See, all of this"—he motioned wildly at her—"I am sick and tired of going on this roller-coaster ride with you. For months, I had no idea why. And you knew all along, your family knew all along. Were you running some type of game on me? Did everyone have a good laugh at my expense?"

"Get out!" she hissed.

"This is my house. I'm not going anywhere. You're going to

sit here and talk to me about this. You're in denial and that's not helping anyone."

"I'm not doing anything. Get out!" This time she hit him as hard as she could across the face. She had reached to hit him again when he grabbed her and pushed her away. She fell across the bed. Before Lance could react, she picked up the lamp on the nightstand and threw it. "I knew you were trying to kill me."

"Nobody is trying to kill you." He took a deep breath, trying to calm down. "Tia, the baby. We don't need to holler and scream. It can't be good for the baby." He reached back and clicked the lock on their bedroom door. "But we are going to talk about this."

Hearing the lock click set her off and she charged toward the door, like she desperately needed to escape. He grabbed her in a bear hug to try to stop her. She elbowed him in the stomach, and when he bent over in pain, she opened the door and took off downstairs.

Lance moaned as he stood up. "Tia," he called out. He saw the cordless phone was missing from the table in the hallway and that the hallway bathroom door was closed.

Lane was shocked when he heard her screaming, "Help me, Officers! My husband is trying to kill me. He has a knife and he's trying to kill me! Please help me!"

"Tia, what are you doing?" he yelled, banging on the bathroom door.

"Please hurry. We're at 1617 Fountain Lake Circle."

This is not happening, Lance thought. She'd actually called the cops. Everything inside him told him to leave, but Lance knew that if he did, they'd have an APB out on him in the next hour and no one would believe his story. Police would arrest him first and ask questions later. All he could do was walk outside to wait for the inevitable.

Within a minute, two police cruisers pulled up to the house. He walked to the curb to meet them.

"That's him!" Tia screamed from the front door.

"Tia, don't do this," Lance said, turning to face her.

"Sir, we're going to ask you to stop right there," one of the officers said as he approached Lance. Both officers had their hands positioned on their guns, ready to fire if necessary.

"Ma'am, are you okay?" one of the officers asked.

"I will be when you throw him in jail," she cried.

"What did he do to you?"

"He tried to kill me. He's been poisoning me and today he tried to strangle me."

"Tia, you know I didn't do that. Why are you lying?" Lance turned to the policemen, desperation in his face. "Officers, my wife is mentally ill."

Mr. Pitre, their nosy old neighbor, peered over the bushes. "Lance, is everything all right?"

Lance wanted to scream, *Does it look all right?*

"Sir, I'm going to ask you to go back inside your house," one of the officers told Mr. Pitre, and he scurried away.

The other officer pushed Lance up against the car. "Sir, you're under arrest. You have the right to remain silent."

"I didn't do anything!" Lance protested as he squirmed to break free.

The officers threw him down on the ground and roughly pulled his hands behind his back. "Anything you say can and will be used against you in a court of law."

"I don't believe this," Lance mumbled as they snapped handcuffs on him. They yanked him to his feet, then threw him in the back of the car.

Lance noticed his wife standing in the doorway. He expected to see a victorious smirk. Instead, she now looked confused, as if she had no idea what was going on.

At least he did, finally.

Chapter 36

In all his thirty-four years—even during his rebellious teen years, when he'd stayed out past curfew, used a fake ID to buy beer, vandalized a neighbor's house—through all of that, Lance had never seen the inside of a jail.

So that he was now sitting behind bars for simply trying to talk to his wife had Lance at a loss for words.

He had been detained four hours, long enough to learn that he was being booked in. They'd fingerprinted him, taken his belongings, and thrown him in a cell with crackheads, rapists, and murderers.

The guards weren't the least bit sympathetic. One of them had even called him a "wife beater." But one had at least told him he would be next up for his one phone call.

The question was, whom in the world was he supposed to call? Brian was out of town. Lance's mother would have a heart attack and never forgive Tia. Despite everything, Lance knew Tia was sick, so he couldn't say 100 percent that he was ready to walk away from his wife and child. So, no, he couldn't bring his mother into this madness. He thought about people from work, but as the boss, that was the last thing that he needed.

He debated calling a few other friends, but besides Brian, he didn't hang out with a lot of people and definitely not anyone he could call to come bail him out of jail. So, that left him with only one option. Someone who was friends with a bail bondsman. Someone who would come right away to set him free.

"Kingston, you ready for your call?" the guard said, opening the cell door.

"Yeah," Lance said, trudging over to the phone. It was late, but he didn't have a choice. He punched in the number and felt like the scum of the earth when he heard the automated voice say, "You have a collect call from an inmate at the Harris County Jail. Do you accept the charges?"

After a brief hesitation, Crystal said, "Yes."

Lance sighed in relief. "Crystal?"

"Lance?" She sounded as if he was the last person she expected to be on the other end.

"Yeah, thank God you accepted."

"I almost didn't. But I thought it may be my cousin. I know she has some warrants for parking tickets. Lance, what in the world is going on? Why are you in jail?"

"I'm so sorry to call you. I just don't know who else to turn to."

"Lance, what are you doing in jail?"

"It is a very long story. But I assure you, I didn't do anything."

"Well, of course you didn't," she said automatically. "But who said you did something?"

Lance didn't have the energy to think of a lie. "Tia."

"Lance, what happened?" Crystal asked, her voice filled with worry.

"We had a big argument. She called the cops and said I tried to kill her."

"What?"

"Yeah, I know, it's crazy. But I'm losing my mind down here. Do you think you can call your friend Mike, the bondsman, and have him post bail and you come get me out?"

"Of course. He's used to late-night calls so I'll get him right on it and I will get you out of there as soon as I can."

"Crystal, I don't know how much my bond is, but I will get it back to you right away."

"Boy, hush. I'm not thinking about that." He heard a lot of rumbling, and he had no doubt Crystal was already moving toward the car to come to see about him.

"Thank you so much."

"I'm walking out the door now. But, Lance, you know you can always count on me, no matter what."

He knew what he was letting himself in for, but at this point he didn't really care.

Freedom never felt so good.

That had to be the longest ten hours of his life. Lance found himself worrying about Tia. But then he silently cursed. Tia was the reason he was in this predicament. So why was he worried about her well-being?

“So where to now?” Crystal said.

Lance looked over at the woman who had been his savior today. He felt really bad having to turn to her. “Crystal, I can’t thank you enough.”

“I told you, don’t worry about it. For some reason, I think you would do the same for me.”

He thought about it. She was right. He would have, without hesitation. After all, they had a history together.

“So, again, where to?”

That was a good question. Lance couldn’t go home. And he sure couldn’t go to his mother’s house. She’d have too many questions, and he wasn’t ready to give her any answers. “A hotel, I guess.”

She turned up her nose. “I wish I would take you to a hotel.”

“Nah, seriously, I can’t go home right now.”

“Then you’ll come to my place.”

He knew that was coming. “Crystal, that’s not a good idea.”

“Lance, it’s five in the morning. I know you’re starving, tired. Do you even have your wallet?”

He thought about it. He hadn’t taken anything when he left but his cell phone, which had been clipped to his waist. He had no driver’s license, no money, no credit card. Nothing.

“Now, if you really want to, I can pay for the hotel for you. But seriously, it doesn’t make sense. Come on over to my place. Let me fix you something to eat, you can sleep in the guest room—I promise, I won’t touch you,” she said slyly. “If you want to talk, we'll do that. If you don't, you don't. In fact, I have to be at work in three hours, so I won't even be there. You can have the house to yourself all day. No pressure. Girl Scout's honor."

"You were never a Girl Scout."

She laughed. "You know me so well."

She was right. He did know her well, and for a moment Lance found himself wondering what life would be like with her. Crystal didn't suffer from any mental illness, she wasn't hiding any devastating secrets. She was as conscientious as he was about her finances. She was ambitious, beautiful, and successful. Everything he wanted in a woman.

Except faithful.

Did that even matter now? On the list of ideal traits, would he rather have a faithful woman or a sane one?

"Come on in," Crystal said once they'd arrived at her house.

Lance couldn't help but notice the men's shoes that Crystal quickly grabbed from the corner and discreetly carried into the back bedroom. He decided he was in no position to mention them and instead sank onto her plush, oversize leather sofa. Lance was amazed how at home he felt in Crystal's house. She hadn't changed much over the past two years, including the five-by-seven photo of them in New Orleans. When they were together, he practically lived here because it was closer to his job.

His comfort level made him uneasy. *What are you thinking?*

His apprehensions were soon eased as Crystal cooked him a turkey and spinach omelet, cheese-smothered hash browns and toast. He'd eaten as if he hadn't had a meal in days. Actually, when he thought about it, he hadn't. He hadn't had a decent meal, and watching Crystal's plump backside as she worked in the kitchen, he realized he hadn't had any decent loving in a while either.

His eyes were riveted to her backside until she turned around and said, "Hey, do you need anything else?"

He looked away guiltily. "No. What time do you go to work?"

"Actually, that was my job on the phone earlier. It's real slow in the ER, so I don't have to go in."

He eyed her skeptically.

"You know what? I knew you weren't going to believe me." She picked up her telephone, put the phone on speaker, and punched in a number.

"Memorial City ER," a woman answered.

"Hey, Tasha, it's Crystal again. Are you sure you don't need me to come in? I was all set to work today until I got your call."

"Girl, why can't you ever relax? I told you we're fine. I'm overbudget and have to cut some of these hours back, so, no, stay at home, relax, enjoy your day off, okay?"

"Okay. Call me if you need me." Crystal pushed the button to end the call, then turned back to Lance. "O ye of little faith," she said with a playful smirk.

"I didn't say a word."

"Yeah, but I saw your eyes. You forget I know you, too." The look she gave him had all the smokiness of their days together.

"Maybe I should go to a hotel," he said after a brief pause.

"If you don't be quiet . . ." She waved him off. "Now, look, I know you've been through a lot, and I am going to allow you time to just relax and get some rest. You can sleep all day and I won't disturb you. It's been a late night for us both, so I'm going to pull the blinds, block out that sunlight, pretend it's nighttime, and watch *When Harry Met Sally* until I fall asleep."

He chuckled. "Again? You're still watching that movie?"

"You know it's my favorite."

He laughed because he couldn't count the number of times she'd forced him to watch that movie. Lance half expected her to invite him back. Hell, he *wanted* her to invite him back. Instead, she leaned over, kissed him on the forehead. "Get some rest, Lance. And know that everything will get better." With that, she headed to her bedroom.

Despite his exhaustion Lance wasn't sleepy, so he sat in the living room aimlessly watching television, debating whether he should call Tia. He eyed Crystal's laptop, popped it open, then logged on to the Internet. He started researching mental illnesses. He was amazed at the stories he read. The more he researched, the more he recognized all the signs of Tia's bipolar disorder.

By noon, Lance decided to shut it down and try and get some sleep. He was mentally drained and couldn't bear to read another word about the disease that was ruining his life.

Lance tiptoed down the hall. He stopped outside Crystal's room and smiled when he heard the television. That used to be a source of contention with them, her always falling asleep with the television on. But he'd learned to live with it because she had so few other faults.

Lance debated going in to cut it off, but decided to go on to his room. He thought sleep would come easy, but thirty minutes later, he was back in front of Crystal's room.

Lance lightly tapped on the door. When she didn't answer, he slowly eased the door open. "Crystal?"

She was sleeping soundly, buried in her down comforter. She must've been used to sleeping during the day, because the heavy curtains were pulled tight and had it not been for the television, the room would have been pitch-black. He tiptoed over and stood over her, watching her sleep. Lance took in the outline of her body, admiring how beautiful she looked, even in her sleep.

Before he knew it, he gently peeled back the comforter, then the sheet. He immediately felt his manhood rise when he saw the purple satin gown clinging to her body. A part of him wanted to say that she'd put it on for him, but that was how Crystal always went to bed. There were no rags around her head, no flannel pajamas. Every night she went to bed looking sexy.

Lance couldn't help it; he gently ran his hand over the satin, stopping at the center of her thighs. She moaned lightly, then stirred. Her eyes popped open as he took in her silhouette.

"Lance, what are you doing?" she whispered.

"I want you. I need you," he moaned as he ran his hand under her gown and up her leg.

Crystal inhaled deeply as if she was savoring his touch. He leaned in and kissed her neck. "Make love to me," he whispered, trying to rub her breast.

Crystal moaned as her back arched. "Lance"—she grabbed his arms to stop him—"don't."

He stopped. That was the last reaction he ever expected from her. "You don't want me?" The light from the TV illuminated the love in her eyes.

Her eyes watered as she said, "I want you so bad, you just don't even know. But not like this. You don't want this. You're hurting."

"I do," he protested. "I want you."

"No, you don't." She smiled and sat up. "I wish you did, but you don't. Not right now. Right now you want comfort and I'm here. I'm a warm body, but later, you'll regret it."

"I can't go back to her."

"I don't think you should," Crystal said matter-of-factly, "but I also don't think you should make that decision after the day you've had."

His level of respect for her rose a few notches. "You're so wonderful, you know that?"

"If I was so wonderful, I'd be the one you were married to," she said as a lone tear trickled down her cheek. His expression must've given away his thoughts because she added, "What I did was the biggest mistake of my life. I regret it every single day. But the second-biggest mistake would be, right now, letting this happen. I love you, Lance. And it's my dream that one day you can love me back. Today's not that day." She gently caressed his face. "So go get some sleep and I will lie here and try to forget the feel of your touch." She laughed. "And I'll pray that everything works out for the best."

She was right. He would've so regretted this, and he was grateful that she had the sense to recognize that.

"I'm sorry," he said.

"Don't be. It was good for my ego," she joked. "Now shoo, go get some sleep."

Lance smiled as he headed back to his room.

Everything works out for the best.

Lance hoped that would be the case. The only problem was, he had no idea anymore what the best for him was.

Chapter 37

"Sweetie, you've got to stop crying." Virginia Jiles stroked her daughter's hair.

Usually that was comforting to Tia. But today it only made her bawl harder. "Mama, I'm messing everything up," Tia sobbed. "I don't know why I keep doing these things."

Leo slammed his Bible shut. "You know exactly why you're doing this, and I don't know why you and your mama want to sugarcoat this. You went into this marriage under false pretenses. So why would you think it's going to be a piece of cake?"

Tia felt a sharp pang at his harsh words.

"You've lost your man. You've lost your friends. You've lost faith," Leo snapped.

"That's absurd," Virginia said. "Me and Tia pray."

Leo shook his head as if they were a lost cause. "You pray for God to take this disease away, and while I know He's capable of anything, He also gives us a sound mind to make just decisions, and ain't neither one of you been making just decisions when it comes to this marriage." He turned to his sister. "First of all, Virginia, you need to butt out."

"This is my daughter. You need to be concerned about—"

"Let me stop you there. You're always putting down my kids. Yes, I know they're trifling, both of them. But you know what? I did the best I could and I let them go. Yes, I can continue to give them advice, but whether they choose to listen or not is up to them. I'm not going to try to control their lives. I'm just trying to keep my own self together while I'm on top of this soil."

"Well, you might not be concerned about your own kids' lives, but—"

"Oh, I'm concerned, all right. But if they make a mess of their lives, it's gonna be on their own terms."

"So, I'm making a mess of my daughter's life?" Virginia said, crossing her arms across her chest.

"Your daughter is over here. Not at home, working things out with her husband. A husband that she had arrested, and for what? Did he really hit you?" Leo demanded to know.

"No . . . I wasn't thinking rationally," Tia admitted. She'd spent the day balled up in a corner, crying. She'd come to her senses and tried to call the county jail. The only information she could get was that he had been released and the fact that he hadn't come home tore at her insides.

Finally, this morning, Tia called her mother to come get her. Virginia hadn't acted the least bit shocked when she'd told her what had happened, but Uncle Leo was not going to remain silent any longer.

"You never think rationally when you're off medication," he said.

Virginia spoke up. "I told you, that medication—"

"I'm sorry, when did you get your medical degree?"

She rolled her eyes.

Leo continued, leaning forward in his tattered recliner to emphasize his point, "Tia, baby, you know I love you with all my heart. But you were wrong. Dead wrong. And if that man never comes back to you, it will be because you pushed him away."

Never comes back to you. Tia's heart sank at that possibility. Uncle Leo was right. Lance had done nothing but love her, and her craziness was pushing him further and further away.

"Uncle Leo, I'm trying to control my mood swings."

"No, you're not. Because if you were, you'd be taking your medication."

"The girl is pregnant! She can't take medication."

Leo exhaled in frustration. "Now you have seized upon what you consider a legitimate excuse not to take your medication. That's all you needed in the first place. Have you called your doctor at all?"

"The only person she needs to call on is Jesus," Virginia said.

Leo shook his head and ignored his sister. "You need to talk to your doctor. That's who I would be taking advice from."

"Okay, you're right," Tia acquiesced. "I'll call the doctor

and see if there's something safe they can put me on to stabilize my moods. I don't want to be like this, honestly."

He came over and patted her face. "But baby, you are." He rose to his full height and patted his little, scrawny stomach. "I don't want to be as good-looking as I am"—he stroked his salt-and-pepper beard and flashed a crooked smile—"but it's the cross that God gave me to bear."

Tia finally cracked a smile. "Okay, I'll call the doctor."

He grabbed the house phone and handed it to Tia. "But you call your husband first."

Chapter 38

Lance stared at his ringing private desk phone. He'd wondered how long it would be before Tia would call. If she would call at all.

He had borrowed Crystal's car this morning and come to work. He didn't want to get too comfortable lying around Crystal's house all day. Luckily, he had a change of clothes in his office. But truthfully, he could've used the day off. Lance had since locked himself in his office and told his secretary he didn't want to be bothered.

He decided that he was going to a hotel after work, but first, he'd have to go by the house and get his wallet and his keys. That's why he decided to go ahead and answer the phone.

"Lance?" Tia said. She sounded as if she'd been crying.

"Yes?" he said coldly.

"I'm sorry. I'm so, so sorry."

"You're always sorry."

"Are you going to leave me?"

"Tia, I can't do this right now." He hoped that she didn't ask him how he got out of jail because he would have to tell her that he'd had to call Crystal to bail him out. "I have a pending court case. A *court case,* Tia, to prove I'm not some wife beater."

"I'm sorry. I just wish I hadn't done that." She sniffed.

"I wish you hadn't done that, either. Now I have to go to court to clear my name. Hope I don't get a domestic-violence charge on my record. My *clean* police record. Up until now."

"I'll tell them you didn't do anything."

"They're not going to believe you, Tia." Lance knew enough about the system in Texas to know that they prosecuted, even when the woman didn't want to.

"Lance, you're right. I'm sick. I mean, I don't really see it as a sickness, but I know it is."

"It is." He was surprised that she finally admitted it.

"I'm sorry I didn't tell you."

"I can't believe you would go into a marriage with a secret like that." He leaned back in his chair and massaged his forehead.

"Can you come home so we can talk about this?"

Lance sighed heavily. "Look, I'm at work right now."

"Please? We really need to talk."

She was right about that. "Fine. I'll come by there after work. I need to pick up a few things anyway."

"Pick up a few things? So you are leaving me?"

"Tia, I don't know what I'm going to do. What I do know

is that I can't continue living like this. If you won't accept that there's something wrong and allow me to do what I can to help, then I need some space."

"So, you're really gonna leave me. You're gonna leave our baby?"

"I would never leave my child."

"But you would leave me?"

"Look, just chill until I get there this evening."

"Okay, fine." She hesitated. "And, Lance, I love you."

"Okay" was all he could manage before hanging up the phone.

Lance had lived in this house for the last four years. But right now he felt like a stranger. He tossed the keys to Crystal's car on the counter.

"Hi," Tia said when he walked in. "Whose car do you have?"

"A friend's. I didn't have my keys or my car."

Thankfully, she didn't ask any more questions and simply said, "Okay."

Tia wore a long, hunter-green maternity sundress and had her hair pulled back into a ponytail. He wanted to reach out and touch her growing stomach, but decided against it.

As soon as Lance took a seat on the sofa, Tia threw her arms around his neck. "I'm sorry, baby. I'm so, so sorry." She showered him with kisses.

"Tia, stop," he said, grabbing her arms and pulling back.

"No, make love to me," she said breathlessly.

As much as he would love to take his wife and love her

all over this living room, Lance knew that would get them nowhere. Lance gently pushed her away. "Tia, don't. Our problems can't be solved by having sex."

"But it's been so long since we've been together. I know you have desires." When he remained stiff to her touch, she fell back on the sofa. "Unless you've been having those desires filled somewhere else."

"Tia, don't start. I mean, I'm serious. I can't do this with you. Now either we're going to talk about the real issue or I'm leaving."

She made a face. "What do you want me to say, Lance?" Her voice started cracking. "That sometimes I'm crazy? Okay. Sometimes I'm crazy. But it's nothing for us to get all worked up about." She leaned in and started fiddling with his buttons again.

He pushed her off him. "Tia, I'm not playing around."

Tears began streaming down her face. "Lance, I'm trying to make it right, sweetheart. I am so sorry. For everything."

Lance was surprised at his lack of sympathy, but he guessed getting arrested in your own house could harden anyone's heart.

"Please forgive me." She leaned in to kiss him, but he turned his head, causing her lips to land on his cheek. "What do I have to do?" she cried. "I'll get back on the medication, go to the doctor more regularly, whatever you want."

"Tia, you had me arrested! For something I didn't do. Your crazy antics have put my job and my life in jeopardy."

She lowered her gaze. "Please don't call me crazy."

"Tia," he said harshly, "if it walks like a duck, quacks like a duck, and looks like a duck, it's a duck. No matter how much you want it to be a chicken."

She could feel herself losing control. "What does that mean?"

Lance leapt off the sofa and pointed a finger in his wife's face. "It means that there is something wrong with you, you've known it all along, and you lied to me about it!"

"If all you wanted to do was get back at me, what the hell did you come over here for?"

He stood in silence, glaring at his wife. Finally he said, "You know, that's a good question." Then he headed to the bedroom.

Lance half-expected Tia to come up after him, but she didn't. He was at his wit's end. He'd never envisioned leaving his wife and his child. He'd never envisioned turning into his father. But all he and Tia did was fight. Why did he want a marriage like that?

Lance grabbed a couple of suits, then tossed some other clothes and toiletries into a duffel bag.

Sooner or later, you'll leave.

Lance pushed his father's words from his head and headed back downstairs.

Tia was sitting on the sofa, looking forlorn. "Lance, come on, let's talk about this."

"I am through with fighting. I will be at a hotel if and when you decide you want to act like my wife. My *honest* wife." Lance didn't give her time to respond as he walked out the door.

Chapter 39

"Okay, Mother. Your ceiling fan is up, your cabinet is fixed, and I moved those boxes outside. Are there any other domestic duties you'd like your hardworking son to take care of?"

Beverly Kingston was sitting with three of her friends playing bridge. "See, that's why I love having a son," she said sweetly.

Lance made a wry face. "You need to let me hire a handyman for you. This is not how I intended to spend my Saturday."

"Sweetie, I know you make all that money running that magazine," she said, which Lance knew was all for show with her friends, "but why would I waste your money when I have a big, strong son to do all this work?" She and her friends exchanged a bout of laughter.

Lance let his mother brag about him. Thankfully, she hadn't asked questions when he'd shown up early this morning. Even his grandmother hadn't asked questions. Before that, Lance had stayed at a hotel for four days. He hadn't talked to Tia and was beginning to get worried about her. He'd replied to her text this morning, telling her he would be at his mother's and couldn't come by the house as she wanted. She'd called several times, but he wouldn't take her calls. He had to show her he meant business.

Lance was starting to hate that hotel, so after a restless night, he left just before daylight and ended up at his mother's. Although Lance complained about the work she had him doing, the manual labor had been a distraction from all of his problems, so he didn't really mind. He just hadn't expected it to take all day.

"Well, I need to get going. I probably need to go check on Tia." Lance hadn't planned on going home yet. He was going back to the hotel. But if he didn't at least mention his wife, his family would know they were having problems.

Beverly gave her son a significant look. She wanted to make sure he didn't say any more. Heaven forbid that Beverly Kingston's friends find out that she had some dysfunction in her family.

As Lance put away the last of the tools, the doorbell rang.

"I got it," his grandmother called out from the living room, where she had been knitting.

Lance slipped his jacket on, then leaned down and pecked his mother on the forehead. "Good-bye, Mother. I'll call you later." He turned to the other elderly women. "Ladies, enjoy your game of spades."

Beverly swatted his arm. "Boy, you know we don't play that game."

"Yes, we leave that to the people in the hood," one of the silver-haired women quipped. They all laughed as if that were the funniest thing they'd heard all day.

"I hate to break up this laughfest," his grandmother said, appearing in the doorway, "but the fruitcake has officially flipped."

"Mama, what in the world are you talking about?" Beverly asked.

Lance's grandmother didn't answer and instead stepped to one side to let Tia walk into the room.

Every single one of them gasped as Tia—clad in a Stars-and-Stripes, two-piece bikini, her protruding belly exposed—grinned widely, waved, and said, "Hey, everybody."

Lance blanched in shock, then raced to his wife's side. "Tia, baby. What are you doing?"

"Looks like she's standing in our kitchen in a toddler's swimsuit," his grandmother said, shaking her head. "Beverly, ain't you gonna introduce your daughter-in-law to your friends?" she added, giggling at the embarrassment on her daughter's face.

Lance took off his jacket and wrapped it around his wife's shoulders. It wasn't exactly cold outside, but she was shivering, even if she didn't seem to notice.

"I was looking for you," Tia said to Lance. "I can't find my keys." Her eyes were wide as saucers and her hair was matted and all over her head—well, what was left of her hair. Lance noticed huge chunks of missing hair.

Tia caught him staring at the mess. "Oh, I cut it. It was very ugly." She stuck out her bottom lip. "Lance, where are my keys?" she whined.

Suddenly, it dawned on Lance that if she couldn't find her keys, she couldn't have driven.

"How did you get here?"

Tia looked confused for a moment, then said, "I walked."

"All the way here?" Lance asked, dumbfounded. He lived twenty minutes away by car. So it had to have taken her two hours to walk here.

"And she walked in that getup," his grandmother added, running her gaze up and down Tia's body. "I'm surprised the police didn't stop her."

"Lance, where are my keys?" Tia repeated. "I need my keys. I need to go buy some dope."

The gasps were even louder this time, and Lance saw his mother clutch her necklace. Horror blanketed her face, and Lance knew she would never forgive Tia for humiliating her in front of her siddity friends.

"Come on, baby. Let's go. I'll help you find your keys." He took her arm.

"No!" She jerked her arm away. "I need my keys and I know you had them!" she screamed. "You just don't want me to go get any dope! It's not gonna hurt the baby. All you care about is this stupid baby."

"Lance, get her out of here," Beverly said, her voice just above a whisper.

Tia spun on her mother-in-law. "You're in on it, you evil troll!"

Beverly's eyes widened in shock even more. Lance was sure his mother was on the verge of passing out.

"All you old biddies are in on it," Tia said, pointing at each of the women, who were equally horrified by Tia's outburst. "Gimme that," Tia said, snatching one of the women's purses off the back of the chair. She dumped out all the contents on the table where they were playing cards. "You sleazy tramp," she yelled at the elderly woman. "Do you have my keys?" She threw the purse and it hit the woman in the face. The woman yelped as she jumped from her seat. Her two friends jumped up as well and backed up against the wall in fear.

"Gimme my keys before I tear out your tongues and feed them to my cat," Tia growled, cornering them against the wall. Drool dripped from her mouth and a crazed look filled her face.

Even Lance's grandmother no longer seemed amused and had retreated to the corner.

"Tia," Lance said, trying to grab his wife in a bear hug, "baby, come on, let me take you home."

Tia squirmed with a ferocity he didn't even know she possessed. "Get off of me. I hate you! You got that other woman pregnant, and I know you're trying to kill me to go be with her!"

Lance wrestled his wife to the floor, giving the three elderly women time to race out the door. Tia knocked over a chair as she kicked, screamed, and struggled to break free.

"Let me go!" Tia shouted.

Lance felt the tears wet his face as he tried to keep his wife pinned down.

"I called the police," Beverly finally said. Lance hadn't even realized she'd jumped up and gone for the phone. He wanted to ask his mother why she'd done that, to tell her that he would handle this on his own. But the way his wife was fighting him, he no longer believed that.

"You called the cops on me, you slut?" Tia spat at Beverly. "I'm gonna kill you. I'm gonna come over here while you're sleeping and cut your throat wide-open. You're the devil. That's why Lance said he wished you were dead. I wish you were dead, too!"

"Mama, go, please just go," Lance cried just as Tia smacked him in the face. He grabbed her free hand and didn't release his grip.

Beverly didn't have to be told twice. She raced from the room, Lance's grandmother right behind her.

"Ugggh, I hate you," Tia said, viciously squirming.

"That's okay," Lance said as soothingly as possible, tears running down his cheeks. "I love you and I'm not gonna let you go, baby." He pulled her tighter, praying that help would arrive quickly.

Chapter 40

This had been the absolute longest night of Lance's life. He sat in the waiting room of West Oaks Hospital. The police had wanted to send Tia to Ben Taub Hospital, but Lance had heard horror stories about that facility, so he'd begged them to take his wife to West Oaks.

He'd called Tia's mother, and she now sat across from him in the waiting room. She'd been relatively quiet since she arrived three hours ago. She didn't ask for specific details; instead, she just wanted to know if Tia was okay. Now she sat clutching her Bible as she silently prayed.

Finally, when he couldn't take the waiting anymore, Lance said, "Virginia, I need some answers."

"Can we not do this right now?" Virginia said, sniffing. "I need to focus all my energy on praying."

"No! We need to do this now!" Lance demanded.

She abruptly stood up. "I'm going to the chapel. Please let me know when the doctor comes back in."

Before she reached the waiting-room door, the attending physician entered. "Mr. Kingston?"

"Yes?" Lance said, jumping up.

The doctor removed his glasses and massaged the bridge of his nose. "We've finally managed to calm your wife down. She is under heavy sedation."

"And the baby?" Lance asked.

"The baby is fine. Quite frankly, we don't like sedating pregnant women, but we felt your wife's state of mind posed a bigger risk than the drugs."

"Can I see my daughter?" Virginia interjected.

The doctor shook his head. "I'm afraid that won't be possible. This was a major psychotic episode. So she's gonna be out for a number of hours."

"Psychotic?" Lance whispered.

"Don't call my daughter psychotic!" Virginia snapped.

The doctor kept his tone neutral. He seemed used to dealing with families in denial. "I'm sorry, but, ma'am, what your daughter experienced was indeed a psychotic episode. Up until she was sedated, she threatened me and my staff, and her baby."

"She's just tired. And stressed, not to mention the fact that she's pregnant," Virginia said defensively. "She don't need you pumping her full of no drugs."

"Ma'am, I assure you this had nothing to do with fatigue, stress, or hormones. These are all classic signs of mental illness."

The doctor turned to Lance. "Has she been diagnosed as bipolar or schizophrenic?"

"You're just like all those other quacks!" Virginia barked. "Ain't nothing wrong with my baby. She gets sick sometimes and worked up. Y'all put her on these drugs and it just makes things worse! You all in it together, the doctors, the people who make the drugs. You just want more money!"

The doctor sighed, then turned back to Lance as if he didn't have time to deal with Tia's mother.

"Can we get her medical records?" he asked Lance.

Lance nodded, although it dawned on him that he'd never seen his wife's medical records. "I'm sure that won't be a problem."

"You'll do no such thing," Virginia said. "As a matter of fact, I'm going to check my daughter out of this godforsaken place right now."

"You'll do no such thing!" Lance snapped at his mother-in-law. "You know there is something wrong with your daughter, so stop pretending." Virginia stood in shock as he continued, "Maybe you can close your eyes and pretend nothing is wrong, but I'm not doing it, especially when my baby's life may be at stake." Lance turned back to the doctor. "Doc, what do we need to do?"

The doctor seemed relieved to be making progress. "Well, I'll need those records ASAP. In the meantime, we need to commit her for seventy-two hours. That's the maximum we can hold her without her consent."

"Commit?" Virginia gasped as she fell back on the hard sofa.

Lance didn't feel like pacifying his mother-in-law right now. He had more pressing issues to deal with. "Okay, Doc. Whatever we need to do."

The doctor nodded. "Great. I will send the nurse back in with the necessary paperwork."

After the doctor left, Lance turned to his mother-in-law. "Virginia, please understand. You weren't there. You don't know how bad she was."

Tears filled her eyes. "If you do this, I'll never forgive you. And I promise you, Tia won't either." With that, she stormed out of the room.

Chapter 41

Lance was jolted awake by the ringing telephone. *What time is it?* he wondered, glancing around the room, trying to get his bearings. *Hell, what day is it?*

Lance squinted as he tried to shake off the haziness of sleep. It was Wednesday. Three days after he'd checked his wife into the hospital. Three days since she'd uttered a word to him.

The phone was ringing, he realized. "Hello," Lance groggily said, catching the call right before it went to voice mail.

"Mr. Kingston?"

Lance sat up. He was now wide awake. A glance at the clock told him it was 5:00 a.m. Anyone calling for "Mr. Kingston" at that time of the morning couldn't be bringing good news.

"Yes." His heart raced. He knew this was about Tia. He'd begrudgingly left the hospital because the doctors wouldn't allow him to stay with his wife. He'd gone and sat in the lobby all day Monday and Tuesday anyway, but the few times he'd been able to see her, she wouldn't talk to him.

"This is Dr. Lewis, the attending physician at West Oaks. I'm sorry to bother you so early."

"No, no bother. What's wrong. Is something wrong with my wife?" Lance's heart was racing.

"Well, as I told you yesterday afternoon, even though your wife wasn't really responsive to you, she was doing somewhat better since we put her on the medication."

"Yes, I know, and?"

"And, well, she feels like she's fine now and she's leaving."

Lance bolted up from the bed. "What do you mean, she's leaving?"

"Her mother is here and she's taking her home."

"No!" Lance cried. "I'm on my way."

"Mr. Kingston, by the time you get here, I'm sure she'll be long gone."

Lance slumped down onto the small leather love seat in his sitting area. "Why did you let her go? She's not ready."

"Unfortunately, she thinks she is, and as you're well aware, until she's ready to seek help, there's nothing we can do."

"Doctor, we have to do something. My wife is pregnant and mentally ill. I'm worried that she'll harm herself and our baby."

"Trust me, Mr. Kingston, I understand your concern. But I'm sure they told you upon check-in that the maximum they can hold your wife against her will is seventy-two hours."

"Is there anything I can do?"

"Mr. Kingston, I deal with this all the time. Unless your

wife is ready to seek treatment, you're fighting an uphill battle. All you can do if you can't convince her to get treated on her own is to seek a court order and get a doctor to cosign that she is a threat to herself and others. You'll need evidence of incompetence." Lance grew completely still as the doctor launched into legal-speak. "This can include unlawful behavior of any kind, doctors' evaluations, witness testimony, etc. You can also start documenting any odd behaviors, like suicidal ideations, spoken suicidal thoughts, periods of confusion, or being disoriented. Also not being able to handle personal affairs, being a dangerous driver, abusive to family or friends."

Lance groaned. He didn't have time to document and file all of that. There was no telling what Tia would do to herself or the baby by the time they worked things out through the system.

"I understand your apprehension," the doctor continued as if he were reading Lance's mind. "We can try to expedite the matter if you can get her personal doctor on board. Just between you and me, if you can prove incompetence, I have a judge that can get you a court order fairly quickly."

"Okay," Lance acquiesced, feeling as if he didn't have much choice.

"But, Mr. Kingston, this is my personal opinion, from dealing with this type of thing for more than twenty years. Until that happens, your wife needs an ultimatum. You need to stress to her that you will leave and take your child unless she commits to treatment. Sometimes that approach works. Sometimes it doesn't."

At this point, Lance was willing to try anything. “Okay, Doc. Let’s move forward with the court order, and I’ll move forward with an ultimatum.” Lance felt his heart sinking. How had their marriage spiraled so far out of control? Yet if he didn’t take legal action against her, he didn’t see how their marriage could survive.

Chapter 42

"How long have you known you were sick?" Lance's tone was firm. Firm and weary, as if he was fed up with her.

Tia knew it was time to stop pretending. She really wanted to stop pretending. After she learned what she had done, she was stunned at how low she had gone. She had expected Lance to be mad about her leaving the hospital, but he hadn't said a word about that, just told her that he was taking her home.

Now they sat in the living room, his bags packed and parked near the front door, a visual reminder, she assumed, that if she wasn't honest with him, he was leaving for good.

"I was fine up until seventeen," Tia began quietly. "Then one day I just flipped. I didn't know then that I had bipolar disorder. Everyone thought it was depression. The only thing I knew was that something was wrong inside my mind."

"What did the doctors say?"

Tia released a pained laugh. "Please. It was five years before I even went to see a doctor. My mom was horrified at the thought of 'telling our business' to anyone—even a medical professional. Looking back, I was grown and could've gone on my own. But I was on her insurance, and she convinced me that I would break out of this 'spell,' as she called it."

Tia took a huge breath. It felt like a tremendous weight was being lifted from her shoulders. "When my mother finally broke down and let a doctor prescribe some medication, I was placed on this drug called Wellbutrin, which made me go into a severe manic episode. I started hearing voices and thinking crazy things like I was an alien sent here to destroy the world."

"But school?" Lance asked in disbelief. "How did you go to college, then law school, and hold down a job?"

"I became good at hiding the truth. And I finally found some medication that worked."

They spent the next hour with her filling him in on horror stories of her young adult years, of living with mental illness, of hiding it from everyone she knew.

"What I don't understand is why you felt you couldn't tell me," Lance said when she was finally done.

"Because whenever I'm honest with anyone, it gets me nowhere but alone. I loved you and I didn't want to lose you," she said matter-of-factly.

"You know this means our marriage was built on deception?"

"I'm sorry, Lance." Tia dabbed at her eyes. "What can I do for us to fix this?"

"Are you seeing a doctor?"

"Yes, I mean, my main doctor moved away and referred me to Dr. Monroe. I went a couple of times, then stopped, but I've started back. Lance, I want to be normal, I want to give you a normal life."

Lance was unyielding. "And what did this Dr. Monroe say?"

"He's the one that suggested I get rid of the stresses, and he gave me some medication. Only I found out I was pregnant and I was scared to take it. I can't take that medication now and risk harming the baby."

The baby. Lance glanced at her stomach. He suddenly found himself wondering if the bipolar gene was genetic. Would she pass it on to their child?

"Tia, you need to get some help."

"We can go talk to my doctor." She grabbed his hand. "Just don't leave me."

She showered him with kisses and straddled him. "Please don't leave me. I love you. I love you." She planted kisses all over his face. "I'll do whatever you want me to do. I'll go to the doctor, whatever you want." She took his hands and put them on her stomach. Desperation filled her voice. "But we need you. We can't lose you. Promise you won't leave us."

"I'm not gonna leave you, Tia."

"Thank God." She leaned in, starting to remove his clothes. This time he didn't stop her.

Chapter 43

Tia knew she needed to come if she wanted her marriage to survive. But that didn't ease her extreme discomfort.

"So, Tia, are you okay with us talking candidly?" Dr. Monroe asked. Lance and Tia were sitting in his office. He'd cleared his calendar to see them immediately.

"Yes, I am," she said, nodding.

"Doc, I know a little about my wife's condition," Lance began, scooting to the edge of his seat. "But I have a lot of questions."

"Ask away. That's what I'm here for."

"Well, for starters, is this a condition she can be cured of?"

Sympathy filled the doctor's face. "Regrettably, no. Now, here's what you have to be most aware of. There is *no* cure for this condition. Ever. There is recovery. It's like a cancer remission. In Tia's lifetime it will get bad again and it will get good. The goal is less bad than good in quantity and severity."

That was not what Lance was hoping to hear. He swallowed and continued, "Let me back up. Please help me understand, what exactly is bipolar disorder?"

Dr. Monroe nodded as if he had expected that question. "Bipolar disorder is when the lithium levels in the body go out of sync, either becoming excessively high, which causes a person to become unusually energetic, or they drop too low, which then causes severe depression. Lithium is a type of salt that all human beings have in their bodies. In the person who suffers from bipolar disorder, their body makes either too much or not enough. When someone who suffers from bipolar lapses into severe depression, the person cannot physically and mentally 'snap out of it.' Once that person hits the bottom, unless treatment is administered, the results can be disastrous. It is like any other disease in the body. For example, if a person suffers from diabetes, they need insulin to regulate their sugar levels, and if they do not receive the insulin, they will go into diabetic shock, then a coma, and they can die. It is the same with any chronic illness. The difference between bipolar and other chronic diseases is that bipolar affects the emotions."

Tia wished she could see inside her husband's mind. What was he thinking? Did he hate her? Did he wish he'd never married her?

"Well, umm, what about the baby? Will he or she be bipolar as well?" Lance asked.

Just the thought tore at Tia's insides.

"Yes, children are ten times more likely to have bipolar disorder if one of the parents is bipolar."

Lance rubbed his forehead, stressed over the doctor's response.

"But there is still a very strong chance that your child will be perfectly healthy," Dr. Monroe continued. "And if not, at least you know how to treat it."

Her child could be subjected to a life like the one she'd lived? The thought alone made Tia want to terminate the pregnancy.

As if reading her mind, the doctor said, "Unfortunately, you're too far along for an abortion, but adoption is also an option."

"Not for us it isn't," Lance said firmly. "We wouldn't abort and we dang sure aren't giving our child away."

The doctor understood how Lance felt. "Well, I just like to lay everything on the line."

Lance waved that discussion away. "We don't even need to talk about that. Because whatever child God sees fit to give us is who we'll live with."

"Okay. Well, do you have any other questions?"

Lance nodded. "Tia said stress triggers her illness. If she got rid of her stressful job, what's the problem?"

Dr. Monroe maintained his patient tone. "Marriage, moving, or a birth are just as stressful as losing your job, divorce, or a death. These major life events, as they are called, can be critical times for a person with a mood disorder—even one that has seemed manageable up until that time. And those people are especially susceptible when they don't take their medication."

The doctor narrowed his eyes at Tia when he said that. She looked away in shame. "Tia is very well aware of my thoughts on the matter of medication. It is essential that she take her medication. Had she been taking it, I think her recent bout of relapses could've been avoided."

Tia frowned. Shouldn't there be a clause in the psychiatry manual about not blaming the victim?

"Well," Lance continued, "naturally, my wife and I are concerned about the effects any medication may have on our unborn child." He looked at Tia sympathetically. "And honestly, I think my wife's fear about the medication was why she stopped taking it."

"That's understandable," the doctor replied. "Most drugs prescribed for bipolar disorder do carry some risk of birth defects for the baby."

Tia let out an audible gasp.

Dr. Monroe continued, "Yet women who discontinue medication risk relapsing into a manic or depressive episode." He leaned forward, his voice taking on that stern tone that Tia hated. "Let me break it down for you. During the postpartum phase, the relapse rate for bipolar women is as high as fifty to seventy percent. Even more alarming, bipolar women are a hundred times more likely than other women to experience postpartum psychosis, a severe mood disorder."

"What does that mean?" Tia interjected. "I'm likely to hurt my child?"

"I can't speak to that. But I can tell you, women who discontinued mood stabilizers during pregnancy spent over forty percent of their pregnancy in an 'illness episode.' And research suggests that the effects of maternal depression on the fetus can lead to complications both during and after pregnancy."

Lance shook his head, trying to make sense of all the jargon. "Doc, no disrespect, but can you talk to us in layman's terms?"

"The bottom line is that bipolar medications aren't considered as risky during pregnancy as they once were, but they aren't exactly harmless either."

Tia threw her arms up. "And you expect me to put my baby's life at risk?"

The doctor didn't flinch. "We can change your medication to lithium and Haldol, which pose the most minimal risk to the fetus. But I can tell you, there is a high probability that *not* taking the medication will put your baby at an even greater risk."

"Doc, I'm kinda with my wife on this one," Lance said, and Tia relaxed. "If there's a chance our baby could be harmed with this medication, I don't think we should do it."

Dr. Monroe took a deep breath. "Let me explain it like this. You know how when you're flying, they tell you to put on your oxygen mask first before putting on your child's?" He continued, even though neither of them nodded. "They do that for a reason. You have to make sure you're safe before you can take care of your child. It's as simple as that."

A brief silence filled the room.

"Okay," Lance said, making the decision for them. "She'll take the medication."

Tia wanted to scream at her husband. She wasn't a child. She didn't need anyone regulating what she would and wouldn't do. "But, Lance—"

"She'll take the medication if she wants our marriage to work," Lance said sternly, cutting her off.

Tia folded her arms across her chest. Yes, she wanted her marriage to work. Yes, she wanted to get better. But she didn't want to do it at the expense of her child.

But looking at the expression on Dr. Monroe's face, the desperation in Lance's eyes, Tia knew she no longer had a choice.

"Fine," Tia said, defeated. "I'll make sure and take my medication every single day."

Chapter 44

Lance needed a break. From life, from his troubles, from everything. But since he couldn't take a break from life, he at least needed to take some time off from work. Keeping up with Tia, staying on her about her medication every day, was taking its toll on him. But he'd been seeing a difference. Two months after their visit with Dr. Monroe, Tia was cooperative, and even though she still experienced some mood swings, she had not suffered from any violent outbursts or extreme erratic behavior. But little things still sent her into a deep depression. They'd found out they were having a girl, and she'd cried for three days because she wanted a boy—even though she'd never mentioned that she'd wanted a boy prior to that.

Lance was so happy that the ultimatum had worked. Still, he'd moved forward with the court order, just in case he needed it. Sad to say, he couldn't trust Tia. A lot more than two months would have to pass before he took her word for anything.

Lance debated calling home to check on Tia. She'd been unusually quiet this morning and he wanted to make sure she was all right. Yet the company was on the verge of a buyout, and Lance was making a presentation to save not only his job, but the jobs of all his employees.

The company that owned the magazine was downsizing and was trying to decide which of its publications to keep afloat. So Lance and his team had come up with a sound presentation as to why they should be one to survive the chopping block.

Lance pressed the button for the intercom on his office phone. "Hey, Ruby, is the conference room set up?"

"It is. And I just talked with the driver. Mr. Lewinsky and the others just left the hotel and are heading this way."

"Okay, great," Lance replied, his heart beating faster. "Is everything in order?"

Ruby smiled as she appeared in the doorway. "You left me in charge, so you know it is."

He returned her smile. "Yes, that's one thing I do know. Now, let's just hope everyone did what they were supposed to."

"They did. I sent out a status-check e-mail this morning to everyone, and they all reported back that they had their assigned task. Robert has done the presentation and we have it all set up on the projector in the large conference room, so we're ready to go."

Lance sighed with relief. "What would I do without you?"

"Let's say a prayer that we never have to find out. Now, I'm going to go grab you a cup of tea to soothe your nerves before the meeting."

"Thank you. And, Ruby, you've been a blessing, through everything."

She knew what he meant. "I'm keeping you in my prayers every day."

"Thank you."

Ruby returned a few minutes later with a cup of steaming-hot tea. Lance sat back and relaxed as he sipped it, enjoying its soothing effect. Suddenly, his eyes were jolted open when he heard someone scream.

"Get the hell out of my way! You can't stop me from seeing my husband."

"Oh, my God," Lance said, jumping up and racing out of his office. "Tia, what are you doing?"

Tia was wearing her white, plush bathrobe, her hair was wild and untamed, and she clutched a knife in her hand.

"Lance, I can't take this baby. Everything hurts so bad. I have to cut it out. But I can't do it, I can't even cut my baby out right. Why can't I do anything right?" she cried.

Lance was horrified. He gasped when he looked down and saw blood seeping through her robe.

"Tia, what have you done?"

"I just want this thing out!" she cried.

By now everyone had come out into the hallway to witness the unfolding scene. Like him, most people were in shock. At the back of the gathering crowd, stepping off the elevator, was the board chairman, Mr. Lewinsky, and his crew. Ruby saw them, too, because she immediately grabbed Tia's other arm. "Sweetie, let's wait in here," she said, trying to lead her to Lance's office.

Tia snatched her arm away from Ruby and put the knife to her stomach. "I just want it out, Lance."

"Come on, baby. Let's go in my office," Lance gently said as he slipped his hand gingerly onto the knife's handle.

Tia let him ease the knife out of her hand, then led her into his office.

"Ruby, please call 911," Lance mouthed to his assistant. She nodded and shut the door behind her.

"Lance, don't leave me." Tia clutched him tightly. "I'm not gonna hurt her. I'm not gonna hurt the baby. I just want her out."

"Okay, baby," he said, easing her down on the leather sofa. He gently pulled her robe open and was relieved to see the cut was just a surface wound. He'd been worried that she'd pierced the amniotic sac or worse. "We're gonna get her out," he said, gently brushing Tia's hair out of her eyes.

Security entered just as Lance got Tia settled. "Is everything all right, sir?"

"No, but someone's called for help."

"Umm, Mr. Kingston, she parked the car on the sidewalk," one of the guards said.

"Can you go move it?" Lance said, gently rocking his wife back and forth and trying to keep her calm. He motioned toward his desk. "Take my set of keys in case she didn't leave her keys in the car. Damien, can you go wait downstairs for the paramedics?" Lance said to the other guard.

Both men nodded and hurried out.

"Lance, I'm sorry, I know you have a big meeting today, but this baby is trying to kill me."

"She's not trying to kill you. I promise you," he said, his voice soothing. He knew her moods could turn bad. He'd just never dreamed they would be *this* bad.

"I just want her out!" Tia cried. "I want us to get back to being normal."

"Okay, we're gonna get you some help. It's okay. I got you. We'll be fine. She'll be fine," Lance said, tears now streaming down his cheeks as he rocked her. "Yeah, honey, you and the baby are gonna be just fine," he whispered.

Yet he couldn't help but wonder if they'd ever know "normal" again.

Chapter 45

Tia was so mad at the man she'd married. He was the reason she was sitting here, surrounded by a team of people trying to "cure" her.

She was told she was coming to the hospital for them to deliver her baby, but after examining her and keeping her all night, they had entered her room this morning, talking about it was "too soon" to take the baby. And the next thing she knew, Lance had her in the car, whisking her across town to this godforsaken place under the pretense that they were going to see if this place would be willing to deliver the baby early.

Part of her understood Lance's frustration. She knew she had been a beast to deal with the last few months. But the other part of her—the irrational part—was mad as hell.

"Tia, do you understand why you're here?"

Tia continued her pledge to maintain absolute silence. She

hadn't said a word during the last thirty-six hours. It had taken that long for her to come to terms with her husband's having tricked her into coming here. He had actually gone to a judge, gotten a court order, and had her committed. She hadn't meant to flip out when she found out what he was doing, but she had no control over the switch that changed her into a stark-raving lunatic. Tia was also hoping that if she refused to talk, they'd let her go. She knew her rights. She knew she could prove her competency, have that court order overturned, and leave if she wanted. She could get right up and out the door and walk away if she wanted. So then why couldn't she will herself to stand?

As if on cue, her baby kicked. And she remembered her exasperated, exhausted, weary-eyed husband. She remembered his warning when they'd stuffed her into that bare, bland room that felt more like a prison cell than a hospital room. He'd told her that if she left, it was over. That was the reason she couldn't move, why she needed to let these people do whatever it was they were going to do. Lance had made it clear that he would leave. That he would pack his bags—again—and leave her for good. He might even fight her for custody of their child. Although she didn't practice family law, she knew that courts favored mothers. So she had an advantage.

What about crazy mothers? Do courts favor those as well?

"Tia, you understand why your husband is doing this, don't you?" the doctor repeated.

"I understand that he thinks something is wrong," she finally said.

"Do you think something is wrong, Tia?"

Her initial reaction was to say no. But she knew better. Not only did she think something was wrong, she knew what was wrong. And she knew the only way to fix it would be to deal with it head-on.

"I'm bipolar," she said, her voice timid.

"How are you feeling right now?"

"Fine. But I always feel fine—until I flip out." She told the doctor the truth. "I don't understand it. I'm taking the medication and I'm still . . . I'm still crazy."

"Tia, you've got to talk to me. Maybe it's the dosage. Maybe it's the drug. I can't help you if you don't communicate with me," the doctor said.

She saw how much agony Lance was in. Tia's pledge of silence was out the window. She just wanted to be fixed. "My mom always said God would work things out."

"That's the reason God put people like me here, to help His will be done."

Tia released a bitter laugh. How much could one person's faith be tested? If God was so loving, why would He make her the way that she was?

"What is God's will for me?" she said, her voice cracking. "Is His will that I torture my husband? That I wake up every single day not knowing who will climb out of bed? And it's so frustrating because I haven't had any problems for years. Now all of a sudden I can't control who I become."

Her chest was heaving as she struggled to keep her anger at bay.

"We talked about this," the doctor continued. "It was the

stress triggers. It was too much at once. All of that left the door wide open."

Tia glared at him, then buried her face in her hands and sobbed. "Doc, fix me, please?" She felt a small flutter of comfort when Lance scooted over to her and pulled her close.

"You have to help us help you," the doctor said.

Tia sniffed as she nodded. "I want to do better."

"You have to do better," the doctor said gently. "Your baby needs you to be well."

Lance lifted her chin. "I need you to be well, baby. You are my heart and soul, and I just want us to be happy. Can you just stay for a little bit, let them nurse you back to health?"

"Why can't you do it?" she said.

"I don't know how. If I did, I would." He wiped her tears.

Tia sighed in resignation. "Okay, I'll stay. I'll do whatever it takes to get better."

Tia silently prayed for the strength to stay true to her word.

Chapter 46

"I cannot believe he put you here!"

Virginia Jiles curled her lips in disgust. This was her first visit to the West Oaks psych ward to see her daughter.

"Mom, I know you're mad at Lance, but I need you to understand that I at least have to try." Tia didn't feel as if she had made much progress, but both Dr. Berry and her doctor, Dr. Monroe, had told her it might take a few days for her new medication to regulate her system. She'd argued for them to just give her the drugs and let her take them home, promising to stay on them. Of course, they didn't believe her.

Virginia's eyes filled with tears as she looked around the room. A cheap-looking picture of a seascape hung on one wall. The hard sofa and bed looked like dorm-room furniture. The cold tiles made the room feel even more uninviting.

"I'm sorry, Tia. I just can't stand seeing you in here."

"Mama, I was mad, too, at first. But I could've really hurt myself and the baby." Tia also knew that Lance was at the end of his rope, and if she didn't get help, she was going to lose her husband.

Virginia brushed that thought away. "That's ridiculous. If you really wanted to hurt yourself, you would've done it a long time ago."

Tia released a frustrated sigh. She'd never get through to her mother about this treatment. No matter how many doctors had suggested that Tia be hospitalized, Virginia always nixed the idea.

"Tia, you know I really like Lance, but I think this is just terrible how he stuck you in this godforsaken place and just left you here."

"He didn't leave me, Mama. He's come to see me every day. He didn't come today so that you could come, because they only allow one visitor a day."

Virginia suddenly pulled Tia up from her seat and walked her over to the small mirror that hung over the sink. "Look at you, sweetheart. Your hair is stringy. You have bags under your eyes. Your skin is sunken and dull."

Tia stared at her reflection. Her mother was right. She looked horrible, the worst she'd looked in years.

"That's from the medicine they're pumping in you, that's why you look like that. That medicine can't be good for your baby." Virginia spun Tia around. "We are a proud, hardworking family that has always helped themselves. I never turned to the government for no food stamps, welfare, or none of that stuff. We helped ourselves."

"Mama, this is different," Tia said, though she was less sure than she had been just a minute ago.

"Tia, if these doctors knew what they were doing, don't you think they'd done found a cure by now?"

"I . . . I guess you're right," Tia stammered.

"I *know* I'm right. Now, do you want your child coming out deformed and stuff? Do you want to put on even more weight?"

Tia shuddered at that idea. The first time her doctors had put her on antipsychotic drugs, she'd gained thirty pounds. As a former athlete, that had devastated her. She'd worked night and day to take that weight off.

"You already look like you've gotten heavier since you've been here," Virginia continued, pushing on that sore spot. "And that's not just baby weight. That's that medication."

Tia turned to the side and studied her body in the mirror. Was she really gaining extra weight?

"Baby, crazy people belong in here," Virginia pleaded. "You're not crazy. You can get high-strung sometimes, but you're not crazy. Don't let anyone convince you that you are."

Tia's mind was getting jumbled again. Was her mother right?

"They don't want you to get better, Tia. The pharmaceutical companies pay them millions to keep people drugged. Hospitals make millions of dollars off putting people in here. I bet this room is three thousand dollars a day. Do you really want to put that kind of burden on Lance?"

Tia was so confused now. Was she burdening Lance? She'd already racked up thousands of dollars in credit-card debt that he was trying to clean up.

"B-but he had a court order."

"Yeah," Virginia said, pulling out a piece of paper with some notes jotted on it. "I called an attorney, and he said they didn't give you a competency hearing, so technically that order isn't valid. You're entitled to a hearing."

Tia knew that, but . . . "What if they won't let me leave?"

"Oh, once they see the wrath of Virginia Jiles and you tell them you want out, they won't have a choice," Virginia threatened. "I know Lance had to call in some favors to get that court order so fast. I will call that Isiah Carey boy over at Fox 26 and have him report on all these people abusing the system. Trust me, none of them want that kind of publicity."

Tia had no doubt her mother would do it, too.

"Baby, come home. Let me nurse you and my grandbaby back to health. You will be so much more comfortable there, and I will take good care of you."

No, no, no. Tia tried to push her mother's insistent voice out of her head. Letting her mother convince her to run—yet again—was not the answer.

Virginia didn't wait for her daughter to respond as she began gathering Tia's things. "I know you're worried about Lance being mad, but he'll just have to get over it. You just trust me, sugarplum. I've always taken good care of you and I'm not about to stop now."

Tia wanted to continue to protest. She wanted to stay and receive help. She *needed* to stay and receive help. But as her mother dragged her to the door, Tia said nothing. A single tear slid down her face as her mother pulled her through a side door and exited the building.

Chapter 47

"Hey, you know burying yourself in your work is not the way to deal with problems. Especially when everyone has gone home but you."

Lance looked up to find Crystal standing in his office doorway, leaning against the frame, looking beautiful as ever. He hadn't realized how late it was. He'd been so angry and disgusted all week. When the hospital called five days ago and said Tia had left with her mother, Lance thought he was going to lose it. He'd tried to remind them about the court order, but they'd told him how they'd stopped Virginia as she was leaving and she'd acted such a fool that the hospital administrator had said they didn't want the drama, so they let Tia go. Dr. Monroe had called and said they could try to have Tia involuntarily committed to another hospital, but Lance had decided against that draconian option. Obviously, Tia didn't want his help. Hell, she wouldn't even take his calls. Virginia was playing prison guard, saying Tia "needs some space right now."

So, Lance had made up his mind that he was through. He couldn't take this ordeal any longer. He was sick and tired of fighting to save someone who didn't want to be saved.

"Crystal, what are you doing here?" he said, snapping himself out of his thoughts.

"I just came to check on you."

"What do you mean?" Then the reason for this convenient appearance dawned on him. "Did Ruby call you?"

Crystal waltzed into his office. "Don't be mad at her. She's concerned about you. And don't be mad at Damien, the security guard. I worked my magic on him so he'd let me up."

Lance made a mental note that he was going to sit down and have a stern talking-to with Ruby. She had to stay out of his personal business, and she definitely couldn't be reporting anything that happened in his life to Crystal.

"Seriously, I called her to check on you." Crystal flashed a sly smile. "You know, since you haven't returned any of my calls since I bailed you out of jail."

"I'm sorry about that," he said apologetically. "It's just, umm, it's been crazy."

"I figured that. I was just worried about you."

"Well, I'm holding up." Really he wasn't, but he didn't need to cry on Crystal's shoulder.

Crystal held up a P.F. Chang's bag. "I know you're hungry."

"I'm fine." No sooner had the words left his mouth than his stomach grumbled, as if speaking up since Lance wouldn't.

Crystal chuckled as she set the bag down on his desk and took the Chinese food out. "Shrimp lo mein, your favorite. And I got some salt-and-pepper prawns."

Lance groaned at the mention of his favorite dishes. He was starving. He had been so preoccupied all day, and there was no sense pretending that he wasn't hungry.

"Here, let me fix you a plate." Crystal didn't give him time to reply as she whipped out a plastic plate and utensils. For a moment he lost himself in being taken care of. It felt good. Tia hadn't so much as fixed a peanut-butter sandwich in the past three months.

"You want to talk about it?" she said after she had both of their plates fixed and was sitting across from him.

"Not really." He bit into a shrimp. "Let's talk about Francis, the guy you're seeing." He didn't want to get into Crystal's love life, but he just wanted to talk about anything else besides his own problems.

"Francis is a nobody," she said, waving him off. "Just someone to take me to see Sade since the person I really wanted to go with seems to be off the market." She flashed a teasing smile.

He noted how quickly she changed the subject, and since he didn't want her pressing him, he didn't press her. They made some small talk, then Crystal mindlessly began chatting about her outlandish relatives. For the first time in a while, Lance found himself laughing. Before he knew it, an hour had passed. He was full and actually thankful for the distraction.

"You know, whatever is weighing heavily on you, I'm sure it will all work out," Crystal said as she began cleaning up their mess.

Lance smiled wearily. Crystal must know everything that was going on. He had no doubt that his mother had already shared all of the latest details.

"I don't have any regrets, you know?" Lance knew he sounded pitiful, almost as if he was trying to convince himself rather than her.

"I'm sure you don't." Crystal dumped the plates in the trash.

"It's just that things are kind of hard right now."

"Umm-hmm." She nodded sympathetically.

"And I love her, I really do."

"I'm sure you do. But"—Crystal hesitated as if weighing her words—"nobody would be mad at you if you left. There's only so much one person can endure. I mean, you're a newlywed. This is a time you two should be enjoying each other. The time when life should be bliss before the real problems of family life set in."

Her words stung his heart. Lance couldn't help it. He buried his face in his hands and broke down. "It's too much," he cried. "It's too much. I can't do it. It's killing me. Every day a piece of me dies. It's like she's in this faraway place and I can't reach her. I don't know what sets her off. I don't know what's wrong or how to deal with it. I'm just tired. My job is suffering. I can't talk to anyone and I feel like I'm going crazy."

"You can talk to me," Crystal whispered, easing over to his side. She stood over him as he raised his head and their eyes met.

"I love her, Crystal, but I can't see going through this the rest of my life."

Crystal gently eased her arms around him. "It's okay. You can talk to me."

Lance wrapped his arms around her waist, buried his head in her stomach, and cried. She held him tight as he released the pain that he'd been feeling for the past nine months. He hadn't meant to get so emotional, but it was as if a dam had just burst.

Crystal felt so good to him, stroking his head and whispering soothing words: "It's okay. You've done everything you can."

He pulled back and stared at her. Was she right? Had he done everything? His mother was right. This was not the life he'd envisioned for himself. This wasn't the life he wanted.

Crystal leaned down, lifted his chin, and kissed him softly. When he didn't object, she kissed him harder. For a moment he felt a release from the pain. For a moment he felt . . . free.

Crystal moaned pleasurably as their lips made up for missed time. He ran his hands up under her blouse. His body craved her touch. His libido longed for satisfaction, and both of them threw caution to the wind as Crystal pulled his shirt over his head.

Lance's cell phone rang and he ignored it as he struggled to unbutton his pants. Crystal unsnapped her blouse and slipped it off as the ringing stopped, then started again. Lance glanced at the phone, but the sight of Crystal's voluptuous breasts beckoning for him instantly brought his attention back to her.

He had just reached around her back to unfasten her bra when the private line in his office rang. That caused him to stop in his tracks. His private line seldom rang.

"I . . . I gotta get that," he said, his voice husky.

"Don't," she moaned. "I've been waiting for this moment. I

need you so bad. I just want to feel you." She nuzzled his neck as the shrill of the phone filled the room.

"Okay, okay, hold on," he said, stepping back from her, then fumbling for the phone. "Yeah?" he answered, not caring that his aggravation was showing.

He heard Virginia scream, "Lance, come quick. Tia's having the baby!"

"What?"

"Yeah, we're headed to Sugar Land Methodist." He heard his wife let out a piercing scream in the background.

All the lust he had been feeling drained out of him. He had no question what his priorities were. "Okay, tell Tia I'm on my way." He hung up.

His eyes met Crystal's. She didn't say a word as she pulled her blouse back over her shoulders.

"I'm sorry," he muttered, grabbing his shirt.

"Me, too."

"I gotta go." He grabbed his keys and rushed toward the door.

"Will you call me?" she softly asked.

Lance stopped and turned. He looked at her with a burst of renewed longing. Yet his common sense prevailed. "I shouldn't have let it happen."

Her eyes welled with tears.

Lance silently cursed as he made his way to his car. He couldn't believe he had been about to cross that line with Crystal. He wasn't stupid. He knew that had been Crystal's plan all along, to give him a sympathetic ear until she got what she wanted. And he'd almost allowed himself to fall for her cunning. The same cunning she had used when she cheated on him.

Almost.

"Almost doesn't count," he muttered as he tried to shake off his guilt. The important thing was that he hadn't. More important, he was going to be by his wife's side as she brought their child into the world. After all was said and done, that's all that really mattered.

Chapter 48

If someone had told her that labor felt like this, Tia would have had her tubes tied a long time ago.

"Tia, we need you to push."

Tia glared down at her ob-gyn at the foot of her bed. Two nurses were assisting her in the birthing room. Tia's mother stood at her side, clutching Tia's arm. She'd been sitting at home with her mother when the first contraction hit. She'd sucked it up, thinking it was false labor. But then another, more painful one had come—followed by her water breaking.

"Do you hear me, Tia? Push," Dr. Comeaux repeated.

"Not yet. Not until Lance gets here." She bit down on her bottom lip to quell the pain shooting through her body.

"You did call him?" Tia asked her mother for the umpteenth time.

"Yes, baby. He's on his way," Virginia said, rubbing her daughter's arm.

Tia was so angry with herself. If she hadn't been so stubborn, Lance would have been there with her when she went into labor. He'd be here right now. She had no one to blame but herself if he didn't show up at all.

"I can't bring this baby into the world without Lance here," Tia cried.

"Well, it looks like you might not have any choice," Dr. Comeaux replied. "You're seven centimeters dilated."

"Can't you give her something to slow the labor down?" Virginia asked.

"She's too far along," the doctor said. "This baby is coming whether we want it to or not."

"But it's too early," Tia grunted.

"Unfortunately, the little one doesn't have a calendar. She's ready to make her grand entrance now."

At a new onslaught of pain Tia sat up, screamed, then fell back against the bed again.

"What if Lance doesn't make it?" she panted to her mother.

"Then he'll see the baby when he gets here," the nurse interjected.

"This is all my fault," Tia cried.

"Tia, I need you to focus," Dr. Comeaux sternly said. "That's all that matters."

Virginia stroked her daughter's hair. "Sweetie, I will stay with you until Lance gets here, so you'll be fine. So, just do as the doctor says and focus."

Tia sniffed. She was crying from the pain—both in her heart and in her body. "Wh-what if he doesn't come?"

"Now, you know that's not going to happen," Virginia soothingly said. "I told you, I talked to him. He's on his way."

"I always make such a mess of things. I . . . agggghhh!" Tia doubled over in pain.

"Tia, this baby is coming." Dr. Comeaux put her hands on Tia's thighs.

"Noooo." Tia tried to tighten her muscles to keep them from contracting. Of course, that didn't work and only sent another racking burst of pain through her body. "Where's Lance?" she moaned.

"I'm right here," he said, dashing into the room.

He was slipping a hairnet on his head and had already squeezed into too-small scrubs.

Tia wanted to scream for joy. "You came?"

"Of course I did." He went to her side and took her hand.

Virginia quietly eased out of the way.

"Lance, I'm so sorry," Tia said. "For everything."

"Babe, I'm not thinking about that," Lance said, wiping sweat from her brow. "Right now all I want you to think about is this baby. You're about to give me the best gift in the world."

"I thought you said me marrying you was the best gift." She sniffed.

"Okay, second best. But focus. You have some serious work to do." He pointed toward her waist.

He didn't have to tell her because the next jolt of pain made her jerk upright.

"Come on, babe, breathe," Lance coached.

Tia pushed and screamed, pushed and screamed, until she heard the wail of a newborn.

"Ladies and gentlemen, we have ourselves a precious baby girl," Dr. Comeaux announced.

Tia fell back against the bed, utterly spent.

Lance was beaming down at the baby. "She's beautiful. She's as beautiful as her mother."

Those words made Tia burst into tears.

Chapter 49

Tia felt as if her world were crashing in. Every piece of her body ached and her mind was going into overdrive—convincing her that what she'd just done was her biggest mistake ever.

"Hey, baby girl," Virginia said as she eased the door open. "How are you feeling?"

"Okay, I guess."

"The baby is adorable."

"She is beautiful." Tia couldn't believe that she had played a part in creating such a beautiful specimen.

"I can't believe I'm a grandma."

"I can't believe I'm a mother," Tia said as she tenderly gazed at her infant daughter. "Where's Lance?"

"He's in the waiting room talking to his mother and grandmother."

"Is he still upset with you?"

Virgina shrugged. "If he is, he hasn't shown it. But I imagine I've worn him out." Tia hadn't had any episodes during the week she'd spent at her mother's house. She'd slept almost sixteen hours every day. Her mother swore it was a side effect of the medication she'd been taking.

"Oh, Lance is a strong man," Virginia said, waving her off. "He'll be all right."

Tia tried to adjust her behind, wincing at the pain that shot up her body as she moved. Finally, she settled, then said, "He doesn't deserve me. He doesn't deserve this life."

"Hush with that foolish talk. You've given him the greatest gift that God has for us to give. A life."

Tia smiled at her baby, sleeping peacefully in the Plexiglas bassinet. Even though she was six weeks early, Lauren Tionne Kingston was perfect. Perfect in every way. Tia wished that she could see into her mind. Make sure that it was right. That it didn't contain whatever crazy gene Tia'd been cursed with. She wished that she had some way of knowing that twenty years from now, her baby girl wouldn't suffer as she had.

"Knock, knock," the nurse said, sticking her head in the door. "Sorry to disturb you, but I need to take this precious little bundle for some more testing."

Tia nodded, giving the nurse permission to take the baby, then watched as she wheeled her away. Once she was gone, Tia turned to her mother.

"Mama, when did you first notice something was wrong with me?"

Virginia immediately stiffened, then began fluffing her

daughter's pillow. "Tia, you know I don't like talking about that stuff."

"That's the problem, Mama. We never talk about it. I have an illness, and your trying to pretend that I don't is not changing anything." Tia leaned back against the pillow. She was so drained—from everything. "I should've never left that hospital. You've been in denial, which put me in denial. You have a sick child. It runs in our family, and if you don't talk about it, the cycle is just gonna continue." Tia didn't know where all of this was coming from. She just knew that she was tired and wanted more than anything else to save her marriage. Seeing her baby made her realize she owed it to Lance to try to face this issue head-on.

"So you're saying this is my fault?"

Tia sat all the way up in her bed. "Mama, that's not what I'm saying at all. Four in ten Americans have bipolar disorder."

Virginia waved her off. "Don't go quoting all those crazy statistics to me. You can't tell me that God ain't powerful enough to exorcise this from your body."

Tia sighed. She debated just letting the issue drop. But that's how she'd always handled it. Not anymore. It was time for a come-to-Jesus meeting with her mother.

"Mama, God made me how I am, flaws and all. And instead of accepting God's will, you want to pretend that I'm something that I'm not. I should've gotten help a long time ago."

"So you *are* saying it's my fault?"

"You're not hearing me," Tia said, frustrated.

"I took you to the doctor. I took you to a lot of doctors."

"And you didn't like what any of them had to say. Every time one of them tried to get you to listen, you wanted to argue that I was just going through a spell." Tia pointed to her head. "This is not a *spell.*"

"Like you're the only young woman that has had problems," her mother said with an attitude.

Tia's eyes held a lifetime of sorrow. "Mama, I tried to commit suicide twice by overdosing on pills. There's nothing normal about that."

Tears filled her mother's eyes. "I just want the best for you."

"I want the best for me, too. But this isn't how to get it. I'm not depressed. I'm not just going through something. I'm sick. I have put my new husband through hell."

Virginia clutched her daughter's hand. "But he stayed, Tia. He stayed. Nobody else did."

"You're right. I don't know why he stayed. But he doesn't deserve this. I should have told him. I should have done what he asked me to do."

Virginia let Tia's hand drop. "Well, we will never see eye to eye on that. If you had told him, you wouldn't have that beautiful baby—because he would've left."

Tia was silent as she weighed her next words. She almost didn't say anything, but decided this matter needed to be addressed. "Like you left Daddy?"

Virginia shot icy daggers at her daughter. "This has nothing to do with me and your father. Your father was messed up from that war."

"Maybe he was. Maybe he was predisposed to the illness. I

just know between him, Uncle Junior, and me, something is not right in our family."

"So now you're all messed up because I left your father?"

"Mama, don't be ridiculous. I know Daddy turned violent. To both of us. I understand, you left to protect me. But something was wrong with him mentally. When you left, you left that fact behind, too."

"He was a mean, ornery man. He didn't have no mental illness. He was just messed up from all those chemicals in the war. He was fine before then."

"Okay, maybe he was. But the fact remains, he wasn't fine after the war and he didn't get help. None of us have gotten the help we need. We can try to pretend all we want, but the fact remains, nobody ever dealt with it."

"Oh, please. Everyone has someone crazy in their family," Virginia huffed.

"And most people sweep it under the rug and no one ever gets help. I want to stop the cycle. Why can't you understand that?"

Virginia threw up her hands in disgust. "Fine, then, Tia. Get help. Go talk to some stranger and tell him all your business. Let some quack pump all these drugs into your system. See how well that works for you." Virginia took a deep breath, then in a calmer tone said, "I told you all you needed to do was take it to God."

"I've *been* taking it to God. But God helps those who help themselves."

"Don't quote the Bible to me. I know the Bible," Virginia said tersely.

Tia blew an exasperated breath. "All I'm saying, Mama, is I want to stop running. I want to stop being a victim. I want to start *living*."

"Don't you think I hate to see what you go through? It tears at my soul. If I could give my life for you, I would."

Tia rubbed her aching abdomen, which was wrapped in gauze. This conversation was wearing her out, but she needed to finish it. "I know that, Mama, and I love you for that. All I can ask now is that you help me fight my battle. That you help me live a normal life. Can you do that?"

Virginia slowly nodded as she brushed her daughter's hair out of her face. "I just want you to get better and live happily ever after."

Tia squeezed her mother's hand. "Me, too, Mama. Me, too."

Chapter 50

"Hey, is that your little girl?"

Lance turned toward the woman who had come up behind him at the nursery window. "Yep, that's my princess." Lance flashed a pleasant smile at the silver-haired woman standing next to him. She looked vaguely familiar. "I assume you're visiting someone, since you're not walking around in one of those horrid hospital gowns."

She chuckled. "Yeah, I'm just a visitor. My baby-birthing days are long gone." She pointed to a little, pale-skinned baby at the end of the row. "That's my grandson right there," she said proudly.

"He's adorable."

"That he is. That he is."

They stood in silence, watching the babies for a few

moments, before the woman turned back to him. "I'm Cheryl. Cheryl Murray."

"Lance Kingston." He shook her hand. "Nice to meet you."

"You, too. And, ummm, I hope you don't think I'm being too forward, but I was in the waiting room the other night when you came in."

Lance remembered the woman now. She'd sat over in a corner knitting most of the evening. "Oh, I'm sorry, things were a little hectic. I didn't even realize it."

"No, problem. I just, well . . ." She hesitated as if unsure if she could continue. "Well, I couldn't help but overhear some of your conversation. Is your wife mentally ill?"

Lance froze. How was he supposed to answer that question? He couldn't believe he'd been so callous as to have that conversation with someone else in the room.

The woman must have sensed his uneasiness because she quickly put in, "I really don't want to get all in your business. It's just that, well, my husband is bipolar and I can kinda imagine what you're going through."

Lance was stunned. The woman was so well put together. Her hair was immaculate, and although she had to be sixty, she looked as if she could grace the covers of a fashion magazine. She looked like the last person you'd expect to ever be living a nightmare as he was.

"No, it isn't easy," Lance finally said.

"I want to encourage you to find a support group." She took out a card and handed it to him. "It literally saved my life."

Lance glanced down at the card for the Loving and Living Support group. If the situation didn't get better with Tia, he was definitely going to check them out. He'd shown up to be by her side when she delivered the baby, but he had no idea where they would go from here.

He tucked the card in his back pocket. "Can I ask you a question? How long have you been married?"

"Twenty-two years."

"Wow, and he's been sick the whole time?"

She nodded. "We didn't know in the beginning. We were married for six years before he was correctly diagnosed."

"Why did you stay?"

She smiled wearily. Her eyes bore the look of a woman who had been to hell and back. "I've asked myself that more times than I can count. And I have friends from the support group who didn't stay with their mates. They had a lot of guilt over leaving, but they didn't stay. But whether you should stay or go is a decision only you can make. I can tell you, if your wife makes you unhappy, you shouldn't stay. If you are staying with her out of pity, you shouldn't stay. If you are hoping that someday she will be 'normal'—don't stay. If you don't love this person with all of your heart, don't stay."

He glanced through the nursery window at his daughter, who was sound asleep. "I love my wife. I do. But I don't know how to deal with her disease."

She nodded as if she could definitely relate. "I love my husband despite his faults. I learned to turn my head when bipolar Thomas was speaking and patiently waited for the more rational

Thomas to return. Our relationship is not based on drama, pity, or unrealistic hope. If you love a bipolar person, your world can be turned upside down in a moment. You have to learn to ride the waves of the ups and downs like a pro surfer."

Lance didn't know if he could do that. He didn't know if he *wanted* to do that.

"Sometimes, she says and does some horrible things," he said. He almost felt strange talking to a perfect stranger, but it felt so good to have someone he felt knew exactly what he was talking about.

"Oh, I know. Thomas has called me some names . . . whew." She fanned herself. "The devil himself couldn't come up with some of the vile stuff Thomas has said. But you have to remember that bipolar people will sometimes say awful things, but understand that is the illness talking, not the person. Don't take it personally, it isn't about you." Cheryl spoke as if she'd been through it dozens of times.

"I just feel so helpless," Lance said. "I try to help her and it seems to only aggravate her more."

"You have to give them space when they need it. Often, when a bipolar person begins feeling down, they just need space. Trying to help by staying close and cheering them up will likely make matters worse."

Lance took in all that she was saying. "You know, I didn't find out she was ill until recently. She knew. Her whole family knew. But no one thought that was something I needed to know."

"Would you have married her anyway?"

Lance thought about her question. Would he have? Or would he have run—like every other man Tia had loved?

"I think I would have still done it," he found himself saying. Then with more conviction, he added, "I know I would have."

"When you love a bipolar person, you have to accept them just as they are. You cannot 'cure' them or 'fix' them. What you can do is love them unconditionally."

Unconditionally. Did he have that power inside him? Lance glanced at his daughter sleeping soundly. He didn't know the answer to that question.

He did know that he wanted to try.

Chapter 51

Anyone standing outside their home, peeping in right now, would think the Kingstons lived a picture-perfect life. Lance leaned against the doorframe and watched his wife as she held their child—their beautiful, adorable baby girl.

Tia caressed the baby's face. They'd been home a week now, and while no major issues had flared up, something wasn't right. He felt it and he knew Tia felt it, too. Lance had heard her on the phone last night, crying to her mother that she felt no connection to the baby. Lance didn't know what Virginia had told her daughter, but it had been enough to calm her down.

"Please, hush baby, please," Tia moaned. The baby was whimpering and squirming, and Tia was getting frustrated.

"Hey, she's probably just gassy," Lance said, walking over to take the baby.

"No," Tia said, pushing the baby toward him in defeat.

"She just doesn't like me." Her eyes were red and puffy from crying.

"That's ridiculous. She loves you." He cradled the baby in his arms. "It's no reason to get upset."

"Yes, it is. I'm her mother. This is supposed to feel natural and it doesn't feel natural."

"Baby, you've had a rough few months. You love this child and this child loves you. You're probably just exhausted."

Tia gave in. "Yeah, that's it," she said, although it didn't sound as if she believed it.

"Why don't you go take your medicine and lie down?" Lance knew she hated to be reminded about her medicine, but until he was confident that she took it on her own, he made it his business to check every day. The doctor had sat both of them down before they left and told them how crucial it was that she stay on the medication. Tia had promised the doctor that she would. And Lance had promised that he would make sure she did. "My mom and grandmother will be over here soon, and I'm sure you don't feel like them hemming and hawing over you."

She pulled herself up off the sofa. "You're right. I really don't feel like company, but I know they want to see the baby."

"Exactly, so you go in the back and lie down, and me and my princess will sit here. I'll feed her and she'll do what she does best," he said, tickling her foot. "She'll poop. Then her grandmother and great-grandmother will arrive in time to clean her up, then spoil her some more."

Tia handed him Lauren's bottle, seemingly grateful for the reprieve. "Lance, thank you for staying to help me through this."

He held the bottle jointly with her. “I’m not going anywhere, babe.” He leaned in and lightly kissed his wife before she made her way to their bedroom. Lance walked into the kitchen to warm the baby’s bottle. When it was heated, he tested it, then sat down to feed her. He’d just gotten her to sleep when the doorbell rang.

“Doggone it,” he mumbled, sitting the baby in the swing set. “You know they’re gonna come in here trying to wake you up,” he whispered to his daughter.

Lance walked over and opened the front door.

“Where’s my grandbaby?” his mother said, rushing in.

“Your grandbaby just went to sleep, but don’t worry, she’ll be up in an hour.”

“But we want to play with her.”

“You can play with her when she wakes up,” Lance firmly replied.

Both of them ignored him and headed straight toward the swing set.

“Look at her. Just precious.” Beverly turned to her mother. “Mother, who does she look like to you?”

Lance’s grandmother leaned in and studied the baby. “A wrinkled prune!”

“Mama!”

“A *cute* wrinkled prune. There, is that better?”

“Okay, Grandma.” Lance pointed outside. “Let’s sit out back on the deck.”

His family reluctantly followed him outside. Lance left the patio door open so he could hear his daughter if she woke up.

"How is Tia doing, Son?" his mother asked once they were settled around the patio table.

"Okay, I guess." He sighed.

"I see the baby is putting on some weight. That's good," his mother said. "Are you breast-feeding her?"

"Well, I'm not," Lance joked.

"Very funny. You know what I mean."

"I know y'all ain't breast-feeding that baby!" his grandmother exclaimed.

"And why not?" Lance asked.

" 'Cause your wife got some big ta-tas. She go to try and stick all that in that baby's mouth and be done choked the poor thang."

"Mother, I'm gonna start leaving you at home," Beverly warned.

"Hey, I'm just saying. Lance probably even has a hard time getting them thangs in his mouth." His grandmother chuckled.

"I'm just going to pretend you didn't say that, Grandma." He shook his head. "But to answer your question, no, we're not breast-feeding the baby. You know, because of Tia's medication."

His mother and grandmother exchanged uneasy glances.

"So how are you handling all of this?" his mother asked.

"I'm doing okay. Now that I actually know what I'm dealing with, I can handle it a little better. I just make sure she takes her medicine and talks with her doctor whenever she needs to."

"You probably should get your own therapist," Beverly said. As hoity-toity as she was, she wasn't the least bit ashamed about going to therapy and felt that everyone could benefit from talking to someone. "Or even look for a support group of your own."

"As a matter of fact, this lady at the hospital gave me the name of a support group, so I plan to check it out. I imagine there may be some difficult days ahead."

"Well, you let me know if we can do anything to help," his grandmother said, patting his hand. "Well, let your mama know because I can't be dealin' with no crazy folk."

Lance shook his head at his grandmother. Everything was a joke. He was about to say something when he noticed the distressed look on his mother's face. "Mama, what's wrong?"

She dabbed at the corner of her eyes with a handkerchief she pulled out of her purse. "It's a shame you got to be dealing with all of this."

"Mama—"

"No." She cut him off. It was as if she had been waiting to get some things off her chest. "I don't understand this arrangement. I know this isn't the life you envisioned." She pointed toward the inside of the house. "That woman is crazy and wouldn't nobody on God's green earth blame you if you left and took that baby with you. You got enough stress in your life with your job. Now on top of providing for your family, you got to do all the housework, the cooking, the shopping, and take care of a newborn."

"Mama, that's just for now," Lance said wearily. He would never admit it to her, but he'd thought about some of those very things.

"You don't know how long she'll be like this. If she'll ever get better. You don't know if one day you'll wake up and the child will have flipped out again. And I can't believe you would even think about leaving that baby with her. What if she does something to her?"

Lance sighed. He couldn't explain it. Despite the hell Tia had put him through, despite the fact that she'd lied to him from the very beginning, Lance loved her. "I love her . . . in spite of." That had almost become his mantra.

Both his mother and his grandmother shook their heads. "You know there are more rocky days ahead," his mother warned.

"We'll find the strength to make it through."

"You sound like a Hallmark card," his grandmother interjected.

Lance leaned forward to stress his point. He needed to get a few things clear. "Look, I love you two with all of my heart. But Tia is my wife now. I'm not bailing on her. I'm not giving up. I'm going to help her battle this disease."

His grandmother couldn't believe what she was hearing. "You always have been a nurturer." She turned to her daughter. "You remember that time he found that kitten stuffed in a trash can? He brought that dang thing home and had a fit until you agreed to let him nurture it back to health."

His mother nodded, glaring at her son. "And no matter what I said, he wouldn't let that scrappy thing go."

Lance stood up. He'd had enough. "You know what? Let me make something clear. Tia is not *some scrappy thing* I'm trying to nurse back to health. She's not some charity case I'm taking in. She's my wife and now the mother of my child, and if you can't accept that, then too bad, because she's in my life to stay." Lance faced off with his mother. The way her chest heaved, he could tell he'd struck a nerve.

"So you mean to tell me when you dreamed of happily ever after, it was with some woman who may or may not go crazy and kill you, your child, and everyone else," Beverly said with a sneer.

"And don't say she ain't capable of it," his grandmother added. "You know what she told Crystal, and you saw what happened at our house when she dang near attacked everyone in your mother's bridge group."

Beverly softened her tone. "Son, I've heard about people like this. They have multiple personalities, they lie, cheat, steal, even kill."

His grandmother nodded. "Um-hmm, and wasn't that Charles Manson and the Unabomber crazy in the head, too? We gon' be looking for you and she'll have chopped you up, made you into meatloaf and try to serve it to us at Sunday dinner."

"Grandma, you're being ridiculous and disrespectful, and I'm not going to stand for it anymore." Lance pounded the patio table.

Beverly put her hand on her son's arm to calm him down. "Your grandmother is being over-the-top, but what she's trying to say, what we're both trying to say, is we feel like you deserve so much better."

Lance was about to respond when he caught a glimpse of his wife out of the corner of his eye. She was standing in the patio door, tears in her eyes.

"Tia . . ." he said, racing over to her.

Beverly put her hand over her mouth in shock. "Oh, sweetie, I didn't . . ."

Tia turned and ran off before Beverly could finish her sentence.

Chapter 52

Throughout her life, Tia had good days . . . and bad days. But it seemed as if lately she was having only bad days. And today had to be the worst day of them all.

You deserve better.

"Are you okay?" Lance had been trying to talk Tia out of the bathroom for the past hour.

She finally broke down and opened the door.

Lance took her into his arms and hugged her tightly. "I'm so sorry, baby." He guided her to the bed. "I put my mother and grandmother out and told them if they continue to disrespect you, they are not welcome here."

Tia knew she had to look a mess. She wiped her nose with her balled-up Kleenex. "They're right, though."

"No, they're not." He shook her gently and waited for her eyes to meet his. "You listen to me. We deserve each other. And

I don't care what anyone says. We can beat this"—she waited sadly as he struggled to find the right word—"this illness."

Tia knew he was being careful, trying to make sure he didn't say the wrong thing to set her off. She hated that he felt he had to tiptoe around her. She felt like a failure. She had hoped the medication would make her mood swings better. She'd been taking it faithfully since she left the hospital. It was a lower dosage, but it still was only making things worse. Now she found herself more depressed than ever. She couldn't even breast-feed her baby because of that medicine. Suddenly, it dawned on Tia that the medication was probably why she couldn't connect with her child. She needed to stop taking it so she could breastfeed and, hopefully, grow close to her daughter.

"Can I get you anything?" Lance asked. "Some water, tea, food?"

She shook her head. "No, I'm fine." She looked around their bedroom. "Where's Lauren?"

"In her room. She's still asleep."

Once again her child had gone to sleep without her assistance. In fact, Lance or her mother had changed Lauren, fed her, bathed her, and played with her since she'd gotten home from the hospital.

"Come on, let me get you in the bed." Lance pulled back the covers and helped her slide underneath. "I know it's still early, but you need to get some rest."

"Can I ask you a question?" Tia asked after she was settled under the covers.

"Of course."

"Do you feel like you got a raw deal?" she asked bluntly.

"Tia, don't pay my family any attention."

"No, seriously."

He hesitated, thinking. "Well, I can't say that I liked you trying to keep me in the dark, but, no, I don't feel that way." He sat down on the bed and patted her leg. "I love you. I love our baby, and I want to be the stabilizing factor in your life."

She took his hand. "I know you get frustrated. But all of this is frustrating for me as well because, lately, my moods cycle so rapidly that by the time I've sorted out whether it is myself talking, or the bipolar taking over, it's too late and the damage is done."

Lance caressed her hands, grateful that they were talking about this. Dr. Monroe had suggested they discuss it, but Tia never wanted to. "What does it feel like, you know, living with this illness?"

She pursed her lips, thinking. "It is one long, continuous roller coaster that pauses briefly, perched on the top arch, before plunging back down again. Then the same cycle repeats all over again. Imagine the saddest moment of your life. Now multiply that by a hundred. Now, multiply that by a thousand. Then keep going until you cannot multiply anymore. That's how I feel. It engulfs me. I feel it in every pore of my body. It overwhelms me and is totally unbearable. I have dark, dark lows where I cry for no reason, but people think I am fine. I have anger that I can barely control some days, and without the meds I couldn't control it on those days, I know."

Lance was stunned by her words. "Wow. But, Tia, then why don't you take your medicine like you're supposed to?"

She didn't dare tell him that she had yet again decided to stop. "I used to make up all kinds of excuses: they made me gain weight, they kept me drowsy, they made the mood swings worse. But I think it's just because I wanted to be normal." This time her reason was completely different. This time she just wanted to be able to bond with her baby. If she could get the drugs out of her system, she could breast-feed, grow closer, and maybe Lauren would learn to love her mother.

"Tia, you are normal. You just have more ups and downs than the rest of us," Lance said.

Tia harrumphed. "Yeah, right. Normal people don't cuss out people they love. Normal people don't walk across town in a two-piece. Normal people don't have voices tormenting them."

Lance drew back in shock. "Voices?"

Tia could kick herself. That's the last thing she wanted Lance to know. She casually waved. "It's nothing."

"Tia, if you're hearing voices, we need to talk to Dr. Monroe about it."

"It just started and I think it's this medication, mixed with the painkillers. But it's nothing serious." She took his hand again. "Lance, I'm trying, baby. I am. But I can't take you treating me like a basket case."

"I just want—"

She put her finger on his lips. "I know. You just want to help. And you are helping by just loving me." She sighed. "And you know how you can help now?"

"How?"

She forced a smile. "By running to get us something to eat. I'm starving."

Lance seemed to want to keep talking, but he didn't press her. "Okay. I have to go drop a package off at Robert's house for the presentation tomorrow. I'll pick us up something to eat." He stood. "I'll take Lauren with me."

She tilted her head. "Lance, I'm perfectly capable of watching my child."

He looked unsure.

"I'm starving, sweetie."

"Okay," he finally agreed. "I'll bring her in here. I shouldn't be gone more than an hour."

"Don't wake her." She pulled the baby monitor close to her and turned up the volume. "I'll just sit here and read, and if she wakes up, I'll hear her."

Lance nodded reluctantly. "I'll be right back. But you call me if you need anything." He leaned down, kissed her on the forehead, then headed out the door.

Tia sighed when she heard the front door slam. She was alone with her child. No husband, no mother. Just her and her baby.

Tia fought the urge, but after a few minutes she threw the covers back and stepped out of bed to retrieve her child. She pushed the conversation between Lance and his family out of her head because she actually felt a little better. Dr. Monroe had been right. Talking to Lance felt like lifting a weight off her shoulders. Maybe she could live a normal life after all. Step one would be discontinuing her medication so she could strengthen her bond with her baby.

Chapter 53

It's as if he were living a different life. This was the life Lance had dreamed of. This was the life he'd envisioned.

"'. . . down will come baby, cradle and all.'" The sight of Tia singing to their daughter warmed his heart. He didn't know what had happened, but in these last three weeks Tia had done a dramatic 180. He did know she was trying hard, and he could see the results of her efforts. She would still sink into a depression every now and then, but she was miles ahead of the way she used to be.

"She loves that song," Lance said, sliding onto the sofa next to his wife.

Tia leaned over and lightly kissed her husband. "She sure does. It doesn't even bother her that I sound like an *American Idol* reject."

Lance laughed. He'd been checking Tia's pill bottle to make

sure she took her medicine every day, and she had, which seemed to have helped in turning her mood around. "I think you sound great."

"I think you're biased." Tia carefully stood up, cradling the baby in her arms. "I'm going to lay her down. How long before Brian gets here?"

Lance checked his watch. "They should be here any minute now. I can't wait to meet this woman he's bringing. Any woman that can get Brian to even think about settling down must be something special."

Lance had been hesitant about having visitors over, but Tia had assured him that she was fine and, in fact, welcomed some adult company. She hadn't gotten a call, a card, anything, from Lucinda, and Lance could tell that bothered her, so she wanted to meet someone she could possibly be friends with.

"Well, you go check on the food and I'll lay her down."

Tia made her way upstairs to the baby's room, while Lance headed to the kitchen. He'd just taken the shrimp enchiladas out of the oven when she returned to the kitchen. She was wearing a long, royal-blue maxidress, her hair was pulled back into a curly ponytail, and she looked as beautiful as on the day they'd met.

"You need help with anything?" she asked.

"Naw, you did most of the work," he replied just as the doorbell rang.

"I'll get the door."

Tia greeted Brian and his new girlfriend, an older woman

named Jillian, and before long, the four of them were sitting around the dinner table, eating and chatting like old friends.

Lance enjoyed the camaraderie with his friend, and he loved how Jillian seemed to tame the wild side of Brian.

"So, Jillian, what do you do again?" Lance asked as they ate their turtle cheesecake and sipped Moscato.

"I work for the Department of Human Services. I used to work in elderly services, and now they've moved me over with the crazy folks. Hence, the reason I'm on my third glass of wine." Jillian laughed as she held up her glass.

Lance, Brian, and Tia all froze.

Jillian lost her smile. "I'm sorry. Did I say something wrong?"

Brian and Lance exchanged glances, but no one said anything.

Tia glared at Jillian, her lips pursed. But then a smile spread across Tia's face. "Oh, it's no biggie. I'm just one of those crazy folks," she said, her voice laced with sarcasm.

"Excuse me?" Jillian said, looking confused.

"Babe, I, um, I guess I should've told you," Brian said, putting his hand on her arm.

"Told me what?"

"That I'm crazy," Tia interjected before turning her fire on her husband. "Because it's obvious Brian knows. I mean, just how much have you told him, Lance?"

"Tia, not now . . ."

"What?" Tia said, getting upset. "I mean, obviously, you sit around talking about me with your boy. Do you laugh at my expense? Do you tell him all the stories about the crazy lady you married?"

Lance inwardly groaned. This could not be happening. They'd been doing so well.

"I . . . I am so sorry," Jillian said. "I didn't mean anything by it."

"Oh, it's nothing for you to be sorry about. But I'm sorry us crazy folks drive you to drink."

"Tia . . ."

Jillian looked horrified. "Seriously, I meant nothing by it."

"You meant every word, you self-righteous tramp."

Jillian's mouth dropped open.

"Tia!"

"Don't Tia me," she said, snatching her arm away from Lance. "You brought her here to humiliate me."

"Tia, I wasn't trying to—" Jillian began.

"Shut your old ass up!"

Jillian gasped.

"I am so sorry," Lance told her.

"Don't apologize for me." Tia looked back and forth between Lance and Jillian. "Oh, I get it. You're apologizing to her because you're screwing her." Tia pushed back from the table. "How dare you bring your whore into my house, have me fix dinner for her and everything."

"Tia"—Lance stood with his wife—"babe, calm down."

"I told you about telling me to calm down." She pushed away from him. "They told me you were trying to play me. They've been telling me all along."

"Who is they?"

"The voices." Tia nodded as if she were finally figuring out some complex puzzle.

Brian finally stood. "Umm, look here, we're gonna get going."

Tia turned to Brian and smiled. "So soon?"

Jillian remained fixed in place. Lance couldn't blame her. He was shocked himself.

"Brian, I'm so glad you came by," Tia said, walking around the table to hug him. "Next time, please leave my husband's whore at home." Tia spun and walked out of the dining room.

Lance was frozen in his spot. Finally he said, "Jillian, I can't apologize enough. I mean, as my wife said, she's ill. I mean, we thought she was getting better, but obviously . . ."

Jillian nodded in understanding as she grabbed her purse. She couldn't get out of there fast enough.

"Man, I'll call you," Brian said as they headed to the door. He shot Lance one last sympathetic look on the way out.

Lance closed the door and ran his hand across his face. What the hell just happened? How did Tia go from singing lullabies to full-blown crazy in hours? And what was she talking about with the voices? His mind raced back to the last time she'd mentioned voices. He hadn't done anything about it then, but he was going to do something about it now.

Chapter 54

Lance hated going behind Tia's back, but these voices she claimed to be hearing concerned him. The first time she'd mentioned them, she'd blown it off and he'd let the matter drop. Then she'd been doing so well these last few weeks that he took her at her word. But after that fiasco yesterday, he realized that it had all been wishful thinking. This voices problem was serious. She'd flipped out before, but this was the first time she blamed voices. Lance had tossed and turned all last night and decided he would try to talk to Dr. Monroe to get some answers.

"Hi, Mr. Kingston, just a few more minutes and Dr. Monroe will be on the line," the receptionist said, coming back on the line. "Do you mind continuing to hold?"

"No, I'm fine."

Lance drummed his fingers on the steering wheel. He was in the parking lot of an Olive Garden, picking up dinner. Tia had been in bed all day. Lance had waited to call when he left the house because he didn't want to risk Tia's walking in on the call. She'd refused to talk to him last night—just kept telling him to go talk to Jillian. She'd even slept in Lauren's room last night. But this morning she'd gotten up as if nothing were wrong. She did apologize for overreacting, once again blaming it on the medication, saying it made her loopy. But other than that, she hadn't mentioned Brian or Jillian and had changed the subject when he'd tried.

"Mr. Kingston, how are you?" the doctor said, finally coming to the phone.

"Okay, I guess. Do you have a couple of minutes?"

"Yes, sir. I just finished up with a patient."

"Look, Doctor, my wife had an episode last night."

"What kind of episode?"

"Well, it's like this switch just flipped and she turned into an unreasonable, jealous tyrant. But the thing that concerned me the most is she said that she's hearing voices. I thought only schizophrenic people heard voices."

The doctor answered in a grave tone. "That's a common misconception. Actually, about twenty percent of bipolar people hear voices. They're called auditory hallucinations."

This situation was getting more and more complicated. "Doc, is my wife a threat to herself?"

"I wish I could answer that. But what I do know is that we have to get your wife stabilized on her medication. I could alter her dosage, but it does no good if she's not taking it in the first place. You have to stress the importance of that."

"As far as I know, she is taking it. I mean, I check her pills every day. And she had been doing better, but yesterday she just turned out of nowhere."

"Classic signs that she's off her meds. Let's get her in tomorrow if possible. And if she is indeed taking them, I'll look at changing the dosage again."

"Okay, thanks, Dr. Monroe."

"No problem. By the way, how's the baby?"

"She's wonderful. Tia was having a hard time bonding with her."

"That's understandable. Even the average woman can have issues and deal with postpartum depression, so it's not unnatural for Tia, who already has heightened emotions, to have problems. It's just important to watch her and keep someone around. Have you gone back to work yet?"

"I have. Tia's mother has been coming by to help out."

"Well, if you say she's been hearing voices, then I need you to make sure someone stays with her around the clock—at least until she's over the postpartum part or we get the new medication in her system."

Lance thanked the doctor, promised they'd see him in the morning, then immediately hung up the phone and called Virginia.

"Hi, Virginia, it's Lance. I was just wondering if you can come stay with us for a couple of weeks."

She cautiously replied, "Why, what's wrong?"

"I just spoke with Dr. Monroe." He ignored her snort. "And, well, we both think Tia needs someone here all the time, at least for a little while. Caring for a baby is difficult and I'm sure she can use your help and would enjoy having you here."

"That's no problem, but has something happened?"

He debated telling her about the voices, but he'd learned by now that his mother-in-law would think up an excuse, so he didn't bother. "I just think having you here would be good for Tia. If you can't do it, I'll hire a live-in nurse."

"That won't be necessary," Virginia said quickly. "Of course I can do it. I'll pack some stuff and just plan on staying when I come tomorrow."

Lance breathed a sigh of relief. "Thank you very much."

Lance had just hung up his phone when he noticed his light blinking, alerting him that he had a text message. He read it, then debated whether he should reply. He owed Crystal a reply, but right now, he couldn't deal with that. He deleted the message, then tossed the phone into the console and went inside to pick up his food. He'd almost messed up with Crystal. To make his marriage work, Lance knew that was a chapter he needed to keep closed.

Chapter 55

She had been doing so well. For three weeks Tia had felt normal. Sane. She felt closer to the baby, thanks to the breast-feeding. Of course, she could only breast-feed when no one was around, but it definitely seemed to be strengthening her bond with her daughter. Everything had been great.

Until yesterday.

Yesterday, the voices had come back and Tia couldn't shake them.

You're so worthless. You'll never make a good mother. You shouldn't have had a baby in the first place. Why would you want to create another you? She's probably crazy just like you.

The voices had her scared. She'd had numerous ups and downs over the years, but never had the voices been digging at her nonstop like this.

Did you see the sixes in her head? You know she's the devil's spawn. Having that baby is the dumbest thing you ever did. But then again, you're dumb. You can't get anything right.

The voices had convinced her that Lance was sleeping with that Jillian woman. She'd tried to tune them out, but all through dinner they'd reminded her how together Jillian was, how pretty she looked, how sane she appeared. And by dessert Tia was convinced that Lance was going to leave her for that woman. But she'd managed to keep her suspicions at bay. Until Jillian had made her stupid comment about crazy people. That had set her off.

Tia was on the brink of tears because she so desperately wanted these feelings to go away. She wanted more than anything to get better. Maybe going off her meds wasn't such a good idea, she thought. But then again, what choice did she have?

Tia ran her hands through her hair. This situation was all so confusing.

"What's wrong with Lauren?"

Tia jumped at the sound of Lance's voice. He walked in and quickly set the bags of Italian food down on the dining-room table. She realized that Lauren was bawling her head off.

"She won't shut up," Tia cried, rocking back and forth on the sofa. "She woke up right after you left, and nothing I did could get her to go back to sleep. She won't take her bottle. She's just screaming." Lauren was in her bouncer on the floor, yelling at the top of her lungs.

"She's a baby, that's what they do," Lance said, walking over to the bouncer and picking up his daughter. Lauren screamed louder.

"Lance, get her away from me, get rid of her." Tia didn't know how long Lauren had been crying. It felt like hours. "I can't take it. Just make her stop crying."

Lance didn't argue as he grabbed a bottle and took the baby upstairs.

Tia immediately relished the peace and quiet. She sat for a few minutes, feeling better. She eyed the bag of food and realized how hungry she was. She walked over to the table and began digging in the bag. She pulled out the first container, then screamed, "Lance!"

Lance came running downstairs. "Keep your voice down. I just calmed Lauren down and got her to sleep."

Ha! He can get her to stop crying, but you can't. You're so pathetic.

Tia pushed the voice away.

"Now what's wrong?" Lance asked. "Why are you screaming like that?"

Tia hurled the tin container at him. "That's what's wrong! I asked for chicken Alfredo. You got spaghetti." She pulled the can of Similac out of the Wal-Mart bag. "Oh, but I see you got the right formula."

That's because he loves the baby more than you.

"It's obvious he loves the baby more than me!" Tia snapped.

"Who are you talking to?" Lance said, then paused. "Are you taking your medication?"

"Don't start with me and this medication. So now you're the medication police?"

"Okay, Tia," he said sternly, "you need to calm down."

His tone snapped her back to reality. She took a deep breath. *Don't do this. You were doing so well.* "I'm sorry. I'm just stressed. It's just normal baby stress."

Lance was studying her carefully. "I asked your mother to come stay with us for a few weeks."

"What? Why? I've been doing fine. I'm just a little stressed today."

"Last night was not fine. And besides, I need to get back to work full-time. The magazine schedule is about to get hectic."

"Why can't you stay home with me?"

"Come on, Tia, you know I can't. It's a crucial time at work. We talked about this. I've already been on this flex schedule too long as it is."

She sat back and folded her arms. "You're the boss."

"Which is why I have to be there."

"What's more important, me and your daughter or that stupid job?" she snapped.

"Don't do that, Tia. I have to put a roof over our heads."

Tia stood up abruptly and started pacing the room. "Okay, okay, I know. I'm sorry. I think I just need a drink."

Lance huffed, "Tia, you cannot drink. You're on medication. The alcohol with the medication is not a good mix."

She wanted to tell him that was how much he knew. She was going on week four without medication. "Okay, Dr. Kingston. I'll wait for you to give me a release form to take a drink."

He wants to run your life. But you're so trifling, you need someone to run it.

Tia put her hands over her ears. "Shut up," she screamed.

Lance stared at her in horror. "I just talked to Dr. Monroe. He wants to see us in the morning."

"I'm not going to talk to that quack!" she screamed.

"This is not open for discussion, Tia. You were doing well, but it's obvious something isn't right. We're going to talk to Dr. Monroe in the morning if I have to drag you there." He glared at her, then spun around and walked out of the room. Tia heard Lance stomp upstairs. A few minutes later, he returned with a bottled water in one hand and her medication in the other.

"Take it," he demanded.

"I already did," she said softly. She felt drained, and the ups and downs were taking their toll.

"You're lying," Lance said, thrusting the medication at her.

Tia was about to protest when she slid to the floor in tears.

"You promised me you wouldn't lie anymore." He sounded so disappointed in her.

"I'm sorry, Lance. I haven't been taking my meds, but it's because I've been breast-feeding. I need to bond with my baby. She didn't like me and I wanted her to like me." Tia sobbed.

An exasperated Lance knelt down next to her. "Babe, you can't do that. You know that. You're no good to either of us if you're off meds."

Tia sniffed as she looked up at her husband. Lance was such a good man. Why had God sent her someone like him? Why had God not given him the type of wife he deserved?

She wondered if Lance regretted the day he stopped her at the hotel. Did he regret sending her flowers? Did he regret marrying her?

Lance held the medication out again. "Please."

Tia wiped her eyes, then nodded as she popped the pills into her mouth.

Chapter 56

Tia watched her mother walk around the living room, singing and cooing to the baby. Those were all things Tia should be doing, but she couldn't bring herself to nurture her own child. She'd tried, and for a minute she'd felt as if it were working, but it had all been a facade. Now every time she picked up Lauren, the baby cried uncontrollably. Tia felt sick to her stomach. She had failed at her marriage, and after only one month she was failing at motherhood.

She'd taken the pills and she still felt distant. Granted, Tia didn't expect them to work overnight, but she had hoped she would wake up today feeling better. Instead she felt more lethargic than ever.

"Do you want to rock her?" Virginia asked.

Tia pulled her legs up under her and scooted away on the sofa. "She doesn't like me."

"That's hogwash. You love your mommy, don't you, poopoo?" Virginia tickled the baby's chin. "You hold her. I'm gonna go and fix her another bottle." Virginia held up the empty bottle. "She devoured this."

Tia took her baby. Lauren didn't cry and, in fact, immediately snuggled close to her. But why did Tia still feel empty? Why did she not feel any motherly connection?

"Mama, your cell phone is ringing," Tia called out when she saw her mother's phone buzzing on the coffee table.

Virginia raced back into the living room and grabbed her phone. "Hello?" Her eyes widened. "What?"

"Oh, my God," Virginia said, her voice panicked. "Okay, all right, all right. I'm on my way."

"What's going on?" Tia asked when Virginia hung up the phone.

"That was Curtis. Leo's clumsy behind slipped down at the senior center and they think he done broke his leg. I gotta go to the hospital." Virginia paused, remembering what Lance had told her. "Oh, no." She looked at the baby, then at Tia. "Maybe you two should come with me."

"That's ridiculous, Mama. I'll be fine." Tia was weary, but she refused to believe that she couldn't take care of her own child for a couple of hours.

"But Lance told me . . . he told me not to leave you . . ."

Tia glared at her mother. "What? He told you don't leave me alone with my own child? When did he tell you that?"

"This morning before he left."

"How long have you known me, Mama?"

"All your life."

"Am I in a spell right now?"

Virginia studied her daughter. "Well, no, you seem to be doing fine."

"Thank you. So, I'll be fine. Just go check on Uncle Leo and we'll be here when you get back. I'll feed her, and hopefully she'll go to sleep."

Virginia twiddled her fingers nervously. "Well, should I call Lance?"

"I'm not a child, Mama," Tia said, agitated. "I don't need a babysitter twenty-four/seven."

"Okay, okay. Well, I'm just gonna go check on your uncle and I'll be back as soon as I can." Virginia left in a hurry.

As soon as the door slammed, Tia wondered if she had made the right decision.

That's because you suck as a mother.

Tia's eyes darted around the room. Why were the voices becoming louder? She felt as if someone were actually in the room with her.

Tia tried to focus. What was she supposed to be doing? Oh, feeding the baby. She laid Lauren on the sofa, walked into the kitchen, and pulled a bottle out of the refrigerator. She placed the bottle in the microwave and heated it for a minute. When the bell dinged, she took the bottle out and trudged back into the living room.

Tia sat down next to her baby and stuck the bottle in her mouth. Lauren let out a piercing scream.

"What now?" Tia snapped. She felt the bottle. It was scalding hot. How did she forget to test the milk? "Dang it. I didn't mean to burn you."

That's why they didn't want to leave her alone with you. What kind of mother burns their baby with scalding milk?

Lauren continued bawling at the top of her lungs. Tia apologized, tried to blow on her tongue, rock her, but nothing would stop the baby from screaming. The shrill cries were grating on Tia's nerves, driving her mad. Tia laid Lauren on the sofa and began pacing the room.

Just get a pillow. Cover her face. That'll shut her up.

Tia stopped, watched Lauren's legs and arms flailing, and begged her to stop crying.

You're wasting your breath. She doesn't listen to you.

Tia finally stopped pacing, grabbed a pillow off the sofa, and stood over her baby with it.

What are you waiting for? She's probably summoning the devil to come here and kill you.

Tia leaned in, putting the pillow closer to Lauren's face.

Tia, don't do it!

Tia stopped. That was the other voice. The rational one. She glanced at the pillow in her hand, then immediately dropped it.

"Oh, my God," she murmured.

Pick her up. Comfort her.

Tia picked the baby up. Lauren wailed louder.

See, she hates you. You're a horrible mother. She wants to drive you mad. Make her stop crying!

Tia shook her daughter. "Be quiet!"

Shake her and make her shut up! Harder! The little brat is just trying to make you lose your mind.

Lauren's eyes bulged as Tia viciously shook her. She had stopped crying, and fear was etched across her face. That look of fear stopped Tia cold.

Wimp.

"What am I doing? Oh, God, I'm so sorry, baby." She placed the baby on the sofa and scootched into a corner, trying to drown out the voices.

"God, please don't let me hurt my baby, please don't let me hurt my baby." She hoped her prayer would drown out the voices.

Medication. That's what she needed. More medicine. She needed to stabilize herself. Tia jumped up and raced into her bathroom, where she flung the medicine cabinet open and grabbed her lithium, Wellbutrin, and bottle of tranquilizers. She grabbed a bottled water off her nightstand. She quickly removed the cap from the lithium, then popped two into her mouth. She gulped the water, then opened the Wellbutrin and tranquilizers. One of those should work. Why hadn't she been taking these pills the way she was supposed to? Why did she think she was strong enough to function without them?

You're not strong enough to do anything.

Tia tussled her hair and let out a scream. Why did she have

to be cursed like this? Now, on top of everything else, her head was pounding and the baby was yelling louder.

Remember the Vicoden.

That's what Tia needed, recalling the wonderful feeling the painkillers gave her when she was in the hospital.

Tia went back into the bathroom. She fumbled through the medicine cabinet until she found the medicine they'd given her at the hospital. She cursed when she spied only four pills left in the bottle, but she popped those in her mouth and had just placed the empty container back in the cabinet when she spotted one of Lance's old prescriptions.

Tia removed the bottle and read the label: *Percocet. Take one daily as needed for pain.* She remembered Lance telling her he'd had surgery on his ankle a few months before they met. He must have used these painkillers then.

Take one daily as needed for pain.

Tia was definitely in pain.

She removed the top, popped two pills in her mouth. Then, in a greedy manic surge she turned the whole bottle up and swallowed them all, finishing off the water to wash it all down.

Just stay in here. Don't go back out there because you might hurt her.

That was the rational voice, the one Tia wanted to listen to. She hated to leave her baby screaming, but she couldn't risk harming her, so Tia locked her bedroom door, and slid down the back of it.

"I love you, Lauren," she whispered as she waited for her mother, Lance, anyone, to return.

Chapter 57

Lance's heart was pounding. He'd gone ballistic when he found out Virginia had left Tia at home alone.

"Why would you do that?" he screamed when he'd gotten the call an hour ago, especially when Virginia told him that she'd left his house almost four hours ago.

"Leo had an accident, I had to go check on him."

"Why didn't you call me?" Lance bellowed.

"Tia didn't want me to. She said she'd be fine."

"She always says she'll be fine and she never is!" He slammed the phone down. Lance knew he'd have to apologize to his mother-in-law later, but right now he was too angry to care.

Lance bore down on the horn at the driver poking along in front of him. He had been in a business meeting on the other side of town—a good hour from his house. He'd been calling Tia's cell phone and the house phone, and she wasn't answering either one. That wasn't unusual. She'd gotten to the point that she never answered either. He'd finally broken down and called Virginia. He was shocked when she answered the phone and told him that she was at the hospital with Leo.

"They're sleeping," he muttered as he whipped into the next lane. He had a horrible feeling in his gut and hoped he was just suffering from nerves.

Lance was a nervous wreck all the way home and must've said several prayers asking God to make sure his wife and daughter were fine.

When he finally pulled into his driveway, Lance barely stopped the car before he threw it into park and jumped out.

"Tia!" he called out, bursting into the house. "Tia!"

His heart raced when she didn't answer. He stopped in his tracks in the living room. Lauren was on the floor, facedown.

"Oh, my God," he said, racing to his daughter. His heart dropped to the pit of his stomach.

He picked up his baby and cried tears of joy when she opened her eyes and whimpered. Her entire face was red and swollen from crying. Her diaper was soaking and she was shaking. He eyed the blanket on the sofa. It was hanging off, as if Lauren had fallen off the sofa and grabbed the blanket trying to hold on. How did Tia let this happen?

"It's okay, sweetie, Daddy's here. Daddy's here," he said, rocking Lauren back and forth. He held her tightly as he looked around the downstairs for Tia.

Where in the hell was she? How could she leave their daughter just lying on a sofa with no protection from falling off?

Lance wanted to call out to her again, but he didn't want to frighten Lauren any more than she already was. He held her tightly as he made his way back to their bedroom. The door was closed. He shook his head, once again cursing Virginia. Tia had probably gotten tired of the baby and gone to lie down.

Lance reached for the door and pushed at it to open. It wouldn't budge. Something was blocking it. His heart began racing again. "Tia?"

When she didn't answer, fear engulfed him. He quick-stepped into Lauren's room and placed her down in her crib. "Daddy's sorry. I'll be right back." Lauren immediately began wailing again.

Lance took a deep breath and fought the urge to go back and get his daughter. "Tia?" he called out again, pushing the door. When it didn't open, he hit it as hard as he could with his shoulder. It opened, but barely moved because something was blocking it. Lance slid in the room. "Tia?"

He froze when he saw his wife spread-eagled on the floor.

"Oh, God, no!" he said, dropping to his knees. "Baby, baby, wake up, please." Lance put her head in his lap and immediately noticed all the empty bottles of pills. "Tia, baby, noooo," he cried, crawling to the phone. Lance didn't even know how he managed to call 911, but he snapped out of his daze when the operator said, "Sir, the ambulance is on the way. I just need you to tell me if your wife has a pulse."

"Huh?"

"A pulse? Does your wife have a pulse?"

Lance had crawled back over to Tia and was rocking her

again, so he reached down to her wrist, struggling to feel for a pulse. He didn't feel anything and prayed that he simply didn't know what he was doing.

"I can't feel anything," he cried.

When he heard the click ending the call, he dropped the phone. Help was coming and he needed to focus all his attention on getting his wife to wake up. "Please, baby, please, wake up," he cried in agony. He opened her eyelid and sobbed when he saw that her eyes had rolled into the back of her head. He quickly laid her down and began performing CPR. "Breathe, honey. Come on," he said, gently pumping her chest, then breathing into her mouth. "Damn you! You can't do this to us!" he cried when she didn't respond. After what seemed like an eternity, he heard someone call out, "Paramedics!"

"Back here!" Lance cried, grateful that he hadn't locked the front door. He jumped up as they raced into the room. "My wife," he said, pointing at her. "My wife, I think she OD'd."

The paramedics dropped to their knees and immediately began examining her.

"We've got a slight pulse," one of them announced as he began pulling out some medical equipment.

Lance hadn't been much of a praying man throughout his marriage, but he squeezed his eyes shut as he fought off the tears and said, "Dear God, please don't take Tia."

He kept praying as he numbly walked into the other room to grab Lauren. The two of them would have to follow the paramedics to the hospital. He just hoped God was listening to his prayer.

Chapter 58

Lance paced back and forth across the waiting room. His heart was racing. His mother had come to the hospital to gather up Lauren. She hadn't wanted to leave his side, but Lance didn't want his daughter here. Especially not if Tia died.

He glanced over at Virginia, who sat in the corner, her Bible clutched tightly as she rocked back and forth, whispering tearful prayers over and over. Uncle Leo was sitting in the chair next to her, his leg wrapped in a cast, his hands on her shoulders as he prayed as well.

Lance instinctively walked toward them. Leo didn't miss a beat as he took Lance's hand and continued his prayer. When he finished, Virginia kept praying. She was almost catatonic. But Lance didn't have the strength to comfort her right now.

"Why haven't they come and said anything?" he groaned.

"I imagine because they're focused on saving Tia," Leo said.

"They'll let us know as soon as they have something to tell us."

Saving Tia. At that moment everything else seemed so trivial. The plastic flowers, the purple bedroom, the shouting sprees. None of that mattered anymore. All that mattered was that his wife pull through.

"Why would she do this? Why would she try to leave us?" Lance cried.

"She wouldn't," Virginia spoke up. "I know my baby girl. She wouldn't try to kill herself." Lance glanced over at his mother-in-law. This was the first thing she'd said since she'd arrived.

"She overdosed on pills."

"She probably just wanted to get better. She loved her baby. She loved you. She wouldn't try to kill herself," Virginia said with conviction.

She went back to praying. Regardless of how they arrived at this place, Lance had to consider what would happen next. He couldn't help wondering if he would be raising his daughter on his own.

They all lurched when the doctor walked into the waiting room. He looked exhausted, with a surgical mask pulled down around his neck.

"Is she okay?"

The doctor sighed. "Unfortunately, she's not. She's gone into a coma. We've pumped her stomach, but she's still unresponsive. We've inserted a drip, but all of her veins have collapsed. Honestly, she has only a fifty-fifty chance of survival. And even if she does make it, she could be a vegetable."

Virginia gasped, and Lance had to steady himself by leaning against a wall.

"I assure you, we're doing all we can," the doctor quickly added. "I don't know if you all are praying folks—"

"We are, of course," Uncle Leo interjected.

"Well, medically we've done all we can. At this point the only thing that can help her is a higher power."

Virginia nodded knowingly. "Well, in that case she'll be fine," she said confidently.

How Lance wished that were true.

"Even if she does pull through," the doctor warned, "it's going to be a long road ahead. Your wife is sick. I've gone over her file and talked with her psychiatrist. We've taken her off the medication."

"I don't understand. She'd started back taking her medication."

"I'm not the psychiatrist, but I do know sometimes you have to try different medications before you find the right ones."

Virginia looked as if she wanted to say something. But thankfully, she kept her opinion to herself.

"I still say that the medication did help," the doctor continued. "With all the stress triggers, her case could have been a whole lot worse. I talked with Dr. Monroe, and he thinks she was suffering from postpartum depression. So, she's been through a lot."

That was an understatement, Lance thought. A whirlwind courtship and marriage, a stressful job, losing Mrs. Bailey's case, the pregnancy, and now postpartum depression. All those combined pressures would be enough to send even a normal person over the edge.

"She tried to get rid of the stress, though."

"If she pulls through, we'll try another form of medication."

"If? When. *When,*" Virginia said firmly.

The doctor looked at her sympathetically and nodded but didn't reply. "Well, I have some other patients to check on. She's stabilized, and, Lance, you can go in and see her."

Virginia looked as if she wanted desperately to go in instead, but Lance couldn't allow that. "Let me do this. I won't stay long and then you can see her."

Virginia squeezed his hand. "Tell her I love her."

"I will, but I'll let you come tell her, too."

She nodded appreciatively.

Lance made his way down the hallway, eased the door open, and peeked into the room. If not for the faint beat on the machine Tia was hooked up to, he would have thought that she was gone. But he knew the beat indicated that she was still alive.

"Tia, baby. I hope you can hear me," he said, leaning over her in the bed. "I want you to know that I am here. I love you, and when I told you for better or for worse, I meant it. I'm here. Lauren and I need you. You pull through this and we'll work through everything else. If that means I have to take a leave of absence, I will. Whatever it takes to get through this. I just need you to come home. *We* need you to come home."

He leaned down and kissed her on the forehead. "I love you, baby."

Lance cried silent tears for his wife when she didn't move. If she would just come back to him, she could paint the house with lime-green polka dots for all he cared. Lance just wanted his wife home.

Long after the announcement that visiting hours were over, Lance sat slumped over the hospital bed.

Epilogue

A cornucopia of conflicting emotions continued to swirl around in her mind. But this time Tia didn't freak out.

"So, Tia, when you reflect back on the time you were in the hospital, how do you feel?" Cheryl Murray's tone was compassionate. Not judgmental. It put Tia at ease.

Tia smiled as she pondered the question. She couldn't believe she was sitting in a support group—talking about her problems to a group of people, many of whom were living through the same mood swings as her. Coming here was one of the best decisions she'd ever made.

Tia glanced over and smiled at the realization of *the* best thing she'd ever done—marrying Lance Kingston. Her heart fluttered as Lance reached over and squeezed her hand. His touch transmitted his strength to her.

"Well," Tia began, "I made it. My will to live is obviously

far greater than my will to die." Tears filled her eyes. Lance had been through so much. And still he stuck by her.

Tia had stayed in the hospital for four weeks. The doctors had said she was in a coma, but she heard everything. She heard Lance beg her to come back. She heard her mother and Uncle Leo praying. She even heard Lance's grandmother and mother apologize and beg her forgiveness. She heard it all. But her mind wouldn't let her mouth respond. So she'd lain there, silently praying, crying inside, until one day she just opened her eyes. In another week Tia was strong enough to go home.

At least physically strong enough.

Mentally, she was still struggling.

Tia glanced around at the eight people in the room. They'd also been a source of strength over the last few months. Knowing that she wasn't going through this struggle alone made a huge difference.

"I kept trying to understand why, when everything was going so well in my life, did this sadness, emptiness, and utter despair return time and again to torment me," Tia continued. "I often used to wonder what I had done that was so wrong."

When she'd emerged from her coma, the transformation had been instantaneous. She'd seen Lance and Lauren—her husband and her baby girl—sitting next to her bed, praying for her recovery.

At that moment, her way forward had never been clearer. She wanted more than anything to live, and she committed then and there to doing whatever she needed to do to ensure that she would never leave them.

"How do you feel now?" Cheryl asked.

"For the first time in many years, I feel good about myself. The hopelessness that I had been feeling has vanished. There are miracles, they do take place. We just have to look in the right places." Tia squeezed Lance's hand again.

Cheryl smiled. "You know my motto: 'God is never too late; He's always right on time.' "

Tia nodded. "Yeah. He certainly proved it to me. He gave me my miracle; he gave me back my life."

Despite her miraculous recovery, there was no happily-ever-after for Tia. Each day was a struggle. Some days were more difficult than others. But just like an alcoholic, she'd taken each step as it came.

Over the past six months, Tia had read every book that she could find on positive thinking. It changed the way that she thought about life and being bipolar. It helped her to see that by fighting the illness, she was only making it worse.

"Lance, do you have something you'd like to add?" Cheryl asked.

Lance sat back, relaxing. "I'm just so proud of Tia. I can't pretend to know what she feels. I'm just glad she has learned to accept it and manage it."

"That's right," Tia said. "I know when the signs are setting in, and before it can take a firm hold of me, I go and see Dr. Monroe, he adjusts my tablets, and everything goes back to normal."

"That medication is key," Cheryl said. Several of the other members in the group nodded as well. That had been the central theme that all of them had come to terms with—medicine was key, and that was nothing to be ashamed of.

Cheryl checked the clock. "Well, it looks like we're out of time, but I want to close with this: Imagine if you had a bank account that credited your account each morning with 86,400 dollars that carried over no balance from day to day, allowed you to keep no cash in your account, and every evening canceled whatever part of the amount you had failed to use during the day. What would you do?" She looked around the room.

"Spend it as fast as I could," a young man named Tony said, laughing. He had been addicted to drugs, alcohol, sex, you name it, in an effort to mask his pain from being bipolar. As with Tia, this group had been a lifesaver for him.

"Right." Cheryl smiled. "You would draw out every cent and use it. Well, here is a little secret: You do have such a bank account, and it's called time. Every morning you are credited with 86,400 seconds. Every night it cancels whatever you haven't used to good purpose, it carries over no balances, allows no overdrafts. Each day it opens a new account with you, and each night it burns the records of the day. If you failed to use the day's deposit, the loss is yours. There is no going back, no drawing against 'tomorrow.' So draw on this precious fund of seconds and use it wisely in order to get the utmost in health, happiness, and success."

Everyone in the room was struck by this metaphor.

"Gosh, that was deep."

Tia laughed at the portly old man sitting next to her, Bernie Walton. Who would've ever thought she'd have so much in common with a seventy-two-year-old white man. But Bernie was another who knew her pain. Bernie had attempted suicide two years ago . . . the same way Tia had last year.

"Well, I try to get deep from time to time." Cheryl chuckled. "But seriously, enjoy your evening and remember Romans 8:28: 'We know—' "

" '—that in all things God works for the good of those who love Him, who have been called according to His purpose,' " they all said, finishing Cheryl's favorite scripture.

Tia knew she hadn't been deeply faithful through all of her suffering. Maybe if she had, events would've turned out differently. She shook off that thought. Cheryl had convinced her long ago that God didn't work like that. Even when we thought we were walking alone, He was right there carrying us.

Cheryl had been a godsend. Lance said they'd met the night Tia delivered Lauren. He'd gingerly introduced Tia to her, but Tia had immediately clicked with her and her husband, Thomas, whose bipolar episodes paled in comparison to Tia's.

Tia had tried to get her mother to come to the support group meetings as well. Of course, Virginia still wasn't hearing it. But at least she'd given up her fight to continue denying something was wrong with Tia. She'd just refused to address the issue at all. She continued with her blinders, and Tia could only continue to pray that one day her mother would come around. For now, she came by to visit Lauren, choosing to focus all of her energy on her granddaughter.

Lauren.

Lauren would be one year old in a few weeks. She'd been Tia's saving grace, her strength to keep going in her darkest hour.

Lance's sister, Patricia, had put her singing career on hold to come back and help Tia care for Lauren. Patricia and Tia had hit it off, and Patricia was relishing "aunthood," as she called it.

Lance's mother and grandmother continued tiptoeing around Tia, and she knew they were waiting and watching for the crazy clues. But Tia no longer worried about that. Walking in the shadow of death—and realizing that Lauren would've been the one hurt most—made her realize now that life was not about choosing the easy road; it was about choosing the road most beneficial to you.

"Well, you know, anytime you need to call me, you can," Cheryl said, snapping Tia out of her thoughts. Everyone had stood up and was gathering his or her things to leave.

"Thanks, Cheryl. I know I could never have done it all on my own," Tia admitted. "God knew it, too. He knew that I had chosen a very rough road, and He knew that I would need help, so he gave me the most wonderful family that anyone could wish for."

Lance once again hugged his wife.

"Oh, Lance, I understand congratulations are in order," Cheryl said as they walked toward the door. "I'm extremely proud of your efforts to educate people about treating bipolar disorder. I heard that four-part series you did in the magazine won a prestigious award."

"Yeah, the Edward R. Murrow Award. Tia's story is also up for a Pulitzer in journalism," Lance said, smiling at his wife.

"I hope that the story will help get rid of that *crazy* label so people can see mental illness as a sickness. We'll go see a doctor if we have a pain in our chest, but we won't go see a doctor if something isn't right in our head," Cheryl said. "We write off kids as troubled without realizing that there could be a much greater problem."

"That's what I'm hoping to change," Lance said. "The stigma that goes along with mental illness. We've gotten several letters from families that said they simply thought a relative was an addict or a troublemaker because that's the life they chose. Many never realized it indicated a greater problem. So, if I can help save one family from going through what we've been through this last year, then our efforts will not have been in vain."

Cheryl hugged Lance, then pointed toward the door. "There's your sister and daughter."

Patricia rolled Lauren's stroller in. Lauren was adorable in a cute pink-and-green vest and pants. "Is this a new outfit?" Lance asked, leaning down to pick up his daughter.

"Yep, got it in the store down the street," Patricia responded. "On your credit card, of course."

"Of course," Lance replied a touch sourly, kissing his daughter on the cheek as Tia walked up.

"Ma-ma!" Lauren squealed, wriggling as she reached for her mother.

Tia smiled as she took Lauren out of her father's hands.

"So your auntie used you as an excuse to go shopping?" Tia said, tickling Lauren's chin.

"Moi?" Patricia said, feigning shock.

"Yes, *moi*." Lance shook his head. "What did you buy yourself—with my credit card?"

Patricia's mouth dropped open. "Why in the world would

you think— Okay, I bought these to-die-for shoes," she said, sticking her foot out to reveal the silver flats.

Cheryl laughed. "Good to see you again, Patricia."

"You, too, Ms. Cheryl."

"When are you going back to London?"

Patricia smiled coyly at her brother and sister-in-law. "Ummm, not for a while. I found something I like being better than a singer—for now." She tousled Lauren's hair. "My sweet pea has grown on me and got me rethinking this whole kid ban I had going on."

"Well, we'd better get out of here. They have another meeting about to start," Cheryl said, motioning to the people who had started filing into the room. "You guys take this perfect little baby home."

Lance watched as Tia strapped Lauren back into her stroller. He couldn't help but smile at the sight of his wife. She was so beautiful—flaws and all. And his daughter was perfect. The spitting image of her mother. Lance felt guilty, but he said a small prayer that looks and personality were all that Lauren had gotten from her mother.

But as he took Tia's hand and led her out of the meeting facility, Lance knew one thing: even if Lauren wasn't perfect, even if one day he discovered she had indeed inherited her mother's genes, he would love his daughter, in spite of it. Just as he loved his wife.

A Note from the Author

All across the country, there are families blowing off someone's erratic behavior, dismissing their mental issues with an "Oh, that's just Crazy ______. He's a little special." In some families (including mine), we laugh away the seriousness of the problems facing our loved ones.

I'm hoping that *The Secret She Kept* can help change that.

This is a book that's been on my heart for several years. I've always taken issue with the fact that we'll seek treatment when something is wrong with our bodies, but when it comes to our minds, we don't give it the same care. Years ago, a cancer diagnosis was something that was whispered in many households and neighborhoods. Today, that's rare. And just like we've changed the way we fight cancer, it's my hope that we'll do the same when it comes to matters of the mind.

Of course, when it comes to writing a story like this (especially when you incorporate humor as I do), you have to have people who trust that you can still tell an engaging, entertaining story while educating at the same time. So for those who believed in me (my editor, Brigitte Smith; my agent, Sara Camilli; my publicist Melissa Gramstad; and my publisher, Louise Burke), I give sincere thanks for letting this story be told.

As always, I wouldn't be able to do what I do without a phenomenal support system at home. So once again, I must give thanks to a host of folks. And since this is book number twenty-five, naturally the list may seem repetitive . . . but I couldn't do what I do without these people and for that, I must give thanks . . . again and again and again.

First and foremost, all praises go to God for blessing me with a talent to write.

Much thanks to my husband, Miron Billingsley, who has nurtured and encouraged my dream from the first day I told him that I wanted to be a writer. Thank you to my three wonderful children who take my writing, traveling, and promoting in stride. A million thanks to my unbelievably, awesome mother, Nancy Blacknell, who fusses like crazy, but still steps up to the plate and takes care of my kids when I hit the road. One of these days, I'm going to retire you (insert your sarcastic comment here).

My little sister, Tanisha Tate, who quit as my personal assistant several years ago just because she wasn't getting paid . . . thank you for still being my right hand! You'll get hooked up, too (one day).

Thank you also to my family and friends who never fail to help me hold it down: LaWonda Young, Jaimi Canady, Raquelle Lewis, Kim Wright, and Clemelia Richardson. Thank you for always having my back.

A Note from the Author

To Pat Tucker Wilson, there are no words to describe my gratitude for your just being in my corner, lifting me up and giving your unwavering support both personally and professionally. To my writing twin, Victoria Christopher Murray, this past year has been an incredible journey of highs and lows . . . thank you for sharing it with me and I'm still confident that this is our year! I can't wait for our next tour (I have a raccoon with your name on it!).

To the fantastic Yolanda LaToya Gore . . . a thousand thanks for your unwavering support and phenomenal ability to keep me on track! To Kym Fisher, thank you so much for all that you have done! You are the best!

Lots of love to my literary colleagues who always offer words of advice, encouragement, and just are trying to run this race with me . . . Nina Foxx, S. James Guitard, Nakia Laushaul, Jihad, Norma Jarrett, Jason Frost, Jumita Tillman, and Tiffany Warren.

Once again, I have to say thanks to Regina King, Reina King, and Bobby Smith for standing firm on our movie-making journey. Thank you so much for believing in my stories and not giving up.

I must also show love to Sonny Messiah Jiles, Marilyn Marshall, Lisa Paige, Rochelle Scott, Addie Hyeliger, Carla Rogers, Tamaria Richardson-Williamson, Jacqui McFadden, and to my wonderful Facebook family who do everything from encourage me in my writing to help me with my coffee addiction. I have over twelve thousand friends and there are some that although I've never met, your words of encouragement and love keep me motivated. So a special shout-out to: Sheretta, Betty, Gina, Portia, Juanita, Barbara, Vetta, Lesley, Ina, Rhonda, Melissa, Antoinette, Dee, Jocelyn, Karen, Josie, Bernice, Sharon, AP, Cassandra, Taryn, Paula, Zandra, Yolanda, Jeris, Raquel, Corey, Roxanne, Myra, Jonathan, Deborah, Davina, Autumn, Catherine, Alfreada, Crystal, Simone, Erica, Denise, Lena, GeeGee, Lasheera, Reginald, Kendra, Venetric, Nadra, Jessica, LaShawn, Allison, Ira, and Cristel. (I know I'm forgetting some folks, but I only have so much room!)

A HUGE thank you to all the book clubs that selected my book. You guys are the best. As always, much love goes to my wonderful illustrious sorors, especially the Houston Metropolitan Chapters and my chapter, Mu Kappa Omega and my sister-moms of Jack and Jill. Big thanks also to Davion and Wanda Anderson and Leota Peterson at Serenity Studios in Houston for all that you do to make me look my best!

And finally, I have to say thank *you*. Yes, YOU! Whether you're a new reader, or a returning reader, I am where I am because of your support and for that, I am eternally grateful.

Until the next book. . . . Thanks for the love.

ReShonda

Readers Group Guide

The Secret She Kept

ReShonda Tate Billingsley

Introduction

Magazine editor Lance Kingston thinks he's found the perfect woman in Tia Jiles—a beautiful and philanthropic lawyer on her way to making partner. After a whirlwind courtship, Lance ignores his family's warnings and marries Tia—but after the wedding, her manic behavior clues Lance in to a serious secret she's been hiding. With in-laws who do more harm than good and stubborn resistance from Tia, Lance urges his wife to seek medical attention. But ups-and-downs in her career, plus an unexpected pregnancy, make Tia even more unstable. As he navigates through her illness, Lance faces life-altering decisions as he tries to help his wife when she refuses to help herself.

Questions and Topics for Discussion

1. Lance's grandmother admonishes, "Crazy leaves clues." Before they were married, what clues did Lance ignore about Tia and her behavior?

2. Uncle Leo and Virginia disagree on whether Tia should be honest with Lance. Discuss how each person pulls Tia in a different direction. In your opinion, whose advice should she have listened to? How does Tia let the various people in her life affect her day-to-day decisions?

3. Discuss how Lance's sense of abandonment by his father influences his dedication to Tia. How does his strong sense of commitment both help and hinder him?

4. Tia comes from a family with a history of mental illness, but also one that looks down upon asking for help. In what ways does her family history affect her decisions?

5. Discuss Tia's reluctance to take medication. What factors have influenced her fear of being dependent on prescription drugs?

6. Discuss how the many stressful changes in Tia's life—including marriage, moving, career, and pregnancy—affect her bipolar disorder. Do you think there was anything she could have changed in her lifestyle in order to minimize the stress?

7. Tia and Lance both face temptations that threaten to lead them astray. What were each of their biggest temptations, and what did it teach them?

8. Discuss the role of medical professionals in handling Tia's illness. What could Dr. Monroe have done to encourage her to take her medication, and how should Tia have taken better control of her own health? What do you think was the biggest mistake or oversight in Tia's treatment?

9. Tia is afraid to tell people about her bipolar disorder after the negative reactions of her ex-boyfriends and Lucinda. Do you think Tia saw these situations differently than they really were? Are there instances throughout *The Secret She Kept* where you think Tia had an altered perspective of reality?

10. Tia experiences a string of violent episodes. How could she and those around her have better handled her spells? Do you think the outcome would have been any different? Why or why not?

11. Tia's pregnancy was her biggest challenge in dealing with her bipolar disorder. Discuss how baby Lauren may turn out to be Tia's saving grace in learning to manage bipolar disorder.

12. Do you feel that Lance and Tia belong together? Is Lance better off with his wife, or should he have left earlier on for someone like Crystal? Discuss where you see these characters headed.

13. What do you think was the strongest take-away or message in *The Secret She Kept*?

Enhance Your Book Club

1. According to the National Alliance on Mental Illness (NAMI), over 10 million people in America have bipolar disorder. Visit www.nami.org to learn more about bipolar disorder. If you or someone in your book club know someone with bipolar disorder, share some of the challenges that person faces and ways loved ones can help.

2. Uncle Leo quotes from the Bible to encourage Tia to tell Lance the truth. Have a Bible on hand and give all participants the opportunity to share their favorite scripture passage, prayer, or personal motto.

3. Virgina believes in the power of prayer over medication—whether or not you agree with her philosophy, discuss a time in your life when you felt that prayer was the only answer. How did it see you through a tough time?

4. ReShonda Tate Billingsley often writes about female characters. If you've read any of her other books, compare her previous characters to Lance—how does centering the story around a male character's point of view change the reading experience?

Raymond E. Brown
a RISEN CHRIST in EASTERTIME